DEATHBED AND BREAKFAST

A Pookotz Sisters Mystery

by

Bart J. Gilbertson

For information, email **Cozy Cat Press**, cozycatpress@aol.com or visit our website at: www.cozycatpress.com

COZY CAT
PRESS

ISBN: 978-1-939816-11-5
Printed in the United States of America

Cover design by Cover Shot Creations
http://www.covershotcreations.com

1 2 3 4 5 6 7 8 9 10

For my sister, Billie
Her invaluable contributions and inspiration helped to
bring the Pookotz Sisters and Pleasant Lake to life.
Without her, this book would have never happened.
Thank you!

Chapter 1

Penny Forester and her grandfather Richard arrived to the scenic town of Pleasant Lake, Oregon just as it began to get dark. Penny looked over at Grandpa Dick as they entered the city limits, but he was still fast asleep, slumped against the passenger side door. "Welcome to Pleasant Lake," Penny read to herself from an elaborate sign on the side of the road. "Population 2,051." She slowed the car down to negotiate a long curve to the right that rested snugly against a steep hill. Grandpa Dick began to stir with the decrease in speed and sleepily opened his eyes.

"Where are we?" Grandpa Dick weakly asked adjusting his body to sit up in his seat. "How long have I been out?"

"We're entering Pleasant Lake," Penny answered. "You've been asleep for almost a couple of hours now. How are you feeling?"

Grandpa Dick did not answer right away as they drove into town, the street lamps beginning to flicker with light in the growing darkness. Penny slowed them down even more to the posted speed limit of 25 MPH while Grandpa Dick rubbed the last of the sleep from his eyes.

"How are you feeling, Grandpa?" Penny repeated.

"I'm just fine, Sweet Pea," he responded, patting her right knee affectionately. "But we should stop here for the night."

"Okay."

Penny turned into the parking lot of a small grocery store to their left called Grogan's, and finding an empty space, she slowed to a stop and turned off the engine. She turned to face her grandfather.

"You were squirming and wincing while you slept Grandpa. I could hear you. Are you *sure* you're alright?" Penny pressed.

"I'm just fine. I wish you wouldn't worry so much. You remind me a lot of your mother," Grandpa Dick replied with a soft laugh. He reached over to open his door and suddenly fell back against his seat with a pained expression on his tired, careworn face. "Just the same though, perhaps it would be best if I waited here while you go inside. Why have we stopped here anyway?"

Penny leaned over and kissed Grandpa Dick on the forehead. "Just as I thought," she stated, concern flooding her blue eyes. "You're getting worse by the minute. You stay here and just rest a bit. We've stopped here because, for one thing, we need to fill your prescription vial and it looks like there's a pharmacy inside. Also, if we're staying in Pleasant Lake for the night, we'll need directions to a good motel."

Penny opened the door, got out of the car and walked up the wooden steps to the quaint grocery store. She was about to enter through the doorway when she heard a car door slam shut behind her.

"Wait a minute, Sweet Pea," Grandpa Dick said. She turned to find him standing next to the car. "I've found my second wind here. Besides, I need to get out and stretch my legs a bit."

Penny went back down the steps and grabbed Grandpa Dick's hand. "Okay Grandpa. Just be careful. Don't over do it."

Together they walked up the steps to the store and entered. Grogan's was a small country store with strong wood and stone tones. Three large, black ceiling fans spun lazily from the vaulted ceiling on long poles spaced evenly from front to back. There were three lines of shelves that ran parallel to one another along the length of the building stacked full with canned goods, boxes and bags of various products. Racks of chips, doughnuts, cookies and jerky occupied the end caps nearest them. Along the wall to their right was a tall magazine stand which contained what seemed to be all the current periodicals and newspapers. On the back wall was a Men's/Women's restroom, to the left of which were refrigerated units that contained sodas, juices, water and milk. The floors were wooden throughout. In the back left corner was the pharmacy that Penny had mentioned. However, it did not appear to be open.

"Good evening." They were greeted warmly by a slightly overweight, balding man behind the counter to their left. He gave a customer their change and closed the cash register drawer. The customer thanked him and walked out the door. The balding man smiled and walked around the end of the counter towards Penny and Grandpa Dick with his hand extended. "Welcome to Grogan's. I'm Steve Grogan."

"Mr. Grogan," Grandpa Dick smiled in return shaking his hand. "I'm Richard Forester and this is my granddaughter Penny. You have a very nice store here. I have to say I'm impressed."

"Why, thank you," Steve responded, obviously very pleased with the compliment. "We do our best, though some days are a little harder than others. So you're new to the area?"

"Yes, passing through."

"I see," Steve replied and then arching his left eyebrow inquisitively, "Will you be continuing on, or will you need a place to stay for the night?"

"Actually, we're hoping you might be able to direct us to a good motel," Penny contributed.

"I certainly can. It's only the best Bed & Breakfast in the state of Oregon, maybe even on the entire western seaboard," Steve beamed. He turned and walked back behind the counter and lifted the receiver from the telephone. "In fact, let me call over there to let them know you'll be coming."

"Oh, that isn't necessary," Grandpa Dick cautioned stepping forward. "You don't have to go to all that trouble."

Steve raised his hand and shook his head. "No trouble at all." And then after a moment, Steve spoke into the receiver. "Hello Mildred? Steve Grogan here. Say, do you have a vacant room over there tonight? Oh you do? Wonderful! I have a couple of guests to send your way. Yes. Very good then. Thank you, Mildred. Say hello to your sister for me. Yes, yes. Good night to you too." Steve set the receiver down and looked back up. "You're all set."

Grandpa Dick was flabbergasted. "Wow! I don't know what to say. Thank you very much. Is everyone as kind as you are here in Pleasant Lake?"

Steve smiled and winked. "Maybe you should stay over a few days and see for yourself."

"Maybe we should," Grandpa Dick agreed.

"Well, we'd love to have you. I called over to the Pookotz Bed & Breakfast on the other end of town. That was Mildred Pookotz, the kindest woman you could ever hope to meet. She runs the place along with her older sister, Edna. They have been there for years and have made a good reputation for themselves," Steve explained, walking back around the counter to rejoin Grandpa Dick and Penny. "They'll be expecting you."

"Very good," Grandpa Dick smiled. "I also need to fill a prescription tonight if that would be at all possible."

"Oh drat it all," Steve said, pouting. "You missed our pharmacist by only a matter of minutes. She's already closed up and gone home for the night. Tell you what I'll do. If you leave your vial here, I'll be sure to have it filled and sent over to the Bed & Breakfast first thing in the morning. They can just add the price of the prescription to their bill and I'll settle up with them later."

Grandpa Dick grimaced a little. "Are there any other pharmacies in town?"

"I'm sorry, but no. We're the only one," Steve reluctantly informed. "You see, Doc Meecham's clinic is located directly behind my store, so it just kind of worked out that way."

"Well, then, I'd appreciate it if you could take care of it for me," Grandpa Dick acquiesced, handing the vial over to Steve.

A small bell rang as the front entrance door opened. They turned to see a police officer with a round brimmed hat walk in wearing a dark brown uniform with tan highlights. He carried a club stick on his left hip and a holstered pistol on his right. A shiny, silver badge was just below his right shoulder on his pocket lapel. His hair was dark and just beginning to gray around the edges and he had a full mustache.

"Sheriff! What can I do you for?" Steve greeted.

Penny smiled to herself. She'd heard her grandfather use those words before. *Do you for*. But she never really understood what it meant.

"Evenin,' Steve," the sheriff returned, walking over. "Just stopped by to check in on things. Everything okay tonight?"

"Yep! Quiet as a mouse in a room full of cats," Steve laughed to himself.

"Sheriff Jake Blackwood," the sheriff said, turning to Grandpa Dick, extending his hand in greeting.

"Hello, Sheriff," Grandpa Dick accepted.

"Uh, this here is Mr. Richard Forester and his granddaughter Penny," Steve cut in. "They're passing through, but will be staying over at the Pookotz house tonight."

"You don't say?" Sheriff Blackwood smiled, looking at the two travelers. "You're in for a real treat then. Edna and Mildred are two of the nicest people you'll ever meet, guaranteed. They may seem a bit odd, but they have run that Bed & Breakfast for years and know how to treat a guest right. It's quite an experience."

"So we've heard," Grandpa Dick nodded toward Steve.

Sheriff Blackwood looked at the watch on his left wrist. "Oh, we don't have much time to lose. They'll be serving dinner in about 15 minutes or so."

Grandpa Dick brought his hand up to cover a cough that sounded deep and rough. He winced a little with pain.

"You're looking a bit pale Richard," Sheriff Blackwood noticed. "Are you okay?"

Penny spun around and looked up at her grandfather. He had beads of sweat on his brow and his breaths were shallow. "Grandpa?"

"Yes," Grandpa Dick responded. "It's just been a long day. I really could go for a good meal and some rest though. I'll be okay if we can get me over to the Bed & Breakfast."

"Are you sure you're alright?" Steve echoed.

"Thank you, but yes."

"I'm heading that way anyway. I'm assuming the silver Camry parked out front is your vehicle?" Sheriff Blackwood asked. When Penny and Grandpa Dick nodded in the affirmative, Sheriff Blackwood nodded once. "Very good then. I'd be happy to show you where they're located if you want to just follow me over there."

With that, Sheriff Blackwood shook Steve's hand goodnight and turned to leave. Steve assured Grandpa Dick that he'd have his prescription filled and sent over in the morning and wished them both a good night. They returned the wish and followed the sheriff outside to his cruiser which was parked only a few feet away from their own car.

"Just follow me."

"Will do, Sheriff Blackwood," Penny said.

Sheriff Blackwood sat down in the driver's seat of his cruiser and with one leg out the door, he picked up the handle to his car radio and spoke for a minute with someone else on the other end. Then he lifted his leg inside the car and shut the door. Penny helped Grandpa Dick into the Camry, and soon they were pulling out of the parking lot with Sheriff Blackwood leading them down the town's main street. None of them, however, noticed the black sedan pull out of the same parking lot and follow, while keeping a safe distance.

Chapter 2

Driving slowly down Main Street, both Grandpa Dick and Penny were immediately taken with how beautiful a town Pleasant Lake really was. The whole town was nestled comfortably in the hills with various types of pine, cedar and fir trees scattered throughout. Old metal lampposts painted dark green alternated back and forth on either side of the street with picturesque glass enclosures on top that curved over and lit up the sidewalks. To their right, just across the street from Grogan's was a nice park with a wooden gazebo, as if it had been placed there straight out of a Norman Rockwell painting. An old, steam engine rested on top of a large concrete slab whispering of days gone by. Filtering throughout the carpet of green grass were picnic tables and benches. Towards the back of the park were a large sandbox, some swings, a slide, teeter-totters, and a small merry-go-round...all of which rested against a hill, the very hill they drove around when entering the town.

To their right, kitty corner to Grogan's, was a small white church with a tall steeple which encased a bell. The sign in front read 'Church of Jesus Christ.' There were lights turned on inside which glowed prettily through the stained glass windows. On either side of the street from there, they drove through the part of town where the Library, Bank, and Post Office were located, all of which had closed for the day.

Following that on the right was an old Majestic movie theater with a large, well-lit marquee over the main entrance where they were featuring the classic film, 'Gone with the Wind.' Posters of the same film were encased in lighted glass displays to either side of the ticket booth where there were nearly a dozen people waiting their turn in line. Right next to the movie theater was Flannigan's Burgers & Malts which could have passed for any soda or ice cream shop in the 50's. They were wall to wall with teenagers and young couples. Continuing on was Mario's Pizzeria & Italian Eatery where they caught glimpses of people sitting at tables with red and white checkered tablecloths and drippy candles. Nestled between the pizzeria and a gas station at the end of the street was a small tavern called Slurp 'N' Burp, from which they could hear live music spilling out onto the street.

Lined along the left side of Main Street were various shops and department stores where you could find any assortment of goods and products. Hardware, appliances, clothing, bikes, pets, antiques…you name it, it was there in narrow shops that stood tall and close together. At the end of the street past the last shop on the left was a paved driveway which forked left and right. The left fork led to a modern, state-of-the-art motel which bore the town's name, and the right fork to a car dealership which looked heavy with used models.

Penny heard Grandpa Dick sigh. Turning to look at him, she discovered that he was completely enamored with the little town, his eyes as big as a child's.

"Grandpa?" she softly said.

"Yes, Sweet Pea."

"Everything okay?"

"I was just thinking to myself what a beautiful town Pleasant Lake is," Grandpa Dick commented. "It's perfect."

Penny had to agree. "Yes, it is."

Grandpa Dick let out a deep breath. "If I could pick a place to die and pass over to the next life in, I'd be hard pressed to find a better place than right here."

Alarmed, Penny looked sharply at her grandfather but decided not to say anything. Instead, she reached over and took his hand into her own.

"I love you, Grandpa."

"I love you too, Sweet Pea."

Neither of them realized that they hadn't yet seen the best that Pleasant Lake had to offer. When Sheriff Blackwood turned to the right down a well graveled road at the end of the town, they drove through a thickly wooded area for about half a mile and then emerged into a clearing and one of the most beautiful sights they'd ever seen.

Through the clear night air, they saw ripples of sparkling silver on the dark lake where the moonbeams hit the surface. Resting contentedly at the lake's edge was the Pookotz Bed & Breakfast. It was surrounded by a well tended lawn, various flowerbeds, a small greenhouse, a stone water fountain, a garden, and what appeared to be an aviary. Lined across the front of the charming three story house were two logs lying on the ground, end-to-end with a gap in between them that opened up to a pathway leading to a white picket fence and gate. Parked in front of the logs were three vehicles, all with Oregon license plates. A gorgeous, white latticed arch with vines and flowers adorned the gate.

A large, bright lamp mounted to the uppermost point of the Bed & Breakfast showed the house itself to be painted in a warm, light brown, almost beige color that was trimmed with forest green and a deep burgundy red. All of the framed windows had shutters in the same green shade with ornate flower boxes painted in burgundy that were abundant with all sorts of variations and color of flowers. The uppermost floor's windows were dark, a couple of the rooms on the second floor had their lights turned on, and the entire bottom floor was lit up with warmth that seemed to beckon temptingly to them.

Neither Penny nor Grandpa Dick said a word as they followed Sheriff Blackwood to the parking area. There were really no words for what they were feeling at that moment. Finally, they came to rest before the home and Penny switched off the engine. Grandpa Dick was quiet. Peacefully quiet. His chin rested thoughtfully in the palm of his right hand as he looked out his window at the shimmering lake.

A loud, pounding on the back window caused them both to nearly jump out of their skin and they turned to see Sheriff Blackwood waiting for them to get out of the car. Opening their doors, Grandpa Dick and Penny joined the sheriff outside.

"You have a fine town, Sheriff Blackwood," Grandpa Dick complimented.

"Thank you. We're rather proud of it," Sheriff Blackwood replied. "Well, this way. I'll introduce you to the Pookotz sisters."

The party of three made their way between the two logs and through the archway into the yard beyond. A spacious porch with a wooden railing wrapped around the front of the house and on both sides. A large wooden bench hung suspended by two chains anchored in the ceiling and was softly swaying back and forth in the evening breeze. As they walked up the front steps, an old shaggy dog lifted his head from where he was resting on the porch swing.

"Hey Rufus," Sheriff Blackwood said walking over and patting the dog on the head. Rufus licked his hand and then lay back down, lazily watching them as they approached the doorway. "World's best watchdog,"

Sheriff Blackwood joked reaching up to ring the doorbell.

To the right of the door in extravagant fashion hung a placard that read, 'Welcome to Pookotz Bed & Breakfast. Established in 1862." A lovely, older woman opened the door as light washed over them from the inside. She had her grayish-blue hair brushed out nicely over a light orange shawl that draped her shoulders. She wore a white dress which was interspersed with rich colors showcasing roses, daffodils and daisies. She pushed open the screen door and gave them a dazzling smile.

"Hello, Sheriff Blackwood," she said in a sweet, petite voice. "It's good to see you again."

"Evening, Mildred," Sheriff Blackwood greeted, removing his hat and holding it before him. "I have a couple of folks here who need a place to stay for the night. Steve said you had a vacancy?"

"Of course, of course," Mildred replied. Standing back, she held the screen door open for them. "Please, come inside out of the cold night air dears."

Nodding to her kindly, the three of them entered into the main foyer as Mildred shut the door behind her. She lightly stepped around to stand before them, her arms and hands extended from her sides almost as if she were floating on air. Mildred looked up at them with a warm smile and caring eyes.

"I'm Mildred Pookotz," she introduced herself as she politely shook Grandpa Dick's and Penny's hands in turn. "Welcome to our home. You poor dears looked famished. Have you eaten your dinner yet?"

"No," Grandpa Dick returned. "We've just arrived in town."

They heard footsteps approaching and turned to see another, statelier, older woman walking up to them. She had her gray hair pulled up into a tight bun behind her and was wearing a button down black dress. She came to a stop with her hands folded before her, prim and proper. She had very strong facial features highlighted by Joan Crawford-like eyes and eyebrows. She seemed to have a no-nonsense quality about her, yet when she smiled gracefully at them, they were made to feel at ease.

"Evening, Edna," Sheriff Blackwood said turning to her. "We have a couple more guests for you tonight."

"Good evening, Jacob," Edna replied with a small nod in his direction.

"Please, just call me Jake," the sheriff responded a bit put off.

"I'll do no such thing, Jacob," Edna retorted. "I've known you since you were just a little baby. I called you by your Christian name then and I still do today. It's only proper."

Embarrassed, Sheriff Blackwood's face blushed red and he bowed his head. "Yes, Ma'am."

Mildred looked over to her sister and leaned forward a little. "Edna, now look what you've done. You've hurt poor Jacob's feelings," she said in a soft, concerned tone. "Do you think perhaps we could just call him Sheriff instead?"

Edna thought a minute, then nodded agreeably. "Yes, I suppose that would be fine," and then to Sheriff Blackwood, "Would that be acceptable to you, Jacob?"

"Yes, of course," Sheriff Blackwood answered looking sheepish.

Edna turned back to greet Grandpa Dick and Penny with a smile on her face. "I'm so sorry," she said in a much kinder voice. "I didn't mean to ignore the two of you. I'm Edna Pookotz. Welcome to our Bed & Breakfast."

"Thank you," Grandpa Dick returned. "This is my granddaughter Penny, and I'm Richard Forester, although everyone just calls me Dick."

"Oh!" Edna faltered, her face drawn. Forcing a small smile, Edna reached over and shook his hand. "Nice to meet you...Richard. Won't you join us in the dining room? You both look as if you haven't eaten in days."

"Well, I believe that's my cue," Sheriff Blackwood spoke up. "I really should be getting home to Cathy and the kids. You folks enjoy your stay here. You're in good hands."

"Goodnight, Sheriff Blackwood," Penny said. "Thank you for your help."

"Yes, goodnight, Sheriff," Mildred said with a kind smile. "Drive safely."

"Goodnight, Jacob," Edna added.

"Sheriff," Mildred whispered to Edna.

Edna rolled her eyes. "Very well then. Goodnight, Sheriff."

Sheriff Blackwood nodded, and placing his hat back upon his head, he turned and walked out the front door.

Chapter 3

"Now," Mildred said, clasping her hands before her, "let's get you two seated at the dining table and fed, shall we? Then we'll get you settled into your room afterwards. I'm assuming you have some luggage you'll need to have brought in as well?"

"Yes, in the trunk of our car," Grandpa Dick answered a bit weakly. "I really need to sit down though. I'm feeling a bit haggard after today's driving."

"Certainly, Richard," Edna responded. "This way, please."

Edna abruptly turned and led them down a few steps into a cozy little parlor to the left where a small fire was crackling and sizzling in the corner fireplace. Facing the fireplace were two plush, tall chairs with a small table and crystal lamp set up between them. Underneath was a large circular rug that nearly covered the entire wooden floor of the room. The ornate lamp was turned on at its lowest setting and together with the firelight cast a mellow hue over the dark green walls which were covered in paintings. On either side of the fireplace was a framed window where the curtains had already been drawn closed for the night. A large painting almost the size of the fireplace itself, was mounted above the fireplace mantle. It was of a stately gentleman with wavy white hair, large sideburns and striking facial features. In fact, it wasn't too hard to recognize that Edna reflected these same features. Underneath the painting was a small tag with some writing which they weren't able to decipher from where they were standing.

"Who is that?" Penny asked pausing to look at the painting.

Mildred walked to her side and smiled softly. "That is Ozymandias Pookotz, dear," she answered in her sweet little voice. "Our great, great grandfather."

"He built this house in the 1800's," Edna picked up where Mildred left off. "He was one of the founders of Pleasant Lake years and years ago." Edna had walked around the two chairs, and with great affection, she reached up and touched the base of the frame around the painting.

"He established the Bed & Breakfast in 1862 and it has been a landmark of Pleasant Lake ever since," Mildred added with tones of reverence in her voice.

"Wow," Penny said under her breath.

The brief moment of silence that followed was rudely interrupted by the sound of someone snoring. Edna turned and saw a man slumped down in the chair to her left, his socked feet crossed in front of him and his hands folded over his belly. His eyes were closed and he was in a deep sleep. He opened his mouth and let go with another loud snore. Edna shook her head placing her hands on her hips, and leaned over the sleeping man.

"Mr. Buchanon," she called out to him. The man's eyes remained closed. "Mr. Buchanon!" Edna repeated louder this time. The man sat up with a start and began rubbing his eyes. "Mr. Buchanon, there you are. Did you not hear us announce dinner?"

"I'm sorry," he replied. "I must have dozed off here."

"Well, Felix is running a bit behind tonight…again," Edna announced with displeasure. "So no harm done."

Then motioning towards Grandpa Dick and Penny, she introduced them to Mr. Buchanon. Standing, he turned to face them. He was a sharp looking young man with gel in his blonde hair that was combed back. He wore gray, pin-striped suit pants and a white, long sleeve dress shirt with a black neck tie hanging loosely at his neck. However, upon catching sight of Grandpa Dick's face, he momentarily froze, his mouth opening slightly.

"Is something the matter Mr. Buchanon?" Mildred queried.

"Oh no, sorry," he replied with a slight stutter. "I sometimes get a small crick in my back if I stay in one position too long. I'm Aaron Buchanon. It's nice to meet you."

Penny quickly looked up at her grandfather, but the expression on his face told her that he didn't seem to recognize the man.

"Mr. Buchanon only arrived about 30 minutes before you did," Edna informed them. "He'll be joining us for dinner as well."

Having made a full recovery, Aaron nodded and smiled. "Yes, dinner sounds good. Lead the way."

Edna walked back over to the other side of the parlor indicating for them all to follow her with a wave of her index finger which they did. She led them down a hallway towards the rear of the house. There were framed pictures of all sizes along the length of the hallway on both sides showcasing all sorts of things. People, animals, places, cars, and landscapes both in color and in black and white. Some were extremely old and others fairly recent. At the end of the hallway, Edna stepped into a large room and motioned them all to enter.

Walking in single file, they found themselves in the dining room where there were already a few others seated at the table conversing among themselves. They looked up as they entered. It was a beautiful room. The ceiling was higher here than it had been in the hallway. The walls and ceiling were painted light beige with dark green trim. Two stunning silver and crystal chandeliers hung down, each centered on one end of the table. On the wall to their left as they entered was a long mirror framed in a dark, polished wood hanging above a narrow chest of drawers about waist high that matched the length of the mirror. Sitting on top of this chest were extra plates, glasses, silverware, napkins, a tablecloth and a few candlesticks. On the opposite wall was a large landscape painting of a waterfall spilling into a blue pond with a splash of exotic birds and colorful flowers. The dining room table itself was made of attractive, finely finished hand-crafted oak that stretched the length of the room. It was covered by a long, beige table cloth and surrounded by matching, high-back cushioned chairs.

"It appears we're all here now. Richard, you and Penny can take those two seats over there," Edna motioned to the two chairs at the far end of the table on the near side. As they seated themselves, Edna directed Aaron to sit right next to them. On the other side of the table sat four others already. Across from Richard and Penny was a young couple who were obviously very much in love. To their right were a middle-aged man and a young boy who looked to be 12, maybe 13 years old. Edna sat at the head of the table, while her sister lightly stepped over to her seat at the other end.

"Everyone," Mildred began politely, "This is Richard and his granddaughter Penny." An echo of 'hello' rippled down the length of the table.

The male half of the two lovebirds was the first to respond.

"Hello, Richard," he said sitting forward. "I'm Sam Richards. This is my lovely wife Gwen." Gwen blushed brightly, biting her bottom lip. "We were just married and are on our honeymoon."

"It's nice to meet you both," Grandpa Dick said with a smile, "and congratulations! You can call me Dick."

"Uh," Edna suddenly interrupted. "Richard will be fine. Thank you."

Suddenly without provocation, Sam began to laugh hysterically. The others looked around at each other in confusion and then back to the young groom who was holding his side because he was laughing so hard.

"Perhaps you could fill us in on the little joke Samuel?" Edna finally said a bit impatiently.

"Richard Richards!" Sam exclaimed trying to catch his breath.

Again, everyone looked around in further confusion.

"It's just that Richard is his first name and Richards is my last name," Sam explained and turned to face his young, blushing bride. "Wouldn't it be funny if we had a son and named him Richard? He would be Richard Richards!"

Sam began to laugh again and was joined by Gwen who had a most irritating, nasally giggle.

"Richard Richards," Gwen repeated. "Hee hee hee hee!"

"Yes, yes," Edna looked at the couple with a straight face. "Quite amusing."

"Oh! Oh!" Gwen shouted sitting up. "His middle name could be Richard too. So he'd be Richard Richard Richards!"

As they burst out into a new round of laughter, Mildred spoke up. "Perhaps you could introduce yourselves?" she said nodding at the other two.

Almost forcing himself to tear his gaze away from the silly newlyweds, the middle-aged man slowly stood up and faced Grandpa Dick and Penny. "Certainly. I'm Jim Frank, and this is my son Charlie," he said leaning over to shake their hands.

"Frank Frank," Gwen snorted as Sam joined her in laughter again.

Ignoring the two giggle-bots, Grandpa Dick nodded at Jim and replied, "Nice to meet you, Jim. What are you two up to?"

Jim smiled and put his arm around the boy and said, "Thought I'd take my son fishing on the north side of the lake where the river ends and try to hook a few fat salmon."

"Oh, very nice," Grandpa Dick returned. "I have fond memories of fishing with my father. Some good times."

"I've never been fishing before!" Charlie said sitting up. "I can hardly wait!"

Jim reached over and tapped Charlie's leg. "Show some manners at the dinner table, son."

Charlie sat back, calming himself. "Yes sir."

"And what is it that you do, Mr. Buchanon?" Edna questioned the blonde young man seated next to Richard and Penny.

Aaron shifted forward in his chair. "Ahem…well, I'm an insurance salesman. I work for Family Fidelity Insurance out of Portland. I'm just on my way back there from a convention, and decided this looked like a nice place to stop for the night."

"What type of insurance do you specialize in Mr. Buchanon?" Mildred asked.

"Life insurance mostly. But we also handle automobile and property."

"Really?" Sam chimed in. "The wife and I would be interested in hearing what you have to offer for life insurance. You know, to help get us started off in the right direction."

"If you don't mind," Aaron replied, looking at Sam, "I'm very tired. And after this weekend's convention, the *last* thing I want to do is open another insurance packet."

"Oh sure, no problem," Sam said sitting back.

The swinging door to Edna's left opened and an attractive woman dressed in a black and white maid's uniform walked in carrying a large tray holding glasses of ice water. She began to set them down, one-at-a-time, next to everyone's plate as she quietly circled the table.

"Alexis," Edna spoke up.

"Yes, Miss?" the maid daintily replied.

"Please go into the kitchen and find out what is taking Felix so long."

"Yes, Miss."

Suddenly, the doorbell rang.

"On second thoughts, Alexis," Edna said standing up, "I'll go see to Felix. You go and answer the door."

"Right away, Miss."

Edna disappeared behind the swinging door while Alexis made her way down the hallway back to the parlor and the front door. Mildred stood as well and smiled warmly. "I'd better go to the front door too. She is a dear, but she tends to…well, muss things up sometimes. I'll be right back." Mildred left the room as well.

Penny leaned over to Grandpa Dick grabbing his wrist. "Are you holding up okay?" she asked him.

"Surprisingly, yes," he affirmed patting her hand. "Good enough to have a nice meal anyway."

"Good. Just checking."

"Thank you, Sweet Pea."

Chapter 4

Mildred walked back in, accompanied by a beautiful woman. She had long, auburn hair that hung down to her waist, a shapely body and big, green eyes. She was wearing a black pantsuit with a white, frilly blouse and black, high heel shoes.

"Everyone," Mildred said, reaching up to place her left hand on the back of the woman's right shoulder, "I want you to meet Sabrina...oh, uh, I'm sorry dear, but what did you say your last name was again?"

Sabrina turned to look at Mildred. "Riggs".

Mildred smiled and nodded. "Oh yes! Sabrina Riggs. She is also just passing through on her way to the coast."

After Mildred commenced with the introductions, Sabrina took the last remaining seat next to Aaron while Alexis prepared another place setting.

"So what is it you do, Sabrina?" Mildred asked finding her seat again.

"I'm a free lance photographer, you could say," she said with a small flick of her hair. "I take pictures of just about whatever captures my fancy and sell them to the highest bidder."

"Oh, that sounds like a lovely job!" Mildred smiled.

"Would you mind very much taking a few professional grade pictures of my wife and me sometime?" Sam asked. "We're newlyweds on honeymoon. It would be nice to have something to remember this place by. We'd be happy to pay for them."

Sabrina briskly smiled and replied in a curt manner, "Sure. Why not."

Gwen smiled and hugged Sam close as he leaned back into his chair.

Edna reappeared through the swinging door and remained in front of it, holding it open for someone behind her. "Well, come along Felix! We don't have all night to wait on you. Dinner is late as it is!" she urged. Turning to everyone seated at the table, she smiled in frustration. "I'm so sorry for the tardiness of this evening's dinner."

They all sat and watched as a crotchety old man slowly made his way through the doorway pushing a metal cart before him which held a large tray containing serving pots and platters. He wore large, round, silver rimmed glasses that rested on a huge nose. He was bald except for the sides which he had let grow out enabling him to comb it over the top of his head. As he walked forward, he was slightly stooped over, stepping deliberately. Upon closer inspection, they discovered that he wasn't pushing a metal cart at all, but rather a metal walker on wheels that he had placed the tray on top of.

"Everybody," Edna announced, "this is our cook, Felix Stiffman. He's been with us since, well, pretty much since the beginning."

"Hello, Felix," Penny offered.

Felix continued on without acknowledging her.

"Felix," Edna called to him, but he didn't seem to hear. "Felix! FELIX!"

"What?" Felix exclaimed turning to look at Edna.

"Penny over there said hello to you! It would be nice if you said hello back to her, wouldn't you agree?" Edna prompted.

"Well, of course she did!" Felix snapped back. "I heard her. You don't have to yell at me. I'm not deef you know!" Edna let out a gasp of frustration and sat back down in her chair.

Felix looked over at Gwen, who was holding her husband's arm close to her, and smiled. "Good evening, Penny. I hope you enjoy tonight's dinner. It's an old family recipe passed down through the generations."

"I...I'm not Penny," Gwen stuttered lifting her arm to point at Penny who looked just as confused as she was. "She is."

Felix continued smiling at Gwen. "Oh, don't worry, sweetheart. I'll meet her too in a moment. So Penny, I hope you're hungry tonight." Felix opened two of his serving trays. In one was steaming white rice and in the other, chopped beef in delicious smelling brown gravy.

"Felix!" Edna shouted. "That is not Penny. That is Gwen! Penny is over here."

"Well of course that's not Penny!" Felix burst out turning red. "I know who Penny is! I'm not senile! Not yet anyway. But if you keep yelling at me, who knows!"

As Edna bit her lip fuming, Mildred omitted a little giggle. "You'll have to excuse these two. Deep down they are both really very sweet."

A small laugh of relief was shared by everyone at the table while Felix slowly worked his way around, serving dinner. After everyone had been served, he placed the platters on the chest of drawers.

"I'll leave these out here if any of you would like to have seconds," Felix informed them. "Meanwhile, I'll go and get dessert ready." Felix pulled a smoking pipe out of his pocket and began to bang it against a metal bar on his walker. He continued banging it as he slowly wheeled back around to the swinging door and then disappeared on the other side. They could hear the banging fade away the further he got. Alexis came through the door carrying another tray holding bowls of salad. She made sure everybody got one and then tucking the empty tray under her arm, she went back through the door.

"Well!" Edna huffed. "Now that the circus is over, maybe we could say grace." She bowed her head with her hands clasped before her. Everyone else followed her example and closed their eyes. "Thank you, Lord, for this wonderful feast we are about to enjoy," Edna began. "Help us that it may strengthen and nourish us. Watch over us and protect us that we may pass through the evening in peace and safety to see another day. We pray that you bless Richard, Penny, Aaron, Sabrina, Samuel, Gwen, James, his son Charles, Mildred, Alexis and even that old, ornery coot Felix, even though he should have kicked the bucket years ago to be in heaven with you. Unless, of course, his calling is to a much more southernly region, which wouldn't surprise *me* in the least. In the name of your son we pray, Amen."

Everyone else said their 'Amen' and began eating.

"Wow!" Jim spoke up. "This is delicious!"

"It sure is," Sam agreed.

"Despite his many faults, Felix *is* an excellent cook," Edna replied. "He's been the house cook ever since Mildred and I were teenage girls. He was a good friend of our father's, you see."

"He's the best cook in Pleasant Lake," Mildred contributed. "We wouldn't ever dare think of replacing him."

"As much as I sometimes think it would be better, I have to concur with my sister. He'd be hard to replace," Edna said.

Charlie quickly cleaned off his plate and then turned to his father. "Is it okay if I have some more?"

"Maybe it would be better if you waited until the adults have had a chance to get seconds first, Charlie," he suggested.

"Don't be silly! You go right ahead young man and help yourself. There's plenty for everybody," Mildred advised.

Charlie smiled and looked back up to his father. Jim nodded and patted him on the back. "Go ahead, son."

As Charlie walked over and served up some more beef and rice, Edna directed her attention to Sabrina who was quietly eating her dinner.

"In the confusion, I was only able to get your name, dear," Edna said.

It took a minute for Sabrina to realize that Edna was talking to her at which point she stopped and looked up. "Oh!" she exclaimed, still with a mouthful of food. She put up her hand as she hurriedly chewed and swallowed it. "I'm sorry," Sabrina said, finally washing it down with some water. "I'm Sabrina Riggs. I'm just passing through on my way to a photo shoot. That's what I do; I'm a photographer."

"She sells her photos to the highest bidder," Mildred proffered.

"Essentially, yes," Sabrina added. "I basically work for myself. However, I have built up a regular clientele over the last few years."

"What do you photograph, Sabrina?" Edna asked with interest.

"Just about anything really. Landscapes, families, models, disasters. Whatever a situation may call for."

"Have you ever done any undercover work?" Charlie interjected excitedly. "Like for the police or a private investigator?"

Sabrina hesitated a moment. "On occasion, yes, I have," she replied with a hint of nervousness. She glanced quickly over to Aaron and then back down to her plate. "You know, that *was* delicious. I think I'll have some more of that myself."

"Help yourself, dear," Mildred encouraged.

Everyone had just about cleared their plates when they heard a banging noise beyond the swinging door. A moment later, Felix reappeared with another tray resting on top of his walker holding small glass goblets of pudding. He was still intermittently banging his pipe against the walker.

"Dessert is served," he announced.

"Will you please stop that infernal banging!" Edna more stated than asked.

Felix stopped and looked at Edna. "I only do it so I don't have to listen to your clamoring!" Felix reached down and hit his pipe against the walker with one sharp bang.

"What kind of pudding is that?" Sam leaned forward in anticipation.

Felix turned his attention back to the guests. "Who said that?"

Sam raised his hand.

"Tapioca pudding, my boy," Felix answered and once more slowly circled the table serving everyone a goblet.

"This is quite good!" Sam said after his first spoonful.

"Very interesting," Sabrina reacted after sampling the pudding. "I've never tasted tapioca pudding like this before. It's bold and different. What is this black and gray seasoning you've sprinkled on top here? Is it some type of pepper?"

"Black and gray seasoning, miss?" Felix asked.

"Yes, right on top here," Sabrina showed him scooping some out with her spoon and then placing it in her mouth. She savored the flavor for a second and then swallowed.

Felix thought a minute and then looked down at his smoking pipe. Hastily, he placed the pipe into the front pocket of his shirt and made his way back over to the swinging door. "It's an old family secret," he said moving about as fast as an old man with a walker could. "Goodnight everyone." Sabrina's face turned a shade of green and she excused herself from the table asking for the nearest bathroom. Everyone else quickly inspected their own tapioca pudding.

"So, Richard," Jim said after everyone began to settle down. "We never got to hear what it is that you do for a living."

"I was the Chief Executive Officer of MicaTek, but I'm retired now," Grandpa Dick replied.

Sabrina rejoined them looking a bit better.

"Wait a minute," Sam interjected. "MicaTek, the computer company?"

"The very same."

"You were the big man on campus, the CEO?" Sam continued obviously very impressed.

Grandpa Dick nodded without saying a word.

"Wasn't there a scandal associated with that company?" Jim queried, leaning forward. "Something…something about misappropriated funds?"

"That's right!" Sam sat upright. "It was all over the news about how an executive stole thousands of dollars from the company and they were forced to close their doors because of it."

Everyone looked at Grandpa Dick with renewed interest. Grandpa Dick, now on the hot seat, let out a light laugh and looked at each of them in earnest. "Yes, that's true, but it wasn't me. I swear I had nothing to do with that."

"But, it's possible that you know who *did* have something to do with it," Aaron said.

"No," Grandpa Dick replied. "We never were able to find out who did it. The money was never found."

"Yes, it's true," Penny said in defense of her grandfather. "They investigated the case thoroughly, but they were never able to pin it to anybody. Whoever took the money got away with it. And the company went out of business, putting good, hardworking men like my grandfather out of a job."

"How much money are we talking about here anyway?" Sam asked.

"Just over $750,000 was embezzled. It's still unaccounted for to this day," Aaron contributed. "I read the newspapers too."

Grandpa Dick turned to see everyone's eyes focused in on him.

"Honestly," he said. "I didn't do it."

"Oh this is just ridiculous!" Mildred said, breaking the uncomfortable silence. She stood up and clapped her hands with a bright smile. "Why don't we all adjourn to the living area?"

"That's an excellent idea," Edna agreed also standing. "I'll have coffee and tea brought out."

"Can I watch TV?" Charlie said moving his chair back.

"Television?" Mildred giggled. "I'm sorry, dear, but we don't have a television here."

Charlie looked crestfallen. "No *TV*?"

"There are books, games and puzzles available in the living area, young man. Those are much more constructive to a growing mind such as yours than the boob tube," Edna replied with distaste.

"Come on, it's okay," Jim prompted his son. "We can play a game." Placing his hand upon his son's shoulder, he directed him out of the room towards the living area.

As everyone else began to filter out, Grandpa Dick approached Mildred. "Thank you for dinner. It was very good. I was wondering if Penny and I could be directed to our room. I'm not feeling so well, and would like to lie down."

"Certainly, dear," Mildred replied. "I'll have Alexis come out and help you up with your luggage. She'll know which room is yours if you don't mind waiting for just a minute."

"That will be fine."

Mildred turned to fetch Alexis while Edna conducted everyone else to the living area. After the dining room had cleared, Penny looked at Grandpa Dick with deep concern.

"They all think that *you* took the money, Grandpa!" she exclaimed.

Grandpa Dick smiled. "So what else is new?"

"But you are innocent!"

"It's okay. It's okay, Sweet Pea. When you think about it, that really is nothing compared to other issues right now," Grandpa Dick said with a ragged cough. "All I want to do is rest and get ready for tomorrow's drive. If we leave early, we should be able make it to Portland before Dr. Wright's office closes."

Penny leaned over and hugged Grandpa Dick close. "I hope we aren't too late."

Grandpa Dick held her close. "Me too," he said disparagingly. "You know, you're all I have in this world. I don't know what I'd do without you."

"I love you, Grandpa."

"I love you too, Sweet Pea."

Chapter 5

While everyone else retired to the living area, Jim Frank and his son, Charlie decided to go outside for an evening walk instead. As they walked out the back door, Charlie opened his mouth to say something, but his father placed a finger to his lips with a shushing motion. "Not yet, son. Not yet. Wait until we're farther away," Jim said, quietly walking down the back porch steps. Jim placed his hand on Charlie's back and guided him through the lawn and down to the water's edge. Jim's breaths were coming fast and hard, his eyes beginning to well up with tears. Finally, when Jim felt they were far enough away to be out of sight of the house, he fell to his knees and cried. Charlie looked at his father not knowing why he cried, or what to say.

"Dad?" Charlie mustered up the courage to say.

Jim looked up at his son, tears streaming down his face.

"Dad? What's wrong?"

Jim wiped the tears from his cheekbones and gestured for Charlie to sit down next to him. Charlie did so, his curiosity peaked. He'd never seen his father cry like this before except for one time. That was the night his mother died. Jim gazed out over the lake, watching as the moonlight shimmered across its surface in the cool breeze.

"Regina," Jim said at last, looking brokenheartedly at the water. Charlie lowered his head. Regina was his mother's name. So he was thinking of her after all. "When you made us promise to bring you here," Jim continued, "I had no idea that we'd be sharing a dinner with your murderer."

"Dad?" Charlie said a bit forcefully this time. He was more than just a little worried by this point.

Jim reached over and hugged his son close to him. "I'm sorry, Charlie, I don't mean to frighten you. There are just a few things you don't know about yet," Jim said after a while, wiping his eyes clear again. "It appears I need to trust you with something."

Charlie nodded. "Okay Dad."

Jim took a moment to gather his thoughts, then he positioned his body so that he sat facing his son. "What I'm about to tell you is to remain between us. I want your solemn promise on that."

"I promise."

"You're almost 13 years old now. So I'll trust you," Jim agreed. "Here's the story."

"About two years ago, when you'd just turned eleven, I received a big promotion where I worked. I was moved from the manufacturing floor into management where all the testing of our final product was done before it was sent on to our packaging department. Along with this promotion came a nice raise and an excellent benefits package. However, as you already know son, it couldn't have come at a better time, because shortly thereafter, your mother was diagnosed with breast cancer.

"Fortunately for us, we now had excellent medical coverage. We were doubly fortunate, because the insurance company held up our claim that this was not a 'pre-existing' condition, therefore, we received full coverage. This was extremely beneficial to us as she was able to receive all the treatments and tests that she needed for us to counter her cancer. Despite the good coverage, however, times were still pretty tight, even with my raise, because as time wore on, your mother began to get very sick. To the point in fact, that she had to quit her job and focus all of her efforts in battling her disease. It soon became obvious that her treatments were not working and she would need to have surgery. We were confident though, that this would be successful and that your mother would be able to make a full recovery.

"The week that your mother was to go into surgery, it was reported that the company I worked for, MicaTek, was under investigation for illegal activities, in particular money embezzlement. And we are talking about thousands and thousands of dollars. The investigation was headed up by the IRS, but the FBI was also an interested party. So whatever it was, it was big. However, the guilty party had used a dummy corporation and an alias so effectively, that they were not able to trace it down to its origin. Within two days, the government was there shutting down the entire company. All manufacturing buildings, corporate offices, testing facilities, human resources, management, warehouses...everything was completely closed down. We all showed up to find chains on the doors. Therefore, all salaries were frozen, paychecks were not issued and benefits were stopped.

"The very next day, your mother went into surgery. When the surgeons opened her up, they discovered that the cancer had spread much further and was much worse than they initially thought. They did what they could for her, but in the end, it was just too late. It now had become a matter of time. While your mother was languishing away on her deathbed, the crook who embezzled what was figured to be about $750,000 was getting away with it. In the meantime, we had bills stacking up left and right, no longer able to afford decent medication and treatment for your mother. The insurance company refused to pay for the operation because, as they put it, as of the day of MicaTek's closing, we were no longer eligible to receive benefits. It was the difference of one day. Just *one* day.

"That's when we were informed of a new surgical process for your mother's type of cancer that might give her a chance. It was still considered to be an experimental process, and there were only a couple of specialists in the whole country who would even dare to attempt it. I became desperate. I did whatever I could do to get the needed help. I applied for financial aid using every avenue I knew of. I pleaded with family and friends, anybody to help us. But as you well know, we do not come from a wealthy family and I had to come to the hard realization that it just was not meant to be.

"The months that followed were next to unbearable. I know I don't have to tell you about that son. You were there. You saw how horrible things got for your mother just before her death.

"One night after you had gone to sleep, during one of the last coherent moments of her life, your mother made me promise her two things. The first was that I let her go and to focus my efforts on raising you. Helping you to cope and move on with your life that you may grow up to be a fine man, a man she would be proud of. Like the son she was already proud of. The second thing she made me promise was that after she died, that we would have her cremated. Then she wanted us to bring her here to Pleasant Lake together and scatter her ashes over its waters. You see, Pleasant Lake was a very special place for your mother growing up. There were many times while she was sick that she thought of coming here again. Of the summers she had spent here.

"That's why we're here Charlie. I know I told you we were going on a fishing trip, but I had two reasons for lying to you, and I hope you do forgive me this lie.

I knew if I told you the real reason we were coming here, it would be hard on you. I honestly didn't know if you'd be able to make such a trip. I didn't know if you could hold up under that kind of commitment at your age. Secondly, since your mother had spent considerable time here during her youth, I didn't want to be the bearer of bad news to the locals about her death. I felt it was better to come here, keep our promise and then move on with our lives. Your mother knew Edna and Mildred Pookotz, in fact, and they knew her. She always spoke kindly of them. I didn't have the heart to tell them of her passing.

"Everything was going okay until tonight. It seems that the god of chance has played a very cruel joke on us, for I believe that Richard was the very man who embezzled all of that money, Charlie. Why we were destined to be here together on this very same night I have no idea. But I can never forgive him for her death. I *will* never forgive him for her death. At a time when Regina most needed compassion and love, he was satisfying his greed with no thought for anybody else but himself."

Jim stopped and looked down at his son. Charlie was silently crying. Jim reached over with affection and squeezed his son's shoulder. "I'm sorry you had to find out like this. About your mother, I mean. I'd planned on waiting until you were a little older before we had this talk."

"It's okay, Dad," Charlie sniffed. "I miss Mom. I miss her *so* much!"

"I do too. Every day I miss her."

Charlie moved next to his father and let the floodgates open wide. Jim held his son while he let it all out. He gave him all the time he needed. Finally, Charlie sat up and wiped his eyes.

"So Mom's ashes are in the car?" he said at last.

"Yes."

"Dad?"

"Yes, son."

"Why are you convinced it was Richard who stole the money?" Charlie asked. "You said yourself they were never able to track him down."

"Out of all the executives who were suspected, he was the only one who didn't consent to a polygraph test," Jim replied.

"What's a polygraph test?"

"It's a lie detector test," Jim answered. "And they couldn't force him to take one. He had to volunteer. Which he didn't. The others did, and they passed it and cleared their names. It's believed by many, me included, that Richard Forester embezzled the money. But you can't convict someone of a crime simply because you think he did it. They needed concrete evidence or proof. They were never able to get any."

"Did you recognize him? Richard, I mean, tonight at dinner?" Charlie continued.

"Not at first," Jim said. "He was the last person I ever expected to run into. While I worked at MicaTek, I'd seen him in a few employee videos and his picture was up on the website. But tonight, he didn't look quite the same. In fact, I think he may be sick. He didn't look well at all. I began to suspect it might be him though about the time dessert was served."

"Why didn't you say anything?"

"I almost did. I wanted to. To be truthful, I wanted to rip his face off."

"Dad!" Charlie exclaimed, surprised to hear his father talk like that.

"Sorry son," Jim said with a certain measure of humility. "You know I'm not a violent man."

"He seemed like a nice person," Charlie said, reflecting on the dinner. "His granddaughter Penny, she seemed really nice too."

Jim laughed. "Well, son, there's one thing you're going to find out as you get older."

"What's that?"

"The quiet and nice people are usually the ones who do the worst things to others. You'll see."

Charlie nodded.

"Promise me, Charlie. Promise me that what we talked about tonight stays between us, ok?" Jim looked imploringly at his son. "As far as anybody else is concerned, we're here to fish. That's it. Tomorrow, you and I will head out early and scatter your mother's ashes over the lake. On the other side, so they won't see."

"I promise, Dad. You can count on me."

"I know I can," Jim said hugging his son close. "Besides, it's better that we don't bring any unnecessary attention to ourselves right now anyway."

"Why?"

"Because, as you'll also find out as you get older," Jim said with certainty, "whatever goes around comes around. I believe that with all my heart."

Chapter 6

Aaron Buchanon put a cigarette between his lips and brought his lighter up to ignite it. Taking a long draw, he leaned against the post at the top of the steps and blew out a large cloud of smoke. He snapped the lighter closed and let it slide back down inside his front pants pocket, listening to the sounds of the insects buzzing busily in the moonlight. After taking another puff, he slowly made his way down the steps and walked across the front lawn to a bed of flowers where he stopped and looked down. It was obvious that somebody had put a lot of time and effort into keeping up the grounds here. Everything was perfectly hedged and trimmed, the flowers themselves were expertly tended and in full bloom. He kneeled down next to a particularly beautiful pink one and rested his rear on his heels. *How remarkable*, he thought to himself as he blew a dark stream of smoke on the flower's petals.

A noise to his right made him look up. He quickly surveyed the lawn next to the house up to the point where it ended against a pathway lined with round rocks on both sides. He followed the pathway with his eyes and found it led to another smaller building, a shed perhaps? He slowly stood back up and walked forward using his peripherals while keeping his eyes open to everything in front of him. But he saw nothing. He could not imagine what it was that he heard.

He shrugged and was about to turn back towards the front porch when he heard it again. This time it was much louder and clearer. It sounded like a branch snapping in half. He stealthily whirled around in the direction of the sound. It was coming from the smaller building, or next to it. With squinted eyes, he tried to peer deeper into the darkness surrounding it. But still he saw nothing. He took one last drag from his cigarette and flicked it aside. Enough of this. He was going to find out what it was.

Aaron moved forward at a determined gait, and quickly made his way to the front of the building. There was nothing there. He strode over to the right corner and looked around it into the brush next to the side wall. A loud 'crack!' only a few feet in front of him made him freeze in his tracks.

"Who's back there?" he said leaning forward cautiously. Something like the sound of breathing began to grow steadily louder. Aaron could feel his skin crawl. He decided he didn't want to know what he'd heard after all and began to turn away. With sudden alacrity, two pale hands thrust forward out of the shrubs for him, snatching at his sleeves and pulling him face first into the bushes. Before he could yell out in alarm, a hand covered his mouth and pulled him quickly down to the ground. Aaron pushed and kicked in desperation and tried to scramble away, his eyes wide with fear.

"Aaron! Stop!" a hushed voice said next to him. "It's just me."

Aaron stopped and turned to find Sabrina hunched down in the darkness against the side wall. Relief washing over his face, he slumped with his back against the wall and let out a big breath.

"What the hell, Sabrina? Are you trying to kill me or what?" Aaron breathed. "You scared the living tar out of me!"

Sabrina giggled. "Yah, you should have seen your face. A big, tough FBI man soiling his $100 pair of underwear. Priceless."

"I'm glad I'm here to amuse you, Sabrina," Aaron replied, regaining his composure. "What are you doing here anyway?"

"What am *I* doing here?" Sabrina returned. "What are *you* doing here? I thought we were overlapping each other to avoid detection, and I arrive to find you sitting at the dinner table right *next* to him no less!"

Aaron spun around to face Sabrina. "I thought they were going to stop at the motel tonight. I honestly didn't think they were going to go to this little out-of-the-way Bed & Breakfast. If I'd have had *any* inkling that they were coming here, believe me, I wouldn't have," he said, exasperated. Aaron took a deep breath and calmed himself. "Now. What are you doing here? Surely you must have realized that allowing yourself to get this close to him, your cover would be blown. If he were to see and recognize you later on, he'd know he was being followed. Why didn't you check into the motel?"

"Because I didn't want to lose him," Sabrina answered defensively. "How am I supposed to keep an eye on him from a motel a mile away? And whoever uses the word *inkling* anyway?"

"Then you park in the trees and sleep in the car."

"In the cold?" Sabrina countered. "I don't think so. Besides, he still doesn't know what you look like... ohhhhhh crap."

"I was sitting right next to him, remember?" Aaron reminded her. "We're completely blown now. A hell of a good job!"

Both Aaron and Sabrina turned with their backs against the boarded wall and grew silent. The crickets chirped, the insects buzzed, the woods creaked, and the breeze fanned the leaves in the branches of the trees.

"Now what?" Sabrina finally asked breaking the silence between them.

"I'm thinking."

"I'm sorry, Aaron. I should have slept in the car."

"What's done is done. Give me a minute. I need to think," Aaron muttered. "One thing is certain though."

"Tell me."

"We're going to have to make our move tonight, or early in the morning before anybody else wakes up," Aaron replied.

"Are we even sure he has the money, Aaron?" Sabrina asked turning to face him once more. "Because if he doesn't and we make our move, we could get into a *lot* of trouble."

Aaron looked over at Sabrina with stone cold eyes. "He's the one, Sabrina. He *knows* where the money…" Aaron suddenly stopped and put a finger to his lips. "Somebody's coming," he whispered.

Aaron and Sabrina hugged the wall with their backs and kept low, trying to peer over to the pathway. There was indeed someone making their way up the pathway, very slowly. After a little while, they saw it was Felix ambling along pushing his metal walker before him, step by agonizingly slow step. Felix was muttering something to himself as he approached the building. It wasn't until he was but a few feet away that they were able to make out what he was saying.

"That's not Penny says she. I know who Penny is. If I know who Edna is and I know who Mildred is, then I *know* who Penny is. Consarn it all," Felix was mumbling to himself. "Why couldn't Edna have ended up with the black and gray seasoning anyway? Heh heh heh heh!" Sabrina felt her stomach lurch at the memory of the tapioca pudding and she had to stifle a gasp.

Felix continued forward until he was standing right next to the corner with his back to them. He stopped and leaned forward on his walker. "I should have made Penny pull my finger while Edna was behind me. Heh

heh heh heh! That would've shut her yappy mouth. Would have served her right too. I know who Penny is. I *know* who Penny is."

Aaron looked over to Sabrina and mouthed the words "what the heck?" Sabrina smiled and put her hand over her mouth. Then she made a circular motion with her index finger around her ear and mouthed back the word "crazy."

"Pull my finger," Felix began again. He leaned further over the walker until his backside was poking up slightly into the air. "Don't mind if I do."

Suddenly, Felix let out the most incredibly loud fart, breaking the silence around them. "Yah, Edna! Take that one, you old windbag! Heh heh heh heh!" It didn't take long for the sour egg smell to hit Aaron and Sabrina full on, and they quickly turned their heads away, completely repulsed. It was all they could do to keep from making any noise and being discovered.

"Oh, you want another one sweetheart? Heh heh heh heh! Fine by me!" Felix laughed. A second fart, even louder than the first one, reverberated off the wall around them and had Aaron and Sabrina gasping for air.

"How about one more for the road, baby?" Felix added with another laugh and followed it up with yet another one. "Ah. Much better. Maybe you won't question me again next time, will you? Heh heh heh heh! Because Edna? I *know* who Penny is!"

Felix brought his feet back down to the ground and slowly made his way forward to the building's front door, mumbling all the way until he finally made his way inside and closed the door sharply behind him.

"OH MY GOD!" Aaron exclaimed, bursting out of the bushes coughing. Sabrina was right behind him, her eyes stinging. The two of them began running toward the lake fanning the air around them with their hands.

Chapter 7

The newlyweds followed Edna into the living area holding each other close. Sam leaned over to his wife and kissed her tenderly on the lips much to her liking as she blushed deeply.

"There will be plenty of time for that later, you two," Edna said, interrupting the moment. "And while we're on the subject, I will thank you to keep your nocturnal activities to a very low volume so that others may sleep peacefully."

"Yes Ma'am," Sam nodded with a smile while Gwen giggled.

"Very well then," Edna replied satisfied. Then stopping, she looked around. "Where did everybody else get to? You're the only two here."

Sam and Gwen looked around them. Nobody else had followed them into the living area. They were alone.

"Looks like we get it all to ourselves," Sam said with a knowing wink to Gwen.

"Just behave yourselves," Edna admonished. "I'm going to go help tidy up the kitchen. I'll have coffee brought out if you would like."

"Well, actually, Miss Pookotz," Gwen responded, "neither one of us are particularly big on coffee. Do you have anything with a little more kick?"

"Goodness gracious, child!" Edna exclaimed looking sternly at her. "How old are you?"

"I'm 19," Gwen answered.

"Just because you are a married woman now does not mean you have the right to drink alcoholic beverages. There is still the state law to consider. We could lose our license if we let you two carry on so. Is that understood?" Edna asked placing her hands on her hips.

"Understood," Sam said.

"I mean it. No alcohol."

"Yes, Ma'am," Gwen and Sam echoed.

With a small huff, Edna briskly walked past them leaving them alone.

"I mean it! No alcohol!" Sam mimicked in a funny voice. Gwen laughed and swung herself around to face him still holding both of his hands in hers. Sam went to pull her close to him, but she pulled away waving a finger in front of her.

"No, no, no," Gwen warned. "We are to behave ourselves in here."

"Oh come on. Just one, little kiss?" Sam begged.

"Nuh uh," Gwen devilishly smiled and began to twirl around the room.

Sam groaned as he watched her spin around with her arms extended. He smiled to himself. "I'm the luckiest man alive," he said. On impulse, he stepped forward and grabbed her by the waist pulling and holding her body next to his. Before she could react, he kissed her deeply until she completely surrendered to his will.

"Oh, you bad boy," Gwen whispered when they finally came back up for air. Sam kissed her again. "Later, lover," Gwen said slowly backing away. "Let's find a game to play."

Sam laughed. "You already know what game I want to play."

"I know," Gwen smiled. "But I want to play a board game. Help me find one." Gwen turned and looked around the room. Reluctantly, Sam did as he was asked.

The living area was a large room with a long, green and gold sofa and matching loveseat. Opposite the sofa and loveseat was a plush recliner. There were end tables next to each of these with lamps bearing brown lampshades. There were a couple of small wooden tables with chairs on either side on both sides of the room. A huge, round throw rug was strategically placed in the center of the room that the furniture sat on. The rest of the floor was polished wood. Beautiful landscape paintings adorned the walls. Along the north wall was a large, built-in shelf containing all sorts of books, both hard cover and paperback. Just to the right of the shelf, on the adjacent wall, was an antique wood stove where a fire was already burning, keeping the room warm. Continuing right, on the other side of a picture glass window was a cabinet with wooden doors and brass handles.

Gwen walked over to the cabinet and opened both doors at the same time. Various board games, puzzles and decks of cards were stacked on shelves inside.

"I found them," Gwen announced, beginning to sort through the boxes. Sam walked up behind her and peered over her shoulder. "Let's see here," Gwen continued. "We have Parcheesi, Checkers, Chess, Scrabble, Backgammon, Yahtze…it's Grandma's and Grandpa's collection. Wait! They have a Monopoly board. That'll do."

"You know I suck at Monopoly," Sam said.

Gwen pulled the game from the cabinet and turned to face him. "I know," she replied with a small peck on his cheek, "but we're playing it anyway. Come on." Gwen walked over to the nearest table and pulled up a chair already opening the game and emptying its contents. Sam walked over, sat down opposite her and leaned back in his chair.

"Do you think he did it?" Sam asked after a moment.

"Do I think *who* did *what*?" Gwen answered without looking up.

"Richard. Do you think he stole all that money?" Sam clarified, sitting up.

"What piece do you want?"

"The shoe," Sam answered. "Well? Do you?"

"Who's Richard?" Gwen asked looking up.

"You know, Richard! From dinner tonight. The old man with his granddaughter?" Sam pressed. "He said he was with MicaTek. Seven hundred and fifty thousand dollars? Any of this ringing a bell?"

Gwen rolled her eyes. "You don't have to treat me like I'm an idiot. I remember him at dinner, yes."

"I think he did it," Sam stated. "I think he stole that money, and now he's here to get it."

"Really?" Gwen put down the stack of Community Chest cards and looked at Sam intently. "Why do you think he's here for the money?"

Sam was about to reply when he heard footsteps approaching. They both turned to see Alexis walk by the doorway and towards the parlor.

Sam leaned over and whispered. "Let's go outside. Besides, I need a drink." Gwen nodded in agreement.

They both stood and walked over to the front door and then out onto the front porch beyond. Gwen grabbed Sam's hand from behind and they crossed over the front steps and down to the pathway. They saw a quick movement to their left and observed Aaron Buchanon kneeling before some flowers. Without a word, Sam signaled towards the cars with a single movement of his head. Gwen nodded in agreement. The two quickly and quietly made their way down the path to the gate and then into the parking lot.

"So tell me!" Gwen persisted once they had reached their car.

"Well," Sam excitedly whispered while unlocking the passenger side door, "I think Richard is not a well man. Did you get a good look at him during dinner?"

"No, why?"

"He was as pale as a ghost," Sam replied opening the door. He rummaged through some items on the front seat and then emerged with a bottle of Jack Daniels. "Ah! Here we go."

"So you think he's sick?"

"Very sick. He had the look of someone on their last leg, if you know what I mean," Sam continued taking a swig of the whiskey. "Oh yeah. I needed that. Want some?"

"Yeah." Gwen took the bottle from him and downed a healthy mouthful. "So? Go on, go on!"

"My guess is," Sam said, taking the bottle back from Gwen, "that he's hidden the money up here somewhere and he's come to get it before he croaks."

"To give to Penny?"

"Who else? Better to keep it in the family if you can't use it yourself, right?" Sam said taking another swallow.

"I don't know," Gwen sat down on the front seat of the car, her feet on the ground. "Wouldn't it be safer to keep the money hidden in a safe or something? That's an awful lot of money to hide in a tree or under a rock."

"Not if he's so sick he's going to die. He'd want to make sure that the money goes to nobody else but Penny. Or whoever he wants it to." Sam handed the bottle down to Gwen who took another drink. "If the money is locked up in a safe, somebody else is going to get it. But if he has it hidden out here, in a place only *he* knows about, it's guaranteed safety."

Gwen thought about it for a minute and then nodded. "Yeah, makes sense to me." She handed the bottle back up to Sam. He took a drink and set the bottle down on the roof of the car. Shoving his hands into his pockets, Sam leaned against the side of the car looking up at the clear sky and the millions of stars above him.

"Sam?"

"Yeah, baby."

"What are we talking about anyway?" Gwen asked.

"I think we should find out where he's stashed the money and take it," Sam responded with finality. "He's going to die anyway, right? And it really wasn't his to begin with. I say we sneak in tonight when Penny isn't around and make him tell us."

"That's assuming a lot, lover," Gwen argued standing up. "That's assuming *if* he's taken the money in the first place, and that he's even sick, *and* that he's hidden it out here. You know what they say about assumption."

"No, what?"

"Assumption is the mother of all screw-ups."

Sam stopped and thought a minute. "No, he's sick alright. It has to be it. It has to be! Nothing else makes sense," Sam said growing more excited by the second. "Just think, Gwen. You and I could take a year long world cruise. Shoot, we could just disappear with money like that! No more shoveling manure or bucking bales of hay on my father's farm. We could live right. We could live like royalty."

"I don't know," Gwen returned. "I have a bad feeling about this. But it would be nice to stop worrying about where our money is coming from." She reached over and snagged the bottle and polished it off, feeling its warmth course through her veins. She closed her eyes for a minute. "Okay," she said.

"Really?" Sam took her hand and squeezed it.

Gwen opened her eyes. "Let's do it."

"Are you sure?" Sam was smiling now.

"Yes. *But*, and this is my BIG but...."

"Mmmm sweetheart," Sam responded reaching around to pinch her backside, "you do *not* have a big butt."

Gwen pulled away in irritation. "Sam, I'm being serious! We either do this my way, or I walk away."

"Okay baby, okay!" Sam settled down. "Go ahead and tell me."

"If we find out anything, anything at all that proves he didn't take the money, we back out. Okay?" Gwen asked, looking Sam right in the eyes.

"Of course!"

"And," Gwen interjected, "we don't hurt him or Penny. If he doesn't tell us, then the game is up and we walk away. I won't have it any other way."

Sam nodded resolutely. "We walk away. Agreed."

"Okay then." Gwen sat back down. "What is the plan? How are we going to do this?"

"Well, we have to get him alone. Penny has to use the bathroom or shower or something before bed, right? So we go in then. One of us will watch at the door while the other gets the information from him," Sam said, his eyes afire with anticipation.

"Okay. But what if Penny walks in on us? What then?"

"We duck out the window."

"The window?" Gwen returned incredulous. "That's three stories up! That's the top floor! Are you crazy?"

Sam was already shaking his head. "When we got here this afternoon, I noticed a terrace runs by that window. All we have to do is slide down the shingles to the terrace and then go around to the other side of the house and go into the window of our room. We're on the top floor too. It would work."

"Maybe," Gwen thought. "We'd have to move fast. Sounds dangerous."

"This whole thing is dangerous, baby. But just think of all that money. I want my wife to have a good life with nice things," Sam countered.

Gwen smiled with the thought and then stood up to face her husband. Walking up to him, she draped her leg over his and pressed her body hard against him. They wrapped their arms around each other and kissed deeply.

"Let's get into the back of the car," Gwen whispered into his ear. "I want you. I want you now."

Chapter 8

Edna entered the kitchen to find nobody there and the dirty dishes from dinner piled up rather precariously by the sink. With a small exhale of frustration, she walked over, rolled up her sleeves, placed the stopper inside the drain and started the faucet running. Just as she was submerging the last dirtied plate into the soapy water, Mildred walked in.

"Why do you go to all this trouble? We have a perfectly fine dishwasher right here that you can use, Edna," Mildred pointed out with a soft giggle.

"I *never* use that dishwasher, you know that. It doesn't clean the crystal or the silver right," Edna replied glancing over her shoulder. "I've tried brand after brand after brand of dishwasher soap and every single one of them leaves either spots or a film on the surface. These dishes always come out cleaner if they are just hand washed."

"Well, let me help you then," Mildred offered, accepting a scrubbed plate from Edna and rinsing it off.

"Where did Felix get off to anyway?" Edna asked. "It seems he no longer feels it necessary to clean up after himself anymore. Although it's probably just as well with as good a job he does in cleaning."

"He was heading out to his quarters mumbling something to himself last I saw," Mildred responded taking another plate from her sister.

"Mumbling, bumbling, and grumbling, or any other possible word that ends with 'umbling'," Edna huffed. "That's Felix for you."

"Even humbling?" Mildred offered.

Edna paused for a second. "Okay. *Almost* any other word that ends with 'umbling' then."

Mildred giggled. "Oh, he's harmless."

"Yes, until he accidentally poisons one of our guests and kills them with his pipe tobacco," Edna laughed.

"You know, I think he fancies you."

Edna stopped and looked at Mildred like she'd gone insane. "You can't be serious! Felix and I are like cats and dogs. We just don't mix."

"Opposites attract," Mildred winked.

Edna turned back to her dishes. "You know, Mildred, I always thought I'd be the first one to go senile. But now I'm beginning to wonder."

The two worked together in silence for a little while. Edna finished cleaning the last utensil and began to drain the sink of its water when she turned to face her younger sister again.

"So, did Alexis help Richard and Penny up to their room?" she asked.

"Oh yes," Mildred replied setting her drying towel aside. "They should be settled in by now."

"I wish Alexis would take her responsibilities around here a bit more seriously."

"She's still young, Edna. Don't you remember how we used to be when we were her age?" Mildred countered with a smile.

Edna stopped for a moment and looked down. After a minute she looked back up. "No. Not really."

Mildred laughed. "Well, it was much the same. Dreams and aspirations filling our hearts and heads, keeping us preoccupied when we were supposed to be doing our chores."

"That was *you,* my dear sister," Edna replied with a raised eyebrow. "While you were off skipping through the woods with your head in the clouds, I was here keeping everything in order, helping Mom and Dad run the bed and breakfast."

Mildred laughed again. "Perhaps."

"Perhaps!" Edna was on the soapbox now. "Perhaps nothing! Who was it that used to always leave the aviary door open after the morning feeding? It's a wonder the birds never flew off."

"Me."

"And who accidentally filled the sugar jars with salt and nearly had all of our guests throwing up at breakfast one morning?" Edna continued.

"Oh yes," Mildred smiled. "I'd forgotten about that one."

"Not to mention," Edna pressed, "the time that you recommended the Schwartz family take a canoe out on the lake. The only problem was that the canoe had holes in the bottom of it and within minutes they were floundering around in the water like bacon in a frying pan."

Mildred laughed out loud at the memory of the Schwartz family walking back ashore completely soaked to the bone. Despite herself, Edna began to laugh with her.

"Yes, okay you've made your point," Mildred agreed.

Edna reached over and gave her sister a hug. "It's a good thing I still love you enough to tolerate you. Or I should have recommended you for a private school somewhere on the east coast."

Edna and Mildred made sure that all the plates, glasses and silverware were properly stored, and wiped off all the counters. Mildred thought back on the dinner and turned to look at Edna.

"What an interesting group of people," Mildred commented.

"Yes indeed," Edna nodded, "and not an honest one among them."

"Edna?" Mildred questioned looking at her curiously.

"Well," Edna began, "we have an overly forthright yet obnoxious newlywed couple who I'm certain are just brimming with secrets. A father and son who are going fishing for salmon, only problem is, fishing season doesn't start for another month, and I highly doubt they have a fishing pole between them. Then there's the flashy young insurance salesman who turned down an opportunity to make a sale. Not to mention the quirky photographer who's obviously more than she professes to be. And finally, we have the ex-CEO of a large corporation who was the centerpiece of an IRS investigation into embezzled funds. Yah, we have quite the group of people alright."

"What about Penny, the granddaughter?" Mildred reminded her.

"She's hiding a big secret, something to do with her grandfather," Edna assessed. "Something I've suspected since I met them."

"What could that be?" Mildred asked.

"I have a suspicion that Mr. Forester is not well. Not well at all," Edna confirmed. "I believe he's quite ill. In fact, he's terminal."

Mildred half raised her hand to her mouth in horror. "Oh! The poor dear! Do you really think so? I thought he look extremely pale."

"Yes," Edna responded. "He knows it. His granddaughter also knows it."

"Well," Mildred replied, lowering her hand, "You can't really fault Penny for wanting to keep that a secret. It isn't exactly the type of thing you go around sharing with strangers. Do you remember when old Henry Peabody was walking around town telling everyone about his ingrown toenail? It was bad enough that he was describing his affliction in great detail to the townsfolk, but he was literally scaring away the tourists…showing them his big toenail. It was quite disgusting!"

"Henry Peabody and Mr. Forester are two different people entirely; however, your point is taken," Edna nodded. "But it's been my experience that young teenage girls tend to be quite the chatterboxes, *especially* when it comes to something like this. *Unless…*"

"Unless they've been sworn to secrecy," Mildred finished for her.

Edna firmly nodded in agreement. "Quite right."

"Yes, I suppose something is amiss there. But who are we to pry into their family matter? They are our guests, and as our guests they will be treated as one of our own family members," Mildred said with warmth, in a way that suggested she was content to leave the subject alone.

Edna smiled and took Mildred by the arm. "Of course they will be, little sister. It is, after all, a Pookotz tradition. We're done in here for tonight. Since the hormonal newlyweds are in the living area, what do you say we go and pull up a chair to the fireplace and read a good novel?"

"Oh yes!" Mildred returned the smile. "Let's!"

"Do you know what I adore reading?" Edna asked as they began to walk. "A *good* cozy mystery!"

"I quite agree," Mildred returned.

The two sisters exited the kitchen turning the lights off behind them.

Chapter 9

After Alexis helped Grandpa Dick and Penny up to their third floor bedroom, she made sure they were settled in, giving them her pager number because, as she explained, she was also on call through the night should they require anything. They assured her they would be fine, gave her a tip and thanked her. After Alexis left their room, Penny closed the door and helped her grandfather lay down on the queen-sized mattress.

While Penny unpacked their bags for the night, Grandpa Dick looked around the room. It was exquisite. The window was covered by a thin white, almost see-through curtain with larger, longer, dark blue drapes that hung from a bronze rod up near the ceiling. At each end of the rod, the metal separated and curved away from each other like vines ending in small circles. The entire room was wallpapered in blue with beautifully framed pictures of various flowers and birds, all also the color of blue. On either side of the bed was a tall, wooden nightstand with a small, lacey, handcrafted white and blue cloth on the surface. Each nightstand had matching antique lamps with silver pull chains hanging out of ornate glass enclosures. In the corner of the room stood an old, oak table with a blue cushioned chair on either side of it. Placed squarely in the middle of the table was a copy of the Holy Bible. To its left was another ornate lamp, and to the right, a telephone. In the other corner was a closet where they could hang up their clothes and place their shoes. The bathroom was shared with another room on this floor just down the hallway next to the staircase. It was a warm room. It was peaceful.

"Sweet Pea," Grandpa Dick said.

"Are you okay, Grandpa?" Penny asked.

"Not so good," he replied with a weak smile. "To be honest, I don't know if I'm going to be up to traveling again tomorrow. I just don't think I'm going to be able to handle it." Grandpa Dick's face tightened suddenly as he winced with pain.

"Oh, no," Penny reacted. "The pain is back. Let me get your meds."

"Can't," Grandpa Dick said, resting his head back into his pillow, "My bottle is empty and at the grocery store, remember?"

"But you'll go delirious without your drugs, Grandpa."

"I'll be okay."

"No, you won't," Penny disagreed. "Let me go down and see if anyone has some ibuprofen or something that will help you."

But as Penny turned for the door, Grandpa Dick sat up. "No, Sweet Pea."

"Why not?"

"Because if this is really it, I want to be fully aware of everything around me. I don't want my senses dulled," Grandpa Dick answered, looking appreciatively around the room once more.

Penny rushed back over to his bedside, her face flushed with concern. "What do you mean if this is really it?" she queried with a trembling voice. "Don't *even* talk like that. We're going to get a good night's sleep and then drive to Portland tomorrow to see the specialist, ok?"

Grandpa Dick reached over and patted his granddaughter's hand. "Bless you, Sweet Pea. But I think it's time we faced the facts here." Another sharp pang of pain hit him, causing him to almost double up. He closed his eyes and grimaced, clenching the bedspread in both hands. Penny was beside herself. Her eyes began to water up and her bottom lip quivered.

"Grandpa?" she softly said, wanting to reach out to help him, but afraid that in doing so she'd only cause him more pain.

After a minute, the pain subsided, and Grandpa Dick laid on his side breathing heavily, tears streaming down his cheeks. Penny didn't know what to do or say. All she could do was stand there and try to choke back the urge to cry. Finally, Grandpa Dick turned on his back and looked up at her.

"I'm alright now," he reassured her. "Sit down. There's something I want to talk to you about."

Penny nodded slowly and sat next to her grandfather.

"Stupid cancer. And the doctors are stupid for sending you out like this in your condition!" Penny said. "You should be at home in the comfort of your own bed. Not out here on the road."

"I know," Grandpa Dick replied. "But I only have myself to blame. Your dearly departed grandmother told me years ago to stop smoking, but I never listened. And when this specialist was recommended to me, I had to take the chance even though deep down, I knew better."

"I guess I just don't understand it. Why are we here? This isn't right Grandpa," Penny said. "Even if the specialist could help, he should be coming to you, not the other way around. If this really *is* it, then why take this trip?"

"I know, I know," Grandpa Dick said calmly. "Someday, you'll understand it all, I promise. But there's something else I wanted to talk to you about."

Penny reached a slender hand up to her eyes and wiped the tears away. "Okay, Grandpa."

"We've been through a lot, this family has," he began. "Before you were even born, our family had to endure some rough times. When you were born, your mother passed away, and your father raised you until his death on your seventh birthday. That was when you came to live with your grandmother and me."

"I remember," Penny said. Her father had been killed in a car accident on the very morning of her birthday when he went out to get some last minute items for her party. It was a birthday she would never forget.

"Your grandmother and I did our best to bring you up. You had no other relatives to speak of, so we accepted the responsibility and grew to love you dearly. As if you were our very own daughter. You've grown up to be a beautiful young woman, Penny. I only wish your grandmother were here today to see how lovely you've become," Grandpa Dick continued.

Penny smiled despite herself, though her heart was still heavy.

"Thank you, Grandpa."

"I know this last year has been very hard on you," he started again. "First your grandmother passed on, and then the embezzlement scam investigation started up. When we didn't think things could be worse, I was diagnosed with lung cancer."

Penny felt the tears begin to well up again. "Yes, Grandpa."

"What I wanted to talk to you about is this. After I'm gone, you'll have to rely solely on yourself, Penelope."

Penny looked up. That was the first time she could remember him ever calling her by her real name. He had always called her Sweet Pea or Penny before now.

"You're going to hear some awful things about me," he continued. "Some of it will be true. But I want you to promise me that you'll be strong. That you'll carry on without me, and grow into a fine, strong woman. You've just turned eighteen years old, so legally, you can live out there on your own…as an adult. The world into which you'll be entering can sometimes be a very harsh and cruel one. The secret to living in this world is simple. Do you want to know what that secret is?"

Penny nodded.

"Live up to your *own* potential. Be the best person *you* can be. And never, and I mean *never*, let anyone else tell you that you aren't good enough. Promise me. I want you to say it. I promise."

"I promise, Grandpa."

Grandpa Dick nodded and sank back into his pillow. "Good. I have faith in you Sweet Pea. I know you'll be strong. Capable. I'm very, very proud of you and I love you more than anything in this world."

Penny lowered her head. Finally, she could hold it all in no longer and the tears gushed from her eyes and she wept uncontrollably. She felt her grandfather's hand touch hers.

"Don't cry Sweet Pea," he reassured her. "In a way, I'm glad everything worked out the way it did. I really like it here. Sometimes you don't know why things work out the way they do until it's all said and done."

"I can't help it, Grandpa," Penny cried.

"I know. I don't want you to worry. I've made arrangements for you that will help after I've passed on. I'm not a wealthy man, not any longer. Not since the IRS froze all of my accounts. But I made sure that my little Sweet Pea would be taken care of." She looked over to her grandfather and he winked at her and gave her a small smile.

Then he arched his back in another sudden spasm of pain and began to cough violently. Rolling back on to his side, he brought his knees up into his stomach and cupped his hand over his mouth. The cough was deep and guttural. In a matter of seconds, blood was dripping from his fingers as he fought the urge to cough again. Penny leaped to her feet and ran down to the bathroom and grabbed a towel, bringing it back into the room and to her grandfather. She gave it to him and then sat next to him holding him close. Slowly, she rocked him back and forth against her until the spasm finally stopped and he was lying quietly. His breathing was raspy and deep. His hand relaxed its grip around the towel and he began to sleep. Penny took the towel, wiping the blood from his hands and then checked the bedspread to make sure none had gotten on it. She took his bloodied shirt off as well as his shoes and pants leaving him in his t-shirt and boxer shorts. She moved the covers down past his feet and then back over on top of him. As he rested, she walked over to the window and looked out into the night sky. She had never seen such a beautiful clear sky before.

"I will be strong, Grandpa," she resolved. "I will be capable."

Chapter 10

After leaving Richard Forester and his granddaughter Penny in their room, Alexis hurriedly made her way downstairs and out the back door. She walked along the pathway to her quarters with purpose. In fact, she was so intent on getting to her room that she almost didn't see the two figures standing to her left down by the water. She paused for a minute and looked over in their direction. It was the insurance salesman and the photographer. It wouldn't have struck her as curious, except for the fact that they were very animated in their conversation, and it was obvious that they knew each other. How curious indeed. She silently moved on before they would see her. As she approached the servant's quarters, she could see the light in Felix's room was turned on. He was undoubtedly sitting in his recliner listening to rebroadcasts of his favorite shows from yesteryear on the local radio station. As she passed by his door, she could hear an old episode of "The Shadow" blaring on the other side.

Alexis opened the door to her room and hastily latched it shut behind her. She turned on the corner lamp and strode quickly over to her closet. Opening the door, she snagged a pull chain turning on the light overhead. She stood on her toes as she reached up and started to sift through the papers and boxes piled up on the shelf above her. Her hand came to rest on a cardboard shoe box and she hesitated for a brief moment. Slowly, she pulled the shoe box down off the shelf and brought it over to her bed. She sat down and removed the lid and, taking a deep breath, she extracted a folded newspaper and spread it open over her knees.

"MicaTek CEO Suspected of Embezzling Thousands" read the headline. Alexis peered at the picture on the front page. It showed Richard Forester in a very nice suit, coming down some stone steps in front of a courthouse, reporters all around him. Standing to his right were some MicaTek protesters holding up signs. Alexis squinted and leaned in closer, looking at the faces under the picket signs. She stopped with sudden recognition and her eyes grew wide. It *was* him. She knew she wasn't wrong.

Standing closest to Richard in the photograph holding a sign that read "An Eye for an Eye," was a man she knew. He was there at the dinner table tonight. Alexis smiled and smacked her chewing gum.

Chapter 11

The windows were completely steamed over inside of the newlywed's car, but the approaching Aaron and Sabrina were so immersed in their own conversation, they didn't even notice. Nor did they notice when the car stopped moving and a hand reached up to wipe a spot clear and two faces slowly appeared to watch them walking side by side into the parking area. The two were intensely discussing something, but they were too far away to be understood. Gwen slowly moved her disheveled hair back over her ears and looked down at her young husband with a raised eyebrow. Suddenly, Aaron and Sabrina walked briskly their way and the two lovers quickly ducked down into the back seat of the car not daring to move or breathe.

"So, what are we going to do?" they heard Sabrina say, almost as if she were standing right on top of them.

"Steer clear of that old cook, that's what," Aaron answered.

"Ha-ha...very funny," Sabrina said. "I'm being serious, Aaron."

Sam risked a quick peek and discovered that they were standing face to face right next to the car, not more than two feet apart from each other.

"One of us is going to have to draw Penny out of that room and the other will have to go up there and force the information out of him," Aaron replied with finality this time.

"Yes," Sabrina agreed. "That sounds good. I really don't see any other way. But who's going to do the drawing out and who's going to do the forcing?"

Aaron stopped and thought for a minute. "You're going to have to get Penny to leave the room. She'll be more apt to go with you for something than with me. I can handle the old man."

"Okay then. But seriously, Aaron. *Inkling*? *Apt*? Nobody talks like that."

Aaron rolled his eyes and reached out with both hands to hold hers. "You never used to complain about how I talked before."

Sabrina slowly smiled, leveling her eyes with his. She stepped forward and kissed him on the mouth. "Who says I'm complaining now?" Sabrina said and then kissed him again. "What do we do with the old man once he tells us where the loot is?" she continued.

Aaron stepped back and lowered his arms.

"You saw how sick he was, right? People that sick don't always make it."

"Ooooooh, I love the way your twisted mind works," Sabrina said. "How do we do it?"

"Simple," Aaron said, turning towards the car and then he stopped short. "Wait a minute. This isn't my car." He looked around until he found where he was parked. "This must be those obnoxious newlyweds' car."

"No kidding," Sabrina chimed in as they walked away across the parking lot to Aaron's car. "I give them two months tops before they get on each other's nerves and kill each other off. They were *so* childish. Can you imagine him asking me for a free professional photo of them?"

Sam and Gwen lay there fuming with anger as the voices faded away.

"Those claim jumpers are using the same plan we came up with to steal the money before we can," Gwen hissed. "We can't let that happen."

"Obnoxious? Childish?" Sam complained. "And they've been secretly planning this all along. They're no better than we are. Free? What does she mean free? I offered to pay for that photo! Are they still out there?"

Gwen leaned forward and carefully looked out the window again. Sam smiled up at Gwen enjoying his vantage point. "They're both standing by his car," she reported, looking back down at Sam. When she saw his self indulgent smile, she shot him a look of disgust and quickly buttoned up her shirt. "Play time is over big boy."

"Aw come on," Sam protested, sitting up slightly.

"Are we doing this or not?" Gwen asked as she pulled her pants on.

Sam reluctantly nodded.

"Okay then," Gwen continued as Sam began to dress too. "We wait until they leave and we get to the old man before anybody else can. But now things have changed. Things are different."

"How do you mean?"

"Well, just this. Now there are others who are after his money too," Gwen explained, lacing up her shoes. "And I'm not exactly in the mood to be sharing *our* money with anybody else, if you know what I mean."

Sam sat upright curiously. "Just what are you getting at?"

Gwen's eyes found his and held his gaze long and steady.

"We have to kill him."

Sam looked at her like he'd never seen her before. He could see she was completely serious. This wasn't the same Gwen he was talking to only a matter of minutes ago. After a moment he replied, "You mean that *I* have to kill him."

"Whatever. The point is that it has to be done or getting to him first won't mean a thing. How do we know that he won't fold under pressure and give the money's location to somebody else too?" Gwen continued. "It has to be done."

Sam looked away. "I don't know Gwen. Getting the money is one thing…but *murder*? Killing another human being?"

"We won't be murdering him," Gwen justified. "He's sick, remember? He's going to die anyway. If you suffocate him with his pillow, nobody is going to know. They'll all assume he died from… from…whatever it is that he has."

"Yah," Sam silently agreed. Then looking at his newlywed wife, he nodded his head. "Yah, you're right. He's going to die anyway. We're just helping him along, saving him from more pain and agony. And nobody would know. It could work."

Gwen leaned in and took Sam's hand into hers. "We have to swear a vow between us that nobody will ever find out what we've done. Ever."

Sam nodded.

"Swear it."

"I swear a vow to you that nobody will ever hear it from me what we're about to do," Sam said.

"I swear my vow to you that nobody will find out from me either," Gwen affirmed. Then squeezing Sam's hand, she leaned in further and kissed him softly on the lips. This was the second set of vows they'd exchanged in the same day, though they were on opposite ends of the spectrum.

"Are they still out there?" Gwen asked after a moment moving back.

Sam looked over his shoulder to see nobody in the parking lot.

"No. They've left."

"Good," Gwen said, kissing him again promptly on the cheek. "Let's go. We'll watch the door to their room through ours; thank goodness we're just across the hall, so that shouldn't be too hard. As soon as Penny leaves the room to use the bathroom…"

"Assuming she'll need to use the bathroom," Sam interjected.

"…yes, assuming that," Gwen agreed without missing a beat, "you'll go straight in and get the money's location from the old man, while I watch at the door. Once he tells you, then…well, then…you know…"

"Use the pillow."

"Yes. The pillow," Gwen agreed quietly. "And then those sneaks won't be able to get anything out of him."

Without saying a word, Sam turned, opened the car door and stepped outside as a cool breeze hit him. He stood still, closed his eyes and took in a deep breath as Gwen followed him out and shut the car door behind her. Together, they walked up the path to the house and disappearing inside, they made their way upstairs to their room and waited.

Chapter 12

The two sisters sat quietly in the parlor, each engrossed in a book, reading silently to themselves when after some time Edna tilted her head back and yawned. Mildred dropped her book to her lap and looked over.

"I think I am going to call it day," Edna said sitting up and closing her book.

"I was thinking the same thing," Mildred agreed stifling a yawn of her own. "How is your book?"

Edna smiled appreciatively and looked at its cover. "It's a fun read. I have my suspicions on who the culprit is in this one already though."

"You *always* know who it is," Mildred laughed. "Is there a book where you haven't guessed the killer yet? You probably even know who the killer is in my book too!"

Edna glanced at the cover of Mildred's book. "As a matter of fact dear sister, I do."

"Well, don't tell me," Mildred replied tucking her bookmark neatly into place and closing the book over it. "I don't want the ending ruined."

"Very well," Edna agreed. Reaching over she dimmed the lamp and stood to her feet facing the portrait hanging over the fireplace. "Good night Ozymandias. The house is in your hands now."

Mildred joined Edna and echoed her with another "good night" directed to the regal figure in the painting.

After a moment, Edna turned and walked around the two chairs. "I am going to go and tidy up the living area. Something tells me those two newlyweds have probably left it in a mess."

"I'll come with you," Mildred stated and followed her sister through the foyer to the other side of the house.

Edna stopped short when she saw the monopoly game and its contents still scattered all over one of the tables. "I thought as much," she sighed. "Today's youth just don't have the same morals as when we were young, and no sense of responsibility."

"Oh, they are on their honeymoon," Mildred said. "They should be allowed a little leeway."

"Hmmph!"

"Don't you remember when you and Roland were first married?" Mildred giggled.

"That was different!" Edna snapped. "And we were always respectful to everyone around us...God rest his soul.

"Besides," Edna continued. "They are like anyone else in this house. They have to abide by the same rules as everyone, regardless if they were just married or not."

Together the two sisters put the pieces of the game back into the box and then made sure the room was clean. Dimming the lights in here as well, Edna turned to Mildred and gave her a hug.

"Good night, Mildred," she said. "Sleep well. See you in the morning."

"Good night."

They entered their respective rooms and shut the doors quietly behind them and retired for the night.

Chapter 13

Penny lifted her suitcase up to the table and opened it, carefully resting the top against the lamp. Quietly, she sifted through her things until she found the shampoo bottle, toothbrush and toothpaste, a hairbrush, and a nightgown. Penny gathered the items and held them close to her and walked over to the bedroom door. With a troubled expression on her face, Penny glanced back at her grandfather for a brief moment and then passed through the doorway, down the hallway and into the bathroom at the end of the hall. On the other side of the hall in the room opposite Penny's, Gwen silently watched until Penny closed the bathroom door behind her and then waited until she heard the sound of running water.

"Okay baby," Gwen whispered. "Let's go."

Slowly, the newlyweds crept from their hiding spot and, keeping a watchful eye on the bathroom door, they slipped into the other room where they found Richard Forester sleeping soundly. Gwen swung the door closed leaving it open only wide enough to where she could effectively see the bathroom.

"Go!" Gwen said turning to face Sam. When Sam hesitated, Gwen gave him a shrewd look. "Go!" she repeated, more forcefully this time.

Sam took a deep breath and walked apprehensively over to the bed where Richard lay sleeping on his back. Sam slowly circled the bed to the far side closest to the window and leaned over him, half expecting Richard to open his eyes and catch them red-handed at any second. But Richard did not stir, and his eyes did not open.

"What in the world are you waiting for?" Gwen exclaimed as loud as she dare, growing impatient. "Hurry up before Penny comes back!"

Breathing fast and heavy, beads of sweat dotting his forehead, Sam swallowed hard and leaned over the still form of Richard. Suddenly, Richard's eyes opened and he looked directly at Sam. Stifling a shout of fright, Sam jumped backward. Richard sat upright, anger flooding his features. "What is this? Why are you in my room?" he demanded.

Sam leaped forward and, clasping his hand over Richard's mouth, he forced the old man back down to the mattress. Eyes wide in fear, Richard struggled and tried to scream out, but to no avail. Sam's grip was firm.

"Listen to me old man," Sam snarled. "If you value your granddaughter's life, then you'll tell me where you've hidden the money. We know you took it. So don't play any games with me. You'll tell me right now or I *promise* you, you'll never see Penny alive again. Nod if you understand."

Richard slowly nodded.

"Now," Sam continued. "I'm going to remove my hand from your mouth. If you have any ideas of calling out for help, I guarantee it will be the last thing you ever do. Nod if you understand."

Once again, Richard nodded.

"Good," Sam acknowledged. Then slowly, he lifted his hand from Richard's mouth. Richard made no attempt to call out. "Now tell me."

Gwen watched as her husband leaned down. She saw Richard tell him something in his ear when she heard the water shut off from inside the bathroom. She looked back down the hallway and saw shadows moving in the light coming from underneath the closed door.

"We don't have much time!" Gwen warned. "Hurry! Finish this!"

Suddenly, she heard the latch on the bathroom door being turned.

"She's coming," Gwen hissed. "I'll try to buy you some time. Remember...nobody else can know. Finish it!" With that, Gwen slipped out into the hallway on the other side of the door and closed it behind her.

With trembling hands, Sam reached over and grabbed a pillow. He looked down at Richard who was strangely calm. With unwavering eyes, Richard said, "You better do what you came here to do, son."

Penny opened the door now wearing her nightgown, and drying her wet hair with a towel, she stepped out into the hallway to find Gwen just coming out of her room.

"Oh, hi!" Gwen greeted.

"Hi," Penny smiled in return.

"How are you doing?" Gwen asked a bit awkwardly, desperately trying to think of anything to talk about. Anything that would give Sam enough time to get out of the room before Penny went in.

"I'm fine," Penny replied. "So you and Sam just got married?"

Gwen smiled and let out a breath of relief. Penny had just given her what she needed. "Yes. Yes, just this morning in fact."

Inside the room, Sam walked over to the window and went to lift it open. The window didn't budge. Sam stopped in surprise. He bent down to the window and with a firm hold, he attempted to lift the window again, but once again the window refused to move. "Unbelievable," he said under his breath to himself. Out in the hallway beyond the door, he could hear

Gwen telling Penny all about their wedding and he realized she'd only be able to hold her off for so long. With renewed intensity, Sam grabbed the window and strained with everything he had. He felt the window slowly begin to give. He opened the window enough to where he could slide his hands underneath it and with one last heave, he finally had the window sliding up and open.

"I really should be getting to bed now," he could hear Penny's muffled voice on the other side of the door.

"Uh…are you leaving in the morning?" Gwen quickly stepped forward.

"I think so," Penny replied and then reached down and grabbed the doorknob. "Well, good night."

"Good night Penny," Gwen raised the volume of her voice a little.

Sam scrambled quickly through the window and steadied himself on the slanted tile of the roof outside. With his heart pounding in his chest, he reached up to shut the window behind him. But the window once more held firm and did not budge. "You've got to be kidding me!" Sam growled. He could hear Penny turning the doorknob from the other side of the door. With sweat dripping down his face, he reached up and with one final burst of strength, he pulled the window down and rolled over onto his side out of view just as Penny opened the door and entered the room.

"Never again," he breathed with his eyes closed, "Never again."

Waiting until he was satisfied that Penny had not seen him, he slowly crept down the tiles of the roof to the terrace and made his way around to the back of the house.

Chapter 14

Jim Frank and his son Charlie were just returning from the lake when a movement up on the roof of the building caught Jim's attention. Through squinted eyes, Jim could see the shadowy figure of someone creeping down from the top floor window to the terrace below and then quickly disappear around to the back of the house. He quickened his pace, leaving Charlie behind. After running to the back of the house, he found he was too late. Whoever had been up there was gone now. Cursing under his breath, Jim turned to see Charlie running to catch up to him.

"What is it Dad?"

"I thought I saw something," Jim replied. He looked up to the roof giving it a last once over but still didn't see anything. "I guess it was nothing."

"You saw something up there?" Charlie continued looking up.

"Nah," Jim responded. "Nah, it must have been the dark playing tricks on my eyes. Come on. Let's get some sleep."

He led Charlie to the back door, but inside he *knew* it wasn't the dark at all. He *had* seen someone up there. And it didn't take long for him to register whose room that was up on the top floor. Jim began to grind his teeth together. What if something had happened to Richard Forester? His ire grew and he found himself getting angry. But to his shame, he realized he wasn't getting angry that someone may have harmed Richard. He was getting angry because he wasn't the person who had harmed him. Perhaps he needed to pay Richard a little visit tonight after all.

Climbing the stairs to their second floor bedroom, he waited while Charlie got ready for bed, formulating a plan in his head. Perhaps he should have the old man tell him where he'd stashed the money. It was only fitting that he know. He earned it. After all, he'd paid dearly for it. He paid with his wife's life.

Chapter 15

Penny closed the door behind her and turned to see Grandpa Dick lying still on the bed. She let out a slow breath. He was resting soundly. He needed it desperately after the day he had in the car. She walked over to the suitcase and placed the items she had retrieved earlier back inside. She sat down on a nearby chair and with both hands, she began to brush the snags out of her hair. She was interrupted by a soft knock at the door. Confused, Penny stopped brushing and sat quietly. After a moment, the knock sounded again. Penny stood up and walked over to the door, opening it slightly. On the other side was Sabrina, the photographer.

"Yes?" Penny inquired looking at her curiously.

"Penny, I know this may seem a bad time," Sabrina started. "But…well, I was wondering if you and I might have a word together."

"Now?"

"If you don't mind," Sabrina smiled encouragingly.

Penny turned to see Grandpa Dick had not moved. "Sure, but not here. I don't want to disturb my grandfather," she returned, looking back at Sabrina.

"Oh, of course," Sabrina replied nodding. "We can go downstairs if that's alright."

"Okay."

Penny gave her grandfather one last look and then slipped through to join Sabrina out in the hall, closing the door behind her. The two suddenly heard the muffled voices of the newlywed couple coming from the other room. Sabrina woefully shook her head. "Those two are enough to drive anyone insane," she said with a small laugh. Penny laughed too.

They turned and walked down the stairs. A moment later, the bathroom door opened and Aaron stepped out, watching their shadows disappear down the staircase. He turned and pulled a syringe out of his jacket pocket and tapped it thoughtfully with his index finger. Inside the other room, the two newlyweds were still intensely discussing something. What it was about he wasn't able to tell. He shrugged and stealthily made his way to the bedroom of Richard Forester and deftly turned the doorknob opening the door. With a hard smile, he entered the room.

"Thanks Penny for seeing me like this," Sabrina said when they'd both taken a chair at the table in the dining room. "I just felt it important to tell you something."

"No problem," Penny responded. "What is it? Is something wrong?"

"No, nothing's wrong," Sabrina continued leaning forward slightly. "It's just that…well, I just wanted you to know that you have a friend in me. I felt that everyone was a bit harsh on your grandfather tonight at dinner."

Penny looked down sadly at her knees.

"I believe he was telling the truth," Sabrina kept on. "I know how hard it can be when nobody will believe you. I've been there in your shoes and I just wanted you to know that if you need to talk to anyone, that I'm here."

Sabrina reached out a sympathetic hand to touch Penny's.

"Thank you," Penny replied, looking up. "Sometimes I feel like I am alone, and I do worry about Grandpa Dick a lot. You see…" Penny hesitated, deciding whether she should confide in this stranger or not.

"It's okay," Sabrina reassured her. "You can trust me."

Penny nodded. "Grandpa Dick was diagnosed with lung cancer and he doesn't have long. He's in so much pain. He's coughing up blood and sometimes has a hard time breathing. We're on our way to see a specialist in Portland but I don't know if Grandpa Dick is going to be able to make it. Today's drive was very hard on him."

"I thought maybe he was sick. He didn't look too good during dinner," Sabrina confided. "How long does he have?"

"Not long," Penny answered bursting into tears. "He's in so much pain."

"I'm so sorry, Penny." Sabrina reached out and hugged the teenage girl close to her. *Not long*, she thought to herself. Good thing they were making their move tonight. "Shhh, it's okay. It's okay."

Penny let the tears flow, strangely comforted by this woman she'd met only a couple of hours ago. After a few minutes, Penny sat up wiping the tears from her eyes. "I feel so stupid," she said.

"No don't. It's okay. We all need a good cry once in a while. Especially us girls," Sabrina winked with a small smile. "It's our prerogative to cry you know."

Penny smiled in spite of herself. "Thank you." The two stood up and hugged again. "I'm going to go outside for a little while and get some fresh air," Penny continued. "Thank you again."

"Anytime sweetie."

As Penny turned and walked down the hallway towards the parlor, Sabrina felt a strange twinge of sadness. She liked Penny. She felt bad for how Penny was sure to feel when she found that her grandfather was dead.

Penny slowly walked into the parlor and then over to the front entrance. Opening the door, she continued out on to the porch and down the steps into the yard. It was a tranquil night, insects buzzing busily in the moonlight. The stars were bright and shining. Penny stopped short of a flower bed and knelt down. Reaching out to a couple of Azalea's, she pulled them from the soil and brought them daintily up to her nose taking in their fragrance. Standing up, still holding the flowers to her lips, she closed her eyes.

Aaron was holding the syringe's needle to the exposed skin of Richard's arm when he was suddenly startled by a creaking floorboard outside the door. He fumbled with the syringe and it fell from his fingers and skitted away from him. Quickly, he flattened himself down on the floor and groped around blindly underneath the bed trying to find it, but he found nothing. Cursing his bad luck, Aaron stood up and hurriedly made his way over to the door, opening it just a crack to peek out into the hallway. Nobody was there. He slipped through to the other side, quietly closing the door behind him and hastily began to descend the staircase. He caught his breath in surprise when a face suddenly emerged out of the darkness before him. It was the maid.

"You scared the bejesus out of me!" Aaron exclaimed, holding a hand to his chest breathing heavily.

"Bejesus?" Alexis laughed.

"Yes, bejesus!" Aaron returned in indignation. "You about gave me a heart attack!"

"Well, you shouldn't be sneaking around in the dark like that then."

"I wasn't *sneaking*," Aaron retorted, calming down.

"What are you doing up here anyway?" Alexis asked, her eyes narrowing. "Isn't your room on the second floor?"

"Well, yes it is..." Aaron stammered, thinking fast. "The bathroom on my floor was occupied so I came up here to use this one. Is that a crime?"

"No, no crime," Alexis relaxed.

"What are you doing here?" Aaron returned.

"I was paged just a few minutes ago," Alexis held up her pager. "Mr. Forester needs me."

Aaron wanted to tell her that he knew she was lying since there was no way Richard could have paged her in the last ten minutes, but then his game would be up too. Instead he smiled and said, "I see. Well, I guess I better let you do your job then." Aaron stood aside. "Good night."

"Good night," Alexis nodded in his direction and walked past.

As she disappeared up the stairs, he leaned against the wall once again cursing his luck. Maybe she won't see the syringe he told himself. Somehow, he realized he would have to get back inside the room before morning and find it. Reluctantly, he turned and made his way down the stairs to the next floor.

Penny walked out of the kitchen carrying a glass of milk, turning off the lights on her way out. She slowly walked over to the staircase and saw Alexis coming down.

"Oh, hello Miss," Alexis warmly greeted.

"Hi."

"Just making my nightly rounds, making sure everyone is tucked in okay. What do you have there?" Alexis asked.

"Oh," Penny responded slightly raising the glass. "It's just some strawberry flavored milk for Grandpa Dick. He loves it. Sometimes it helps to settle down his stomach, so I thought I'd bring him some. I hope it was okay that I helped myself to the kitchen."

"Don't worry about it," Alexis smiled. "Well, I'm off to bed myself now. Good night Miss."

"Good night," Penny returned.

Alexis softly padded out the front door and Penny turned and climbed the staircase to her room. Penny opened the door and walked quietly inside. Grandpa Dick was as she had left him. She walked over to the bedside and placed the glass of strawberry milk down on the nightstand.

Chapter 16

"Well?" Gwen asked, her hands on her hips.

"Well, what?" Sam said still catching his breath.

"What do you mean 'well what'?" Gwen returned angrily. "Did he tell you?"

"Listen. I just crawled through a window out on to the roof of this building in the middle of the night, and then scaled said roof *in the dark* all the way around to our window…all without breaking my own neck!" Sam exclaimed. "So you'll have to excuse me if I want to catch my breath and steady my nerves first for a minute."

Gwen pouted and crossed her arms in front of her and began to tap her foot, glaring at her husband. Sam stopped and looked at his distraught wife.

"Okay. Okay! Yes! Yes, he told me!" he said in frustration.

"Did he really?" Gwen responded throwing her arms around Sam, plastering him with kisses. What a moody girl he thought to himself.

"Yes, he did. Really."

"Oh baby!" Gwen squealed excitedly, jumping up and down in his arms. "We're going to be rich!"

Sam smiled and held her close. "I knew he'd taken that money. I knew it!" he confirmed. "There's only one thing that troubles me."

"What's that?" Gwen stopped suddenly, looking at him with one of those 'what's the catch' type of looks.

"He gave it up so easily," Sam said. "It was almost like he didn't even care."

"Is that all?" Gwen breathed in relief. "He was on his deathbed at a bed & breakfast in a town that nobody knows about. He probably didn't care."

Sam relaxed. "Yah, you're probably right."

Gwen moved back a step. "Speaking of deathbed," she probed. "You *did* take care of him, didn't you?"

"It's done," Sam answered, looking down. "And if you don't mind, I'd prefer we never speak of it again."

"Okay." Gwen studied him quietly for a moment and then drew him near, holding him close to her. "So?"

"So *what*?"

"Where is it? Where's the money? What did Richard tell you?"

Sam smiled and reached into his pants pocket. He pulled his hand out and held up a small metal key. "This, my dear, is the key to our fortunes!"

"What does it open?"

"That's what he told me. He said in his bag was a key. And that the key opens a locker located at the Portland International Airport."

"And inside the locker is the money?" Gwen asked.

"That's what he said," Sam returned. "My guess is that is where they were going."

"Oh, baby!" Gwen exclaimed, jumping onto Sam again, her arms wrapped around his neck. "We really did it!"

It was all Sam could do from losing his balance and falling over with Gwen smothering him.

"Nobody must know about this. I'd hate to show up to find an empty locker. I think we should get an early start in the morning. In fact, I really don't even want to stay here any longer," Sam continued. "I think we should leave right away. Right now."

"No," Gwen returned, stepping back again to look her husband in the eyes. "I've been thinking about that. If we're gone when Penny discovers he's dead, it's going to put us under suspicion. We need to be here just like everyone else."

"But…" Sam started to object.

"I know," Gwen interrupted him. "You're worried about those two sniveling claim jumpers, Aaron and Sabrina. I thought about them too and realized that they won't blow the whistle. What are they going to say? *Oh, sorry, we snuck into his room to force the hidden money's location from him and then kill him only to discover he was already dead*? I don't think so. They won't say anything. They can't or they'll be incriminated for his death. No, they won't say a word. Penny will be the one to discover he's dead."

Sam stopped and thought about it for a minute. Gwen was absolutely right. Aaron and Sabrina were their saving grace. He realized, in fact, they were necessary.

"Penny did see you out in the hallway," Sam reminded her.

"We were just talking. Nothing wrong with that. I made it appear that I'd just come out of our room," Gwen explained. "Don't worry. We're completely safe here. But we have to stay here tonight."

"You're right. I need a breath of fresh air though. Can we go outside again for a little while?" Sam asked. "I'm pretty sure I have another bottle of JD stashed somewhere in the car. And I could sure use a hit."

"Sure baby," Gwen responded, holding him close again. Then he felt Gwen's lips on his neck, kissing him. "Later. First things first, though," she prodded, leading him over to the bed. "It is, after all, our honeymoon."

Sam felt all of his inhibitions crumble and he let himself fall to the mattress with her on top of him.

Chapter 17

Aaron quickly and quietly went to his room, entered without turning on the lights and latched the door shut. He turned and closed his eyes, resting the back of his head against the door jam.

"How did it go?" a female voice sounded to his left.

Aaron turned in surprise, and after his eyes had adjusted to the dark, he discovered the beautiful photographer sitting cross legged in a chair next to his bed. Aaron stood upright and walked over to where she sat.

"I lost the syringe."

Sabrina frowned. "Damn it, Aaron!"

"But the maid, what's her name…"

"Alexis."

"Yes, Alexis," Aaron continued. "She went in there after I did. So as far as we're concerned, if the syringe is found, it belongs to her."

"Aren't you afraid she'll say something?"

"No," Aaron replied. "No, she lied about having to go into the room. She won't say a word. She can't afford to."

Sabrina didn't say anything. She slowly stood up and in the darkness walked over to Aaron. The two embraced in a long kiss.

Chapter 18

Penny woke with a start. It was still dark in the room. She sat up stretching and looked over at the digital clock. The blue light display showed it was 1:44 in the morning. She moved her blankets aside. She'd pulled them along with a pillow down to the floor earlier and fallen asleep there. She stood to her feet and looked down to where Grandpa Dick lay unmoving underneath his blankets. Wrapping a bathrobe around her, Penny picked up the now empty glass and walked over to the door. She slowly opened it and then looked back again. "I love you, Grandpa" she said softly.

A silent, dark figure watched unnoticed from the hallway of the second floor as Penny made her way down the stairs to the main floor. After Penny was gone, the figure raised its head and cast its eyes up to the top floor.

Sam lay quietly in bed holding his bride close, her head on his shoulder. He looked at the clock. It was a little before two in the morning. He needed a smoke.

Carefully, he moved his arm from underneath Gwen doing his best not to disturb her. She shifted her head slightly as he moved a pillow under it to support her. But she didn't wake. In the darkness, Sam found his shirt, jeans and shoes and quickly put these on. He grabbed the keys from the nightstand and opened the bedroom door.

He left the room and soon found himself in the parking lot leaning against his car. He put a cigarette between his lips and lit it. Taking in a long drag, he closed his eyes and exhaled a steady stream of smoke. He looked up to the top floor window he'd actually crawled out of like some professional cat burglar.

A quick movement within the window caught his eye. He walked to the other side of the car and edged in closer. It was the foreboding figure of someone standing over the bed, looking down. Suddenly, the figure lunged towards the bed. Sam caught his breath, unable to turn away, spellbound. After what seemed an eternity, the dark figure stood once more. Without warning, the figure turned and bent to the window peering outside. Sam quickly ducked next to his car. Slowly, he turned his head to look up. The figure was still there but did not appear to have seen him. Sam watched and waited, trying to recognize who it was. Then the figure faded back within the room and disappeared. Sam slowly slipped down to the ground and leaned his back against the car.

Finally, after first finishing his cigarette, he rose to his feet and walked back over to the house. He went inside, climbed the stairs to his floor and entered his room where Gwen still slept. Shedding his clothes, Sam crawled back into bed. Gwen sidled up next to him and hooked her arm around his stomach. He held her arm close to him and with a troubled mind, he drifted into a fitful sleep.

Chapter 19

Edna stirred restlessly until finally her eyes fluttered open. What was that? She'd heard a noise. Slowly sitting up in her bed, she strained her ears. Whatever it was, it was coming from the kitchen. What *was* that? She swung her legs over the side of the bed and slipped her feet into some bedroom slippers and draped a nearby robe around her shoulders. She stood and walked briskly over to her door and opened it. The noise was definitely coming from the kitchen. It sounded very much like somebody was using the garbage disposal. Edna frowned and looked back at her clock. At 2:15 in the morning? Who would be using the garbage disposal at 2:15 in the morning?

Edna pulled her robe close and walked out of her room towards the kitchen. Suddenly, a shrill howl echoed off the walls around her as she felt her foot step on something furry. Jumping back in alarm, Edna looked down to see Rufus walking back and forth licking his chops, wagging his bushy tail. Realizing she must have stepped on the poor dog's tail, she knelt before him and reached out. The garbage disposal noise in the kitchen stopped and it grew quiet.

"Come here Rufus," Edna said. "I'm so sorry old boy. I didn't mean to hurt you." Rufus walked up to Edna and licked her hand. "What are you doing inside anyway? Did you sneak in again?" Edna queried, stroking the hairy dog and patting his side. Rufus panted and sat next to Edna still wagging his tail. A crack of light appeared behind Edna as Mildred opened her bedroom door.

"Everything okay?" Mildred asked poking her head out.

"Yes. I'm sorry if I woke you. I stepped on poor Rufus' tail here," Edna replied. Then standing, she faced her sister. "But I heard something coming from the kitchen."

"I thought I heard something too," Mildred said stepping out completely. "Is Felix in there? Sometimes he likes to get an early start on breakfast."

"At 2:15 in the morning?" Edna laughed. "He'd be lucky if he can even remember his own name at 2:15 in the morning. Then again I'm surprised that the old coot can even remember his own name at all!"

Mildred raised a hand to her mouth and giggled. "Yes, I suppose so."

"Still," Edna continued, "I should like to know who it was."

The two sisters walked over to the swinging door that led into the kitchen and entered. Edna reached over and flipped on the light switch. Nobody was there. With questioning looks on their faces, they walked over to the sink where small droplets of water fell from the faucet. The sink was wet.

"Somebody was using the garbage disposal alright," Edna confirmed.

"Strange," Mildred offered.

Edna opened a nearby drawer and reached in snagging a fork. Making sure the wall switch to the disposal was turned off, she inserted the fork into the disposal unit inside the drain and dug around. She pulled the fork out, but it was bare.

"Whatever it was they were disposing of, they did a good job," Edna ascertained. "There's nothing in there."

"Do you smell something?" Mildred asked, sniffing the air. Edna stopped and sniffed as well. There was a very faint, almost indistinct odor. "It seems like I have smelled it before, vaguely familiar. But for the life of me it's too hard for me to place what it is," Mildred continued.

"Well." Edna rinsed the fork off, wiped it with a towel and placed it back inside the drawer. "Remind me to ask Felix if he was indeed in here working when we see him in the morning. In the meantime, I'm going to let Rufus outside and then go back to bed."

"Okay. Me too. I'll see you in the morning, dear," Mildred agreed and returned to her room.

After letting Rufus back out on to the front porch, Edna also returned to her room, closed the door and slipped back underneath her covers. "Weird," she muttered to herself and then closed her eyes.

Chapter 20

Penny did not return to her room immediately. She walked out to the shoreline of the shimmering lake and strolled down its length, soaking in the night air, deep in thought. She thought of Grandpa Dick and her eyes watered. She hated to see him in such pain, but she was extremely grateful that he'd found some peace here in Pleasant Lake, even though some of the guests at the bed & breakfast were less than cordial to him at dinner. How dare they accuse him, a good, hard working man of embezzling all that money? If they really got a chance to know him, they would have known better.

After some time, Penny made her way back to the statuesque building. Being sure to be quiet, she entered the building again. She found her way back to their room on the top floor. She took a deep breath and locked the door closed behind her. She really needed to get some sleep for the long drive ahead tomorrow.

Penny once more looked over to where Grandpa Dick lay. He was like a rock. She decided to continue sleeping on the floor and pulled her blankets close about her. Soon her weariness overtook her and she slept.

Chapter 21

The sun was just coming up over Pleasant Lake
when young Billy Corbitt was pedaling his way down
the gravel drive leading to the Pookotz Bed & Breakfast
on his dirt bike. This was nothing new to him as he'd
delivered out here many times before. However, today
was different in that he'd never been out here so early.
He was told he needed to bring this particular bag out
as soon as possible. So, he quickly downed a strawberry
poptart and some chocolate milk, pulled his red
baseball cap snugly down on his head, and waited until
Rita Crumb, the pharmacist, handed him the bag to be
delivered. Without any delay, Billy hopped on his bike
and sped his way down Main Street and now here he
was.

Billy skid his bike to a stop in a shower of gravel
and dismounted. Pulling the white pharmacy bag from
the plastic green milk crate he'd fastened to the
handlebars, he walked through the latticed archway and
up the pathway to the porch. Rufus greeted him at the
bottom of the steps wagging his bushy tail back and
forth.

"Hi Rufus!" Billy said, patting the dog on his head.
"How are you this morning?" Rufus sniffed anxiously
at the bag in Billy's hand. "Oh no," Billy said, yanking
the bag away. "This isn't for you. This is medicine for
one of the guests. But, I do have something for you."
Billy reached into his pocket and tossed a small piece of
left over poptart down to the gray and white dog who
quickly wolfed it down and then sniffed around on the

ground to make sure there wasn't any more. Billy smiled and patted Rufus on the head again and then ran up the steps two at a time to the front door. Reaching up, Billy pushed the doorbell and waited.

After a minute or so, the door opened and Mildred stepped out.

"Well, good morning, Billy!" she said with a big smile. "You're here bright and early. You have a delivery for us?"

"Good morning. Yes, Mr. Grogan and Mrs. Crumb said I was to bring this out here right away," Billy answered, handing over the white bag to Mildred. "I think it's medicine for somebody."

"Oh yes. This would be for Mr. Forester," Mildred replied, accepting the bag. "The poor dear is not well, not well at all."

Billy was hit with the smell of cooking bacon and his eyes perked up. Mildred noticed and laughed.

"Do you want to come in and have some of Felix's famous bacon?" she offered.

"Yah!" Billy smiled in return.

Mildred opened the door to let the young boy in. Billy removed his baseball cap from his head before he walked through the doorway and held it in his hands before him.

"My! Such a perfect little gentleman!" Mildred exclaimed. "Run on back now to the kitchen and tell Felix that he's to give you some bacon, Billy."

"Okay, thanks!" Billy ran past Mildred and down the hall to the swinging door.

"But not too fast," Mildred admonished. "We wouldn't want you to slip, fall and hurt yourself."

Billy slowed down, but walked briskly through the door into the kitchen to find Felix busy at work cooking breakfast. Felix turned to see the young boy enter and raised a finger to him.

"What in tarnation are you doing in my kitchen? Can't you see I have a job to do?" Felix asked.

"Mildred said I'm to come back and get some bacon," Billy answered.

Felix sighed and began to mumble something to himself under his breath.

"Can I have some? Please Felix?"

"Very well, then," Felix grumbled. "Come here. You said the magic word, so I suppose I can afford to give you a few pieces."

Felix held out a paper towel with some strips of bacon which Billy gratefully accepted. Billy had just taken his first bite when a high-pitched scream pierced the morning air, causing him to drop the paper towel and its contents to the kitchen floor.

"What in the blazes did you do that fer?" Felix asked turning to face the boy.

"Didn't you hear it?" Billy returned.

"Hear what?"

"Someone just screamed!"

Felix shook his head. "I didn't hear a scream."

But there was fear in Billy's eyes. So Felix grabbed up his walker and made his way over. Billy uneasily followed Felix as they walked into the hallway. No sooner than the swinging door had closed behind them when a second scream sounded, this time much louder and longer than the first.

"I heard that one," Felix acknowledged.

Edna and Mildred appeared as well.

"What in the world?" Edna exclaimed, concern lining her face.

The two sisters hurried themselves up the stairs towards the source of the scream. Billy ran past Felix and up the stairs as well, to the very top floor where it appeared that all the other guests in the house had just gathered.

Standing just outside the door to her room was Penny. She was as pale as a ghost. Her hands were cupped under her face and tears were streaming from grief stricken eyes down her cheeks.

"He's dead!" Penny exclaimed. "Grandpa Dick is dead!"

For a moment, nobody dared to move or speak. And then Penny's eyes rolled back and she collapsed unconscious to the floor.

Chapter 22

A collective gasp echoed through everyone standing there as Edna and Mildred rushed to Penny's aid. Sabrina also dropped to her knees beside Penny, putting the teenager's head in her lap. Everyone crowded around looking down at Penny, eyes wide with worry.

"Somebody wet down a towel and bring it here," Edna instructed. "Quickly!"

Gwen hesitated for a second, but then ran to the bathroom and did as Edna directed. She soon returned with a dampened towel and handed it down to Mildred who in turn placed it tenderly over Penny's forehead.

While they tended to her, Aaron shifted his attention to the bed where the still form of Richard Forester lay. Moving forward a step, he solemnly and slowly walked into the room. Sam quietly followed.

Jim turned to Charlie. "Son, wait here."

"But, Dad," Charlie began to protest.

"No, Charlie. In fact," Jim said firmly, noticing Billy standing at the other end of the hallway, "I want you to go down there and wait with him. Is that understood?"

Charlie nodded and walked down to stand next to the other boy. Jim winked at his son sadly and then entered the room behind Sam. Aaron by this time had made his way over to the foot of the bed.

"Is he dead?" Sam asked.

Aaron raised his hand to silence him and moved in for a closer inspection. Richard's eyes were open and he was facing the window. He did not appear to be breathing, and he was not moving. Aaron moved his hand slowly back and forth in front of Richard's eyes but nothing happened. Taking a deep breath, he reached down while Sam and Jim looked on and with two fingers he probed for a pulse on Richard's neck. He stood still for a moment and then moved his hand back.

"He's dead," Aaron confirmed.

"Lord have mercy," Mildred said raising a hand to her mouth.

"Alexis!" Edna called out looking around the hallway area. "Alexis?"

"Yes, Miss?" Alexis responded stepping forward.

"Oh, good, you're here," Edna replied. "Go call the Sheriff and let him know what's happened. Tell him to bring Doc Meecham with him when he comes up. Well, go on, child!"

"Right away, Miss." Alexis turned and left the hallway.

"Mr. Buchanon," Edna continued. "Perhaps it would be best if you, Mr. Frank and Mr. Richards all rejoined us out here in the hallway. I doubt very much if Sheriff Blackwood would like to have anything in the room disturbed before he has a chance to look around."

"Quite right," Aaron nodded in agreement. "Of course."

As Jim and Sam both turned to walk out, Aaron risked a quick look around, even bending slightly to look under the bed. The syringe was nowhere to be seen. He shook his head and followed them out into the hallway.

"We really should get Penny off of this cold floor and into a warm bed," Sabrina suggested.

"Let's take her downstairs," Mildred spoke up. "We can lay her down in my room on the bed. It will keep her secluded from the Sheriff and his men while they're working. That way, I can keep an eye on her."

"Yes," Edna agreed. That's a good idea. How do we get her downstairs?"

"I'll take her," Jim offered, kneeling down.

"Very well," Edna said, standing.

Jim carefully moved his hands underneath Penny's arms and legs, and after he was sure he had a secure hold on the teenager, he lifted her close to his chest and then stood to his feet. Everyone cleared a path as Jim made his way down the hallway and then slowly carried Penny down the stairs to the main floor.

As everybody filtered down behind him, Aaron hung back and took one last look into the room hoping to find the missing syringe. But once again, it was nowhere to be seen.

"Forget something?" he heard someone say.

Turning, he found Sam looking at him.

"No," Aaron replied. "Just hard to believe that's all."

Sam nodded. "Yah, it's a shame."

"A shame," Aaron agreed. Then without another word, he walked forward and brushed by Sam and went down the stairs. Sam turned and followed.

Mildred entered her room and hastened over to the bed, moving the covers back. Jim followed her over and carefully lay the still unconscious Penny down on the sheets as Mildred propped up a soft pillow under her head.

"Oh, the poor dear," Mildred said as she moved the covers back over the teenager. "The poor, poor dear."

Edna appeared by the bedside and slowly shook her head. "She's had quite a shock. Doc Meecham can see to her when they arrive. In the meantime," she continued turning to face everyone who'd congregated at the doorway, "we should let her get some rest. Let's go to the living area."

Slowly, everyone moved away from the door and into the living area where Felix, standing behind his walker, was already waiting.

"What's going on? What happened?" Felix inquired.

Nobody answered him, but instead quietly filed into the room. Sam went over to the loveseat and sat down with Gwen right next to him, leaning against his shoulder. Sabrina sat down as well on one end of the longer couch with Aaron standing just behind her. Jim and his son Charlie sat on the other end of the couch while Billy walked over to the window and leaned against the sill. Edna sat on the recliner while Mildred remained behind with Penny.

"Somebody better tell me what's happening!" Felix exclaimed, growing agitated.

"Penny's grandfather passed away last night," Aaron responded.

"Oh," Felix calmed down. "I'm sorry to hear that." And noticing the distraught mood of all the others, he continued, "I'll go and finish breakfast."

"That will be fine, Felix," Edna agreed. "When Alexis returns, I'll send her in to help you. Maybe it would be nice if we could have some coffee and juice brought out. Also, Sheriff Blackwood will be here soon with some other officers I'm sure. Be sure to have some extra made up for them too please."

Felix nodded and made his way over to the kitchen.

"I feel bad for Penny," Sabrina said after a moment. "She really loved her Grandpa. You could see they were close last night at dinner."

"You could see that he was pretty sick last night at dinner too," Aaron said. "Does anyone know what was wrong with him?"

"Penny told me that he had cancer," Sabrina answered looking up.

"Cancer?" Jim said, turning to look at Sabrina. "When did Penny tell you this?"

"Well, last night," Sabrina responded. "Before...that is to say, she and I bumped into each other before I went to bed."

"Alexis," Edna spoke up as Alexis entered the room. "Did you call the Sheriff?"

"Yes, miss," Alexis confirmed. "He and Doc Meecham will be here shortly."

"Thank you, Alexis. Please go help Felix in the kitchen and set out some coffee, juice and something to eat on the dining room table. I think for today, everyone can just help themselves, so don't worry about setting any places for breakfast. Just be sure to have plenty of plates, silverware and napkins out," Edna further instructed.

"Okay, miss," Alexis said and then briskly left the room.

"He must have died from his cancer then," Gwen offered, still leaning against her husband who sat quietly.

"If he indeed did have terminal cancer," Jim agreed, "then I'd have to say so. He did look very pale last night."

"So, that's who the medicine was for?" Billy asked.

"What medicine?" Edna asked back.

"Billy delivered a prescription this morning," Mildred answered for him as she walked into the room. "That's why he's here. It was for Richard."

"Oh, I see," Edna responded. "How's Penny doing?"

"She's resting. She appears to be alright," Mildred replied, sitting down in one of the chairs by the wooden tables. "The sweet dear. What an awful thing to happen to a young girl."

"When we talked last night," Sabrina reflected, "Penny was extremely concerned for his health. She also told me that he was coughing up blood and having difficulty breathing. They were on their way to see a specialist in Portland for his condition, but apparently the drive here was very hard on him."

"Apparently *too* hard," Aaron added.

"He must have died in his sleep," Gwen said.

"Perhaps," Edna said as everyone turned to look at her.

"Perhaps?" Gwen responded. "I think it's pretty obvious."

"Well," Edna continued, "Sheriff Blackwood and Doc Meecham will be here soon. They'll examine Mr. Forester and we'll have our answer then. But until then, we really won't know just what happened to him."

"What do you mean we won't know?" Sam sat up silent until now. "I also think that it's pretty obvious. The old man was sick with cancer, he was near to passing out at dinner last night and finally his body gave up on him in his sleep. He died. Just *died*. That's all."

"What about all his money?" Charlie spoke up, but then regretted it immediately and shrunk back into the couch as everyone turned to look at him.

"Charlie!" Jim exclaimed with a frown.

"No, he's right," Aaron said stepping forward. "Everyone here is thinking it. We might as well get it out into the open."

"Of course, you'd say that," Sam returned.

"Don't tell me that you haven't been thinking about that money too!" Aaron retaliated.

Sam's face grew red and he was about to respond in kind but Sabrina cut him short. "No, he *is* right. I'd be lying if I said I wasn't wondering about that money too now that he's dead."

"Just what exactly is being suggested here?" Jim asked sitting up.

"Nothing is being suggested," Aaron replied. "Just that everyone in this room believes he embezzled that money. Even our kindly hosts."

"Well, it certainly isn't our place to assign guilt to a man we hardly even knew," Edna stated. "I don't believe talk of this kind will get us anywhere."

"Yes," Mildred joined her sister. "The poor man has passed on. The least we can do is to show a little compassion. Besides, our main concern right now should be for Penny, not for money that he may or may not have stolen."

Everyone sat in chagrined silence then. Alexis walked in abruptly to announce that breakfast was served as requested when the doorbell sounded.

"That will be the Sheriff," Edna said, standing to her feet. "Alexis, please show them in." Alexis turned to do as she was asked. "I think it would be best if everyone remained inside as he may have some questions to ask. Except for you, Billy. You should be going on back now."

Billy started to object but seeing the stern look in Edna's eyes decided against it. "Yes Ma'am."

"Uh, just a moment," Jim said, also standing. "Do you think it would be okay if Charlie goes with him? I really don't feel he should be here during all of this."

Edna nodded in agreement. "Yes. Billy, is it okay if Charlie stays with you today? You can show him around Pleasant Lake."

Billy looked over to Charlie. "Sure. I can do that."

Charlie looked up to his father who nodded for him to go with Billy. Charlie stood and hugged his father and the two boys turned and left.

"He'll be okay, Mr. Frank," Edna reassured him. "We can call over to the Corbitt's later this evening after things have settled down a bit."

Everybody else stood up when Alexis reappeared with Sheriff Blackwood. Another elderly, balding man with nicely groomed white hair ringing the sides of his head followed him in. He wore a neatly pressed suit also the color of white and carried a black leather bag by two handles that were snapped together at the top. A silver chain hung from inside his vest and curved down to the left pocket of his pants. Silver rimmed spectacles rested on his nose over a well trimmed white mustache. His dark green eyes looked saddened.

"Jacob…Jedidiah," Edna greeted each in turn.

"Hello Edna," Sheriff Blackwood returned the greeting. "We came as soon as we could."

"Really, Jacob," Edna huffed noticing the wide brimmed hat still on his head.

"Sorry, Edna," Sheriff Blackwood replied. "I'm here on business today. This is not a social call."

Edna let out a short breath but decided not to push the issue. "Everyone," she said, turning to face the others. "This is our good Sheriff, Jacob Blackwood, and our town physician, Jedidiah Meecham."

"Just call me Jake," Sheriff Blackwood stipulated.

"And I'm Jed," Doc Meecham stated. "But everyone around these parts just calls me Doc."

They all nodded in greeting as both Sheriff Blackwood and Doc Meecham shook everyone's hand in turn. Another police officer, also wearing a tan uniform with dark brown trim similar to Sheriff Blackwood's walked into the room. He was much younger and thinner with curly, sandy blonde hair and stood a good four inches taller than anybody else in the room. The gun strapped to his hip looked to be too big for him; in fact, he looked just like a tall, lanky child, unable to hurt a fly.

"Boss," he said, pulling his hat down from his head upon seeing Edna's disapproving look. "Where do you want us?"

"Everybody," Sheriff Blackwood said, This is Deputy Moss." And then, turning back to Edna, he continued, "I'm sorry Edna, but where is the body?"

"On the top floor in the Blue Room," Edna answered. "He is as we found him. We've done nothing with him."

"Very good," Sheriff Blackwood turned to leave. "Doc, are you coming?"

"First, I want to check on the young lady," Doc Meecham replied. "I was told there's a granddaughter?"

"This way please, Doc," Mildred indicated towards her room. "She's lying down in here. She's resting just now."

"Go on up, Sheriff. I'm going to tend to her first, and then I'll be there directly. Don't let anyone move the body," Doc requested, shooting a nervous glance over to Deputy Moss.

Sheriff Blackwood nodded. "I'm sorry everybody, but I'll probably have some questions for you, so I'm asking that you all remain on the premises. I do apologize for any inconvenience that this may cause. Let's go, Ross," he said, turning to his deputy. The two officers left the room and began to climb the staircase up to the top floor. Mildred showed Doc Meecham into her room where he promptly began to examine Penny.

"Wait a minute," Sam spoke up after they had left. "The deputy's name is Ross Moss?" He let out a little snicker.

"Let's get something to eat," Edna suggested, ignoring Sam's question.

As they passed through the hallway, they could see a couple more officers standing outside the front door talking. Upon seeing them, Edna instructed Alexis to bring them each a cup of coffee and to offer them a plate of food which she readily did.

When they arrived to the dining room, they found the table was setup buffet style with large, covered metal containers holding scrambled eggs, sausages, bacon, biscuits, toast, hash browns, pancakes and french toast. Stacks of plates, napkins and silverware were placed at each end. On the chest of drawers against the wall they found coffee, juice, milk and water with glasses and cups ready to go.

"Oh, man, that smells good," Sam said taking in the array.

"It sure does," Jim agreed picking up a plate.

Sabrina also grabbed a plate and worked her way down the table, taking the time to inspect each container before serving up a helping. Despite the somber mood, everyone was soon eating a hearty breakfast.

Chapter 23

As the two officers approached the bedroom door which was open at the top of the stairs, Sheriff Blackwood suddenly began to feel sick in the pit of his stomach and slowed down.

"Are you okay?" Deputy Moss asked, noticing his hesitation.

"Yah," he responded, a hand on his stomach. "It's just that I haven't eaten anything yet. Stomach isn't feeling too strong right now. This isn't exactly my favorite part of the job you know."

"Don't worry, boss. I've got your back!" Deputy Moss clapped him on the back, with the palm of his other hand over his handgun. Sheriff Blackwood turned to face his young deputy who was smiling eagerly back at him.

"Ross?"

"Yah, boss?"

"We aren't going in under fire here. It isn't like we're in a hostage situation, and there's nobody else on the other side of this door that we need to worry about!" Sheriff Blackwood exclaimed. "We're simply going to examine a dead body. That's it."

"Oh, sure, boss," Deputy Moss agreed nodding his head.

"So take your hand *off* your weapon and relax."

Deputy Moss weakly smiled and nodded again moving his hand away. "Sorry, boss. It's just that we don't exactly get a lot of action around here, you know? This is kind of exciting when you think about it."

The sheriff shook his head. "Believe me, Ross, you'll come to appreciate the peace of a small town someday."

"I suppose so, boss," Deputy Moss shrugged.

"And don't call me boss."

"Sure thing, bo…errr, sure thing, Sheriff," Deputy Moss hastily amended.

"Give me a pair of gloves," Sheriff Blackwood instructed Ross, holding his hand out, "and don't touch anything while you're in here."

Ross reached into his pocket and procured a pair of latex gloves and handed them over. Pulling the gloves over his hands, Sheriff Blackwood shook his head and stepped through into the Blue Room. It was called the Blue Room simply because it was decorated in all blue. As long as he could remember, that's how the Pookotz Sisters had run the bed & breakfast. Each room was decorated in a certain color, and then of course, that's how they labeled it. In addition to the Blue Room, on the top floor was the Burgundy Room. Down on the second floor were the Green, Brown, and Purple Rooms. Each was done in easy-on-the-eyes dark and light tones with beautiful paintings, upholstery and bedspreads to match. He and his wife Cathy had actually spent an anniversary weekend here at the bed & breakfast in the Brown Room a few years ago which had warm, earthy tones. It was a very good experience for them both and they always thought back fondly on that weekend.

Lying on the bed directly in front of him was the body of Richard Forester. Sheriff Blackwood frowned. It was hard to believe that he'd only just met him and his granddaughter Penny the night before. He himself had guided them out here, and now here he was, lifeless. Sheriff Blackwood felt Deputy Moss move up anxiously behind him looking over his shoulder into the room.

"Ross, I want you to stand guard at the door," Sheriff Blackwood turned and instructed the deputy.

"Aw, boss…" Deputy Moss looked crestfallen.

"No, I mean it! Right now; I don't want anybody else in the room but myself and Doc Meecham when he comes up. Is that understood?"

Deputy Moss was disappointed, but he nodded in agreement.

"Good."

Sheriff Blackwood once again turned and continued forward. He walked to the foot of the bed and looked at Richard. He lay on his back, his head facing the window, eyes still open. Once again, the sheriff felt his stomach grow queasy, but he fought back the feeling. The blankets covered Richard's legs up to his waist, his arms on top of them and by his sides, the palms of his hands turned down. He wore a plain, white t-shirt and from what he could tell without moving the blankets, what looked like boxer shorts. He was extremely pale, his mouth slightly parted and his back tensed into a small arch. His death appeared to be a painful one. The sound of approaching footsteps interrupted his thoughts.

"Oh, heya, Doc," Deputy Moss said as Doc Meecham appeared at the doorway. He handed the town physician a pair of latex gloves. "Go on in."

"Thank you," Doc Meecham replied, stepping gingerly inside the room.

"How's Penny?" Sheriff Blackwood inquired as the doctor joined him.

"The granddaughter? She's sleeping still. She's suffered a shock, but all of her vital signs are good. She'll be just fine," Doc Meecham informed him. "What do we have here?"

"This is Richard Forester, her grandfather," Sheriff Blackwood answered sadly. "It's a real shame. They only arrived in Pleasant Lake last night. I met him over at Steve Grogan's and brought them out here. He did look pretty sickly come to think of it."

"Indeed, he was," Doc Meecham confirmed. "Mildred was kind enough to fill me in on a few things while I was downstairs. He had cancer and, in fact, they were on their way to Portland to see a specialist."

"Is that normal?" Sheriff Blackwood asked. "I mean, for him to be traveling like that in his condition?"

"I wouldn't recommend it. But I suppose if you're sick enough, you might be willing to try anything to find a cure for whatever ails you," was the reply.

Sheriff Blackwood let out a sigh. "It's a shame. The cancer probably got too strong a hold of him last night and did him in."

"More than likely," Doc Meecham nodded. "But that's why I'm here. Let's make it official. I'm going to examine his body."

"Okay. I'll have a look around the room."

While Doc Meecham began his examination, Sheriff Blackwood's eyes began to scan over the room. On initial inspection, nothing seemed to be out of the ordinary. Both of the nightstands to either side of the bed had nothing on them except for the ornate lamps. The wooden closet was open where a few clothing items were hanging. A pair of men's black leather shoes had been placed inside at its base, shoes that Sheriff Blackwood could only assume belonged to the deceased. An unopened suitcase was to the left of the closet on the floor. Moving over to the far wall where the window was, he saw that another suitcase was on top of the table and had been left open. The top of the suitcase was resting against the lamp on the table. Inside the suitcase were more clothing items. Stuffed into the corner were a shampoo bottle, a toothbrush and a tube of toothpaste. Next to the lamp lay a closed copy of the Holy Bible, and to the right was a telephone. Draped over the back of the chair to the left of the table was a long, bathroom towel. A hairbrush had been set on the chair's seat cushion. On the chair to the right of the table, was a pair of white Nikes stacked on top of some blue jeans, a pair of white anklet socks, and a pink shirt. Those would be Penny's. The window was closed, although the curtains had been opened. Sheriff Blackwood crouched to his knees and looked over the floor along the walls and under the bed. There was nothing there except for a blanket and pillow lying to the right of the bed at the base of the nightstand. *That's curious,* he thought to himself. Did Penny sleep on the floor?

"Who did you say this was again?" Doc Meecham asked, interrupting his thoughts.

Sheriff Blackwood stood straight to look at the doctor who was sitting on the side of the bed, his black bag opened and placed next to the body. "His name is Richard Forester. Why?"

"That's what I thought you said," Doc Meecham replied. "This man is famous. Or rather, *infamous*!"

"How do you mean?"

"Don't you remember? The big embezzlement case last year? MicaTek?" Doc Meecham asked.

With sudden realization, Sheriff Blackwood looked down at the corpse and gasped. "That's right! I do remember. That was him?"

"I believe so," was the answer. "Not only that, Sheriff, but I suspect foul play here."

"Why's that?" Sheriff Blackwood, now very curious, stepped forward.

Doc Meecham shook his head. "I can't confirm anything yet. I still need some time with the body. I have to say, this one is rather confusing. Let me do a little more work here first, and then I'll show you what I've found. However," Doc Meecham looked up, "I'd give the room another once over. Look for something, anything that might be out of the ordinary, Sheriff. Something isn't right here."

"He was *murdered*?" Deputy Moss suddenly spoke up from the doorway, his face lined with excitement.

"Now, I didn't say that, Ross!" Doc Meecham emphatically stated.

"And I don't want you to go around saying that either," Sheriff Blackwood reaffirmed. "Anything you hear, anything that's discussed within the walls of this room here today stays between us. I want to make sure that's perfectly clear to you deputy."

"Yes, boss," Deputy Moss nodded. "Stays between us."

As Doc Meecham went back to his examination, Sheriff Blackwood started over again. Taking his time, he methodically searched through the items hanging in the closet, finding nothing but pocket lint and a couple of plastic wrapped hard candies. He opened the suitcase sitting on the floor and inspected its contents. Inside was a pair of men's jeans, a couple of t-shirts like the one Richard was wearing now, a couple pairs of socks and boxer shorts underwear, an electric razor, and a bottle of aftershave. Tucked underneath the clothing was a manila folder with some health insurance paperwork outlining Richard's disease. But once again, nothing out of the ordinary.

Sheriff Blackwood moved over to the table and chairs and carefully looked over the items there. In the suitcase on the table other than what he'd initially found were a cell phone, an iPod with headphones, a bag of red rope licorice, and a small purse containing Penny's makeup, fingernail polish and remover, another brush, and a wallet. In the wallet, he found her driver's license, a social security card, a few pictures of who he assumed to be family and friends, a library card, a debit card, an old high school picture ID card, and $27 in cash. The Bible looked to be undisturbed. The towel on the back of the chair was still slightly damp, obviously Penny had showered or bathed the night before. In the pockets of the jeans on the other chair, were a few coins, a folded piece of paper with the address and phone number for a Dr. Edmond Wright in Portland, but nothing more.

He then focused his attention on the window. He noticed something he hadn't before. There were flakes of blue paint scattered all along the window sill. He looked down at the base of the wall underneath the window and saw more of the same blue flakes on the floor as well. This was curious. It wasn't like either of the Pookotz Sisters to leave a mess like this before allowing a guest into the room. They would have seen to it that it was cleaned up and proper first. Whatever caused this was recent. Very recent.

The sheriff pushed the curtains all the way open and looked at the sides of the window. Flakes of paint had been broken off leaving bare patches of wood underneath. He reached down and tried to open the window. It was snug, and after some considerable effort, he was able to lift it open. This window was not used that often, if at all, and the metal tracks were corroded. Apparently, some time ago, the window had been painted over and nobody had bothered to open it before painting it or since. He believed it was opened last night, and when it was, the now dried paint seal broke resulting in the flakes on the sill and floor. He placed his hands on his hips. He doubted very much that either the grandfather or his granddaughter could have managed such a feat. It would have taken somebody else with considerable strength.

However, in and of itself, that didn't really prove anything. Penny or Richard could have very easily had somebody come in and open the window for them. But that didn't sit right with him. He leaned out the window and peered over the side down to the roof. What he saw confirmed his gut feeling. There were dried dirt smudges on the tiles, probably from the bottom of somebody's shoes. He shook his head. Somebody had opened this window and then crawled through it. Coming in or going out, he couldn't be sure. No...he was sure. It had to be going out. The window would have had to have been opened from the inside. There was no way it could have been opened from the outside. Whoever it was, they'd opened the window, crawled outside, and then pulled the window closed behind them. Foul play indeed.

"Ross," Sheriff Blackwood called out.

"Yes, boss?"

"Go down and have one of the officers on duty bring up the camera. I think we're ready for pictures now," Sheriff Blackwood instructed. "Also, check to make sure that the ambulance is here. If it isn't, call my wife over at the station to make sure it's on the way. And remember, not a word yet to anyone."

"You got it, boss."

"Don't call me, boss."

Deputy Moss headed downstairs. Doc Meecham didn't say a word, but continued on with his examination. Sheriff Blackwood walked over and peered over his shoulder. He noticed a small pink residue on the pillow case next to Richard's mouth.

"What's that, Doc?" he asked, pointing at the residue.

Doc Meecham stopped long enough to look at what the sheriff was pointing at. He shrugged. "I don't know. Probably something he drank or ingested that trickled out of his mouth while he slept. Could be cough syrup, Pepto-Bismol, just about anything really."

"Well, I found no cough syrup or Pepto-Bismol with any of their belongings," Sheriff Blackwood returned. "Although there was a bag of red rope licorice. Remind me to keep that pillow case so we can test the residue for content."

Doc Meecham nodded and continued his work.

The sheriff walked over to the other side of the bed where the blanket and pillow remained on the floor. He carefully picked these up, inspecting them for anything, but finding nothing. He set them at the foot of the bed and then knelt down to look underneath. He found nothing but dust. Standing back up, he looked at the nightstand. There was nothing there. Wait a minute, there *was* something there. He looked closer at the wooden surface. It was faint, but there was a small, dark circle in the wood. It looked like a glass or cup had been set there, and the condensation coming off of it left behind a ring, which suggested to him that whatever was in the glass was cold. Maybe whatever the glass contained caused the residue on the pillow case. But there was no glass or cup there now. Sheriff Blackwood once again gave the entire room a stringent search, but came up with nothing more than he had before.

He heard Deputy Moss returning with another officer. Deputy Moss informed him that the ambulance had arrived and was down in the parking area. Sheriff Blackwood once again had him post guard and then he instructed the other officer what he wanted him to take pictures of. While the officer set about his task, Sheriff Blackwood rejoined Doc Meecham at the bedside.

"Any idea when he died Doc?"

"It's still too early to tell at this juncture," Doc Meecham replied.

"Cause of death?"

"That's what puzzles me," Doc Meecham admitted. "But I can confirm one thing here."

"What's that?"

"It was a wrongful death."

Sheriff Blackwood closed his eyes and hung his head. He let out a deep breath and then opened his eyes again. "I thought so. Okay, Doc. Show me what you've found."

Chapter 24

Downstairs, the house was bustling with activity. Word had gotten out that there was a free breakfast prepared in the dining room, so all of the officers on site were going in and out of the house carrying plates and cups. Others were standing outside in two's or three's, talking about this or that with small smiles of appreciation to the two sisters for their hospitality. Some of the male officers watched Alexis admiringly as she quietly blushed and went about her business of making sure every coffee cup stayed full.

Mildred made sure the door to her room remained closed so that Penny could rest undisturbed, then she found Edna who was shouting instructions to Felix in the kitchen. Upon seeing her sister approaching, Edna turned in exasperation to face her.

"Oh, for Pete's sakes!" Edna exclaimed. "You'd think they called out the entire National Guard for this. I had no idea we had this many police officers in Pleasant Lake!"

"It does seem everyone on the force is here today," Mildred agreed.

"How long are they going to be here?" Felix demanded. "If I'd had known they were going to be eating us out of house and home, I'd have called in sick!"

"Oh, hush, Felix!" Edna retorted. "You've never been sick a day in your life. Our own misfortune, I suppose."

Grumbling to himself, Felix returned to his duties.

"Where is everyone else?" Edna directed back to Mildred.

"They've all migrated back to the living area," Mildred replied. "The dining room got to be too busy. Officers coming and going."

"Exactly!" Felix burst out. "And do they say thank you to the cook? No! It's only 'can I have some more please'?"

Edna let out a small sigh, but said nothing to him.

"Perhaps we should go see how they are doing," Mildred continued.

"Yes," Edna agreed, and then to Felix, "If you need anything, just send Alexis after one of us."

"Oh, you can be sure I will!" Felix grunted.

The two sisters made their way into the living area where their guests were quietly seated. Empty and half-full plates remained on the tables in the room where they'd left them. They all turned and looked up at the approaching sisters.

"How long is this going to take?" Gwen asked sitting up.

"As long as it has to I'm afraid," Edna said. "I'm sorry, but that's beyond my control. I know you all have things you need to do, but don't forget that Penny has just lost her grandfather. We should be concerned for her right now."

"I don't want you all to have to change your plans because of me," a timid voice sounded from behind Edna and Mildred. The two sisters turned and moved apart to reveal that Penny had walked up behind them.

"Penny!" Sabrina exclaimed, standing to her feet and walking over. "Are you okay?"

Penny nodded sadly, her eyes downcast. Mildred also walked over, taking Penny by the arm. "You poor dear," she said. "Why don't you come and sit down over here on the couch?" With Mildred and Sabrina on either side of her, Penny once again nodded and walked sullenly over to the couch and very slowly sat down. The others gathered around them.

"It's like…it's like a bad dream," Penny said, choking up. "Is it true? Is Grandpa Dick dea…..is he dea….." She was not able to finish the question as she looking imploringly at each of them in turn. The grave looks on their faces confirmed her worst fears and she burst into tears. Mildred hugged the teenage girl close while she cried. The others lowered their heads silently.

"It's okay, sweetheart," Mildred reassured her. "We're all here for you."

"I know this may not be much to console you, Penny, but your grandfather is no longer in any pain. He's not suffering any more. He's at peace now," Sabrina offered kindly.

"That's right, Penny," Gwen agreed, a bit more matter-of-factly. "He's going to a better place."

Penny sat up, sniffling, and wiped the tears from her eyes with the backs of her hands. "Thank you. I do appreciate what you're trying to do for me."

"Take heart, Penny," Edna added. "You're a strong, young woman. You're going to be okay, you'll see. Mildred and I lost both of our parents at the same time, and though it was very difficult on us, we learned to find strength within ourselves and with each other in order to carry on. You must do the same."

"Yes," Mildred agreed. "Believe me, if we can do it, then you can too, dear."

"I know. I will be strong," Penny nodded, sadly. "It's just that Grandpa Dick was all I had left. I have nobody now."

"What about your parents?" Sam asked, leaning in.

"No, they're dead. My mother died shortly after I was born. I never knew her. My father died on my seventh birthday in a car accident. All my other grandparents are dead too. I don't have any uncles, aunts, brothers or sisters," Penny explained. "It's just me now."

"That's terrible," Jim said. "I too have known loss. My beloved wife Regina has also passed on due to cancer. Breast cancer. It was too far spread for the doctors to be able to do anything for her." A tear formed in Jim's eye and he clenched his fists. "It was too late for her."

"I'm so sorry," Penny responded in a caring tone.

Jim looked back over to Penny. He leveled his eyes with hers and said, "Thank you, Penny. I'm sorry for your loss too."

"We used to know a Regina, didn't we, Mildred?" Edna spoke up then.

Jim drew in a short breath and held it. He couldn't believe he'd actually said her name. His eyes shifted around, nobody seemed to notice. Nobody seemed to care.

"Oh yes!" Mildred agreed. "She was a beautiful young girl. She used to come up here for summer vacation with her parents. She *loved* the lake and the trees surrounding it. Regina would come by the bed & breakfast and help us feed the birds in the aviary every morning."

"I didn't see any birds in the aviary when I walked by it," Aaron said.

"Oh, we don't keep it up any more," Edna pointed out. "Maybe someday we will again."

"I love birds," Penny said.

"Well, maybe we will just have to get some for you to watch over then," Mildred smiled. "You're always welcome to stay here as long as you need to, Penny. You have a family here."

"Really?" Penny managed a small smile.

"Of course!" Edna affirmed.

"Thank you," Penny said gratefully. "Thank you all so much."

In that moment, Sheriff Blackwood and Doc Meecham walked into the room. Both of them had taciturn expressions on their faces. But upon seeing Penny sitting on the couch with everyone circled around her, their expressions softened somewhat.

"I see you have awakened," Doc Meecham said, walking over. "How are you feeling, my dear?" he asked, kneeling before her.

"I feel okay," Penny answered not convincingly.

"Well, you're in good hands with the Pookotz Sisters. They'll take good care of you," Doc Meecham reassured her with a warm smile. "It's good to see you up and about. You have my sincerest condolences, young lady."

"And mine as well, Penny," Sheriff Blackwood said, pulling the hat off of his head, walking up to join them.

"Thank you."

"Where are Alexis and Felix?" Sheriff Blackwood asked then, placing the hat back on his head.

"I'll fetch them," Mildred said taking her leave.

"Is there something wrong, Jacob?" Edna asked.

"I'll tell you, Edna," he replied, "when everyone is here first."

A moment later, Mildred returned with Alexis and Felix in tow. Once they'd joined them and the sheriff was satisfied that everybody was present, he cleared his throat and spoke.

"Firstly, I want to thank you all for your patience with us this morning. I know it's been a long and arduous task, and I further understand that you have things you need to do and lives to get back to. However, I'm afraid I'm going to have to ask you to be patient for a while longer yet," Sheriff Blackwood announced.

"What do you mean?" Sam stood up and stepped forward.

"What I mean is that I'm placing all of you under house arrest in the matter of Richard Forester's death," Sheriff Blackwood stated.

"House *arrest*?" Aaron also stood up, incredulous at what he'd just heard. "You don't place anyone under house arrest unless a crime has been committed."

"Yes, that's true," Sheriff Blackwood agreed. "Or if a possible crime has been committed."

"What possible crime could have been committed?" Sabrina protested.

"You said the crime was in the matter of his death," Jim said. "Are you suggesting that he was…?"

"Grandpa Dick was sick," Penny interrupted. "I woke up this morning to find that the cancer had killed him last night in his sleep."

"That's right," Gwen agreed.

The two sisters also couldn't believe what they were hearing. Alexis and Felix remained silent where they stood.

"Please! Please!" Sheriff Blackwood shouted, waving his hands in the air. "Listen to me! Please!" When he was satisfied that he had everyone's attention, he continued. "We have evidence to suggest that Richard Forester did *not* die in his sleep. He was, in fact, murdered."

"Murdered?" Penny whispered as a deathly silence settled over the room.

"There can be no denying it. The killer…" Sheriff Blackwood paused then, a stone cold look in his eyes. "The killer is right here in this very room. Right now."

Chapter 25

The silence that followed was so dense, that you could have cut it with a butter knife. Sheriff Blackwood quietly stood before them, carefully gauging their reactions and facial expressions. He was hoping for a sign, a clue…anything that might help provide him with an idea of who the killer could be. But what he saw instead were dropped jaws and wide open eyes of disbelief.

"I'm sorry, but did you say that he was murdered, and not only that…but that one of *us* is the killer?" Sabrina was the first to speak.

"I can't believe what I'm hearing," Sam added.

"Jacob, I hope you haven't gone too far this time!" Edna exclaimed as Penny buried her face in her hands sobbing. "House arrest? *Really*!"

"I'm sorry, Edna. You know I wouldn't do this if it weren't absolutely necessary," Sheriff Blackwood replied.

"You said you had evidence Sheriff?" Jim inquired.

Sheriff Blackwood lowered his head sadly. "Unfortunately, yes, we do have incontrovertible evidence."

"But what? What is this evidence?" Gwen asked.

"For that," Sheriff Blackwood nodded in Doc Meecham's direction, I'll let the good doctor tell you."

With a deeply saddened expression on his face, Doc Meecham stepped forward. "I examined Richard Forester's body and here's what I found." The doctor flipped open a notepad on which he had penciled in some notes and with a clear voice he proceeded. "The deceased was lying on his back, his head facing towards the window. His back was arched slightly and his hands were still clenching the blankets by his sides. There was a pink stain on the pillow case next to his mouth. It appears to have been something he either drank or ate."

"Strawberry milk," Penny clarified.

"Pardon me?" Doc Meecham looked up.

"It was strawberry milk," Penny repeated. "I had brought a glass of strawberry milk up to the room for Grandpa Dick. Sometimes it helps…" Penny choked up suddenly, "…uh…*helped* his stomach when he wasn't feeling too good."

"Yes," Alexis spoke up suddenly from the corner. "It's true. I saw the young miss bringing the glass up to her room."

Doc Meecham nodded. "Strawberry milk." He wrote another small note on the paper. "Well, that clears that up."

"But what is this evidence, Doc?" Aaron persisted.

"I was just getting to that," Doc Meecham responded, once again consulting his notepad. "There was a large contusion on the left side of the deceased's head a couple of inches above his ear which indicates he was sharply struck with some sort of hard, blunt instrument."

"What?" Felix exclaimed, cupping a hand to his ear. "What did you say? A blunt excrement?"

"A blunt *excrement* indeed!" Edna retorted. "Honestly, Felix, don't you pay attention? Who's going to hit someone with a blunt excrement? He said a blunt instrument, you idiot!"

"I'm sorry, but I haven't heard *half* of what he's been saying," Felix returned red-faced. "I'm not the spring chicken *you* are, you know."

Edna tightly clamped her mouth shut and turned away, steaming.

"Uh, well…yes. Let's continue then, shall we?" Doc Meecham shook his head slightly, clearing his throat. "There was considerable swelling there and could have been the cause of his death."

"*Could* have been the cause?" It was Sam this time who spoke up. "I thought Sheriff Blackwood said the evidence was incontrovertible."

"If you'll all just let me finish, I'm sure your questions will be answered in due time. Please! Just hear me out here, okay?" Doc Meecham paused until he got a nod in return from everyone in the room. "Now, besides the lump on the head, I also found a distinctive mark on his inner right arm. It was distinctive to me, that is to say, as I see marks just like it on a daily basis. What I found was a small puncture in the skin where a needle had been inserted. A syringe needle. After searching the room, we weren't able to find any syringes. Therefore, a sample of the victim's blood will be drawn and analyzed which will hopefully shed some light on what that syringe may have contained. It's very possible that whatever was injected into his system killed him."

"I'm sorry, Doc," Aaron interrupted again, feeling a brief moment of relief that they hadn't found his syringe. "But it's *possible*? He said incontrovertible!"

Doc Meecham raised his hands to silence him. "Please! Just listen."

Aaron bit his tongue and patiently waited.

"However," the doctor continued, "what I found next left no doubt in my mind. Just beneath the deceased's jaw line…"

"Could you please stop referring to my grandfather as the *deceased* or the *victim*?" Penny cried. "His name was Richard."

Shamed, Doc Meecham lowered his head. "I'm truly sorry, Penny. I'm afraid I'm not very good at these things. Of course."

"What Doc has been trying to tell us is that Richard Forester was strangled," Sheriff Blackwood took over as Doc Meecham stepped back. "There were marks and bruises on his neck where someone had choked him…with their hands no less. It wasn't even difficult to ascertain what had happened. There can be no question of it."

Sam could feel Gwen's eyes burning holes into him. He turned to see she was staring at him in complete bewilderment.

"I'd say that's incontrovertible alright," Jim quietly said.

"Is there anything anyone would like to say? Anything? Any questions? Observations? Anything at all? Now is the time," Sheriff Blackwood stated, looking at each of them.

Nobody moved. Nobody looked up.

"I have something to say!" Penny was on her feet then. "Shame on you! Shame on *all* of you! You're all so convinced that he'd stolen that money, aren't you? You just couldn't leave it alone, could you? And now a good man lies up there in that room dead for something he didn't even do! What…you snuck into my room while I wasn't there? I hope he told whichever of you killed him to go to hell, because that's where you're going. Straight to hell! And I hope you burn for all eternity!"

"Penny…" Sabrina softly said, reaching out to the teenage girl.

"No!" Penny shot a hateful glance to the photographer. "I don't trust you. I don't trust any of you!"

Penny brought a trembling hand up to her mouth and as the tears began to flow, she ran from the room crying.

"Let me go see to her," Mildred asked, standing.

Sheriff Blackwood nodded his approval. After Mildred left the room, he turned to the rest of them.

"Anybody else have anything to say?"

Nobody said a word.

"Very well then," Sheriff Blackwood said. "We'll be enforcing the house arrest as of right now. You'll all be allowed to make whatever phone calls you need to for the next hour. Work, family members, a lawyer…whatever you feel is necessary. Then I'm afraid I'll need to collect all of your cell phones, blackberry's, iPods or whatever other portable devices you may have with you. I'll be conducting an investigation and speaking to each of you."

"I'm not talking to anyone without my lawyer present," Sabrina stipulated.

"That's your right, Miss Riggs."

"It most certainly is *not* her right!" Edna retaliated. "I'm being held under house arrest in my own home! The Pookotz Bed & Breakfast has had its share of problems over the years, but nothing like this."

"Now Edna…" Sheriff Blackwood began.

"Don't *now Edna* me, Jacob!" Edna said. "You may be the sheriff of our town and the law around here. But this is my home, not your town."

"It's my right to have counsel present with me," Sabrina insisted.

"Why? Is there something you aren't telling us? Any particular reason why you'd need to have a lawyer?" Edna returned.

"What?" Sabrina flung her hair back defiantly. "Are you saying that I killed Richard?"

"I think the question is...are *you* saying it, Miss Riggs?" Edna queried with a raised eyebrow.

Sabrina squinted her eyes in thought for a couple of seconds and then with a small sneer, she said, "You're absolutely right, Edna. I have nothing to hide." Then turning to look up at Sheriff Blackwood she continued, "I waive my right to counsel, Sheriff."

"Are you sure you wish to do that, Miss Riggs?"

"Yah," Sabrina replied, looking back over at Edna. "I'm sure."

"And I'll have words with anyone else here who doesn't have the nerve to answer for *themselves* while they're staying under my roof!" Edna included the rest of them.

"Edna," Sheriff Blackwood raised his voice, "it's their decision. I have very little tolerance for shenanigans like this!"

Edna started to say something, but something in Sheriff Blackwood's tone prevented her from opening her mouth. "Hmmph!" she muttered and then crossed her arms in front of her.

"That's okay, Sheriff," Sam said, sitting forward. "Gwen and I would also like to waive our right to counsel. We can't afford a good lawyer anyway."

"Are you crazy?" Gwen turned to her young husband, clenching his arm with both hands.

"It's okay, sweetheart," Sam continued, placing his free hand over hers. "Really, it's okay."

"I won't need a lawyer either," Aaron added. "I think we should get to the bottom of this as soon as possible."

"Mr. Frank?" Sheriff Blackwood looked over to where he sat quietly.

"Nah," Jim replied after a moment. "No lawyers. I'm sick of lawyers. Sick of due process. All of it. Let's just get it over with."

"Okay then," Sheriff Blackwood said. "For the time being, even though they are under the conditions of the house arrest, I'm giving the Pookotz Sisters and Felix Stiffman a few allowances. They will be allowed to use the phone to both call out and answer incoming calls. They do still have a business to run. And given Felix's advanced years, I don't feel he's a threat to escape or outrun any of us with his walker. Therefore, he's excused from having a police escort from the main house to his living quarters. Edna and Mildred are also excused from any escort as long as they stay on the property grounds. Do any of you have any objections to this?"

A collective "No" resonated among them.

"Very well. However, I'm afraid you're under suspicion as well, Alexis, and will need to abide by the conditions of the house arrest. You'll be free to continue doing your daily chores as your employers see fit. However, please be sure to have an officer escort you to your living quarters. Are we clear?"

Alexis sullenly nodded.

"Will you be seeking legal counsel?"

Catching Edna's look of reproof, Alexis shook her head. "No."

"Then that's that," Sheriff Blackwood stated. "Now, I need all of you to collect whatever forms of identification you have with you. A driver's license or whatever you use, and bring them back to me. Also, if you need to, one of my officers will be happy to escort you to your car to get any personal belongings you may need. You have all waived your right to counsel, but you may still have an hour to make your phone calls. At the end of that hour, we will all meet right back here to go over the conditions of the house arrest. Is *that* understood?"

Everybody nodded their agreement in turn.

"See you all back here in an hour with your ID's and phones," Sheriff Blackwood concluded and then turning to Edna, he said, "Edna, may I talk to you for a minute please?"

Edna stood and walked to the side of the room with the sheriff where he looked at her with a stern expression. "Edna, I should haul you downtown and put you in a cell for the stunt you just pulled!"

"Oh, come now, Jacob," Edna returned.

"I'm only going to say this once. So you better listen," Sheriff Blackwood said pointedly. "I have the world of respect and affection for you and Mildred. But if you get in the way or obstruct this investigation like that again, I will arrest you. I'll do it myself."

"Jacob!" Edna responded aghast.

"I'm being serious, Edna. This is murder. Not some kid stealing a candy bar or soda from Grogan's store. But manslaughter. Please, let us do our job."

Edna pouted slightly, and then nodded her head in agreement. "I'm sorry, Jacob. I'll try my best. I promise."

"It's Jake."

"Don't push it, Jacob," Edna smiled and then reached up to pat him on the shoulder. "I have the world of respect and affection for you too. Ever since the day you were born."

Sheriff Blackwood smiled in return. "Thank you."

As Edna turned to leave, Deputy Moss walked up to the Sheriff.

"What is it, Ross?" Sheriff Blackwood asked.

"Boss, I was wondering...well, aren't they supposed to get just one phone call?"

Sheriff Blackwood laughed and clapped his young deputy on the back. "You watch too many movies, Ross."

"But aren't you afraid if they are allowed to make unsupervised calls that the killer may try to hide his tracks or something?"

"No," the Sheriff answered. "I don't believe there was an outside accomplice involved. The killer is here in this house. This wasn't a premeditated murder. Whoever killed Mr. Forester will want to keep it as quiet as possible. They can have their one hour to make their calls and then we will proceed with collecting their phones. Besides, it will give us time to set up a fingerprinting and profile picture of each of them. We won't need to print the officers on site today for our elimination prints. All of our files down at the office are current."

"Okay, boss. But aren't you afraid that if you give them an hour, that whoever killed Mr. Forester will try to make a break for it?" Deputy Moss continued.

"Well, then, we'll know who did it, won't we?" Sheriff Blackwood smiled.

Deputy Moss hesitated and then smiled back. "Oh, yah."

"Nobody will try to make a break for it. We'll be okay, Ross."

"Should I print Edna, Mildred, and Felix too?"

Sheriff Blackwood emitted a small sigh. "Unfortunately, yes. We need to do this by the book."

"You got it, boss."

Deputy Moss left to make the preparations, leaving the Sheriff by himself. He softly smiled and shook his head.

"Blunt excrement. That was good."

Chapter 26

Gwen was practically dragging her husband up the staircase to their room when they were met and forced to stand aside by two paramedics coming down carrying the corpse of Richard Forester on a stretcher between them. His body had been covered by a thick blanket they'd brought with them. Deputy Moss was right behind them and nodded to the newlyweds as he passed by. "Please, don't enter that room," he warned. They quietly nodded as they watched the procession make its way down the steps. Then with a needle piercing glare, Gwen grabbed Sam's hand and stormed up to the third floor passing a couple more officers on the way. There were still a couple more officers in the Blue Room busy dusting and taking photographs. They briefly looked at the young couple and then returned to their duties. Once they were safely behind the closed door of their room, Gwen turned and angrily pushed Sam, causing him to stumble backwards and fall down to the bed. Her look said it all. Sam could see she was getting ready to unleash her fury on him.

"We agreed to suffocate him," Gwen seethed through clenched teeth as loud as she dare. "Not to strangle him! And what else? Knock him silly and *inject* him with something? Where in the universe did you find a syringe anyway, and what was in it? Oh! Oh!" she exclaimed, on a roll now. "Not to mention you waived our right to a lawyer. How *stupid* is that?"

Sam sat on the edge of the bed and let out a deep breath, burying his face in his hands as he looked down at the floor.

"Well?" Gwen insisted. "I want an answer, Mister!"

"I lied."

"You lied?"

"I didn't kill him," Sam admitted, looking back up. "After you left the room, I just couldn't go through with it."

Gwen stood open mouthed unable to say anything.

"He kept saying things to me like 'you better do what you came to do, son' and 'either you take care of business or I will boy.' He was freaking me out," Sam continued, "so I panicked and did the next best thing. I grabbed the thickest, biggest item I could find and knocked him cold instead."

"You knocked him out?" Gwen returned incredulous. "With what?"

Sam sighed. "The Bible. There was a big Bible sitting on the table there, so I snatched it and swung it down across the side of his head. That's how he got the contusion. I didn't inject him with anything and I most certainly did not *strangle* him. I swear to you it's the truth."

"I can't believe this." Gwen walked over and sat next to him on the bed. "Did you lie to me about him telling you where the money was too?"

"No," Sam confirmed facing her. "That's absolutely the truth. He did tell me. But, sweetheart, I just couldn't bring myself to murder another human being. And I don't think I like myself very much right now for what I *have* done. I'm sorry, but that's who I am. That's the man you married."

Gwen looked across the room quietly for a minute and then softly smiled. "It's okay," she said then. "I doubt if I could have either and, to be honest, I'm actually relieved that you didn't go through with it. And I'm proud of the man I married." Gwen leaned into him as he let out a thankful breath and wrapped his arms around her.

"If you didn't inject him or strangle him, then who did? Whether you did it or not, Richard was still murdered," she pointed out.

Sam told her how he'd gone out to the car later that night for a smoke and how he saw someone in the window. He also told her he wasn't able to identify who it was, but the action of lunging towards the bed would make sense with the fact that they found Richard strangled. And then, of course, there was the conversation they'd overheard between Aaron and Sabrina. It just didn't make sense though that someone would take the time to inject him with something and then turn around and leave such an obvious clue by strangling him too.

"We both know we're innocent," Gwen commented after a while.

"Innocent of murder."

"Yes," Gwen agreed. "Innocent of murder. But there's no way they'll believe we didn't kill him, so we still need to keep this *hush hush* and between us. We were never in that room."

Sam agreed, squeezing his wife's hand in his own.

"There's only one thing that I still wish you hadn't done," Gwen continued a bit irritated.

"What's that baby?"

"You should have never waived our right to counsel."

"I know. I'm sorry. I just thought that since I didn't murder Richard, that we wouldn't need one," Sam returned. "Besides, it's true that we really can't afford one."

"I hope we won't need one when this is all said and done," Gwen replied.

"Let's make our phone calls," Sam suggested pulling out his cell phone. "We only have twenty minutes left. Both our parents should know what's going on."

Gwen nodded and did likewise with her cell phone.

Chapter 27

Aaron gave Sabrina a knowing look and walked from the living area, through the foyer and to the other side down into the parlor. Sabrina took a cell phone out of her pocket and slowly meandered in the same general direction, pretending to be preoccupied with finding a number. She looked briefly over her shoulder, but nobody was paying any attention to her. Shaking slightly, she walked up into the foyer but was cut off by paramedics carrying Richard's body out the front door. She saw Aaron standing down in the parlor by the fireplace looking at her with a paled expression.

"Did you need some things out of your car, Miss?"

Sabrina turned to see the tall deputy standing next to her.

"I'm sorry?" she replied.

"If you need any belongings from your vehicle, now is the time to get them. I'll be happy to escort you down to the parking area. You won't have a chance later with the house arrest in effect," Deputy Moss said.

Sabrina chanced a quick glance over to Aaron. He mouthed the word "Later" and then turned his back on her. Suddenly feeling miffed, she snapped her cell phone shut and shoved it down into her pants pocket.

"Sure, officer," she replied with a bland smile. "Lead the way."

Deputy Moss opened the front door to allow her through and then the two walked down the front porch steps to the path beyond.

"It's hard to believe that we have an actual murder here in Pleasant Lake," he said. "The last time we had a murder was since…well…since I don't know when actually."

While the gangly deputy rambled on about the peacefulness of his quaint and beautiful haven of a town, Sabrina watched as the two men ahead of them bore the corpse of Richard Forester through the latticed archway and into the parking area where an old, station wagon ambulance waited with the back door open. *If only you knew how many of these stiffs I've photographed in my lifetime, you backwoods hick* she thought to herself.

Then she began to wonder what had happened in that room with Aaron and the old man. Strangled? Wasn't that a bit extreme? Aaron did say he was going to take care of him, but she found it hard to believe that an experienced agent like him would employ such an obvious method. He was supposed to inject Richard with a truth serum and then get the money's location from him. But she couldn't fathom that not only would he strangle him, but hit him over the head. And what had happened to the syringe anyway? They said they hadn't found it. Or did they? Maybe they were hiding that from them. Maybe they did have it along with Aaron's fingerprints. She felt a small shiver go down her spine. Maybe they were already totally screwed.

"Are you okay, Miss?"

Sabrina's attention was brought back to the deputy who'd stopped and was intently looking at her.

"Sorry," she answered. "But what did you say?"

"Which one of these cars is yours?" he repeated.

She turned towards a black sedan parked against the tree line on the other side of the parking area and pointed. "I'm in that Lincoln over there."

As they made their way to her car, she wondered when she might get Aaron alone again...if ever. She suddenly felt very alone and very afraid.

Chapter 28

Jim waited patiently for Edna to finish talking with the sheriff and then he approached her. "Edna, I need to call my son. Do you have the phone number where they might be?"

"Certainly, Mr. Frank," Edna responded. Walking him over to a phone sitting on a table in the corner of the room, she picked up the receiver. "I'll call down to the Corbitt's place to see if the boys are there. I've been meaning to call them anyway."

"Thank you."

Edna stood quietly listening to the phone ring on the other end. After four rings, she heard a female voice. "Hello?"

"Hello, Sharon. This is Edna Pookotz."

"Hi, Edna," Sharon warmly returned. "How are you?"

"Well, the Bed & Breakfast has seen better days. We've had an incident up here this morning."

"I thought so!" Sharon said. "We saw the ambulance and the police cars heading your way earlier. The whole town's been buzzing about it. What's going on?"

Edna explained what had happened and that one of her guest's son was with Billy. She asked Sharon if the boys had been by their house yet to which Sharon said they hadn't, but when they did show up, she'd call and let her know. Sharon didn't sound too pleased that her son had been there when the body was discovered, but she did agree to let Charlie stay over at the house with Billy as long as was needed while the matter was being investigated. Edna thanked her and hung up the phone. She called Grogan's and Steve also stated that he hadn't seen the boys yet either, but that if he did, he'd call back.

"It's a Sunday," Edna said, turning to Jim. "Billy probably took Charlie to meet some of the other boys in town. Knowing them, they've probably started up a game of baseball or something. I'm sure he's doing just fine, Mr. Frank. Sharon Corbitt is going to let Charlie stay there with them. They're a fine family and he'll be well taken care of, I can assure you."

Jim smiled his thanks. "I appreciate it. It's a relief to know that Charlie is in good hands and that he won't have to deal with all of this. Thank you, Edna."

"You're quite welcome."

"I better call my work and let them know I'm going to be a while longer here," Jim continued. "So I hope you'll pardon me."

Edna nodded politely and took her leave of him. But then she stopped and watched him inquisitively as he picked up the phone to place his call. A faint hint of recognition flickered in her eyes just then...but it wasn't for him.

It was for Charlie.

Chapter 29

Sheriff Blackwood knocked softly at the already open door to Mildred's room. Inside he saw both Mildred and Doc Meecham trying their best to comfort the distraught teenager who was sitting on the bed wiping tears from her eyes.

"May I come in?" Sheriff Blackwood asked when they turned in his direction.

"Of course, Sheriff," Mildred responded kindly. "Come in."

Sheriff Blackwood slowly made his way over to where they were and he humbly removed his hat and held it before him in both hands. "I'm so sorry for your loss, Penny. It's always hard to find the right words at a time like this. But hopefully you can find comfort in knowing that we are here to help you in any way we can."

"I know. Thank you," Penny nodded.

"Penny," Sheriff Blackwood started again. "When you feel up to it, I do have some documents that I'm going to need you to read and then sign for me. You can have some time, but I'll need that soon. Okay?"

"Okay."

"Also, one more thing," he continued, a bit hesitantly. "But this needs to be said."

Penny looked up at the Sheriff with red eyes. "What?"

"I'm afraid you'll have to abide by the conditions of the house arrest as well. You're more than welcome to consult a lawyer if you wish," he returned.

"Are you saying that *I'm* a suspect?" Penny's eyes narrowed. "You think that I strangled my own grandfather?"

Sheriff Blackwood swallowed hard. "Off the record...no, Penny. I don't believe you could have done that. But on the record, everyone is suspect. Believe me, I feel like such a heel even telling you this, but officially, I'm required to. Please understand."

"I understand, Sheriff."

"Again, I'm sorry, Penny."

"Yah. Okay."

"Mildred," Sheriff Blackwood said, turning, "I'll need Penny to relocate to another room for the duration of this investigation. It seems your rooms are full though. Do you have any ideas?"

"Penny can stay right here in my room, Sheriff," Mildred offered. "I can sleep in my sister's room. I'm sure that won't be a problem."

"That's agreeable to me. Also, please make sure that nobody is to go into the Blue Room whatsoever. Penny will be allowed in to collect her personal belongings with a police escort, but other than that, no one is to enter there."

A beeping noise suddenly interrupted them. Doc Meecham produced a cell phone from a coat pocket and stood up. "They have Richard in the ambulance," he announced, snapping his black leather case shut. "I need to head back to my clinic where they're taking him."

"Let me show you to the door, Doc," Mildred offered.

"If you need anything, Penny, please don't hesitate to ask," Doc Meecham advised and then kindly patted her on the shoulder. "Don't worry. I know it doesn't feel like it now, but everything is going to be alright."

Penny silently nodded.

After Mildred, Doc Meecham and the sheriff all left the room, Penny lay down on the bed and turned on her side with her back towards the door. She curled her knees up to her chest and quietly wept.

Chapter 30

Alexis and Felix entered the kitchen where Felix promptly returned to his chores, shaking his head and muttering something to himself.

"I can hardly believe it. A murder. Here at the Bed & Breakfast?" Alexis said.

"Terrible!" Felix returned. "It's a terrible, terrible thing."

"Has there ever been a murder before like this in Pleasant Lake?" Alexis asked.

Felix stopped and looked up. "Yes, once long ago. That was well before your time."

"What happened?"

"Don't concern yourself with that. Pleasant Lake is still one of the best places to live and very safe," Felix admonished. "Now, go and collect the breakfast containers, all the plates and silver. It's already almost one in the afternoon. We've been so busy that we've missed lunch altogether and soon we'll have to start preparing for dinner."

Without another word, Alexis picked up a damp wash cloth and went through into the dining room where a couple officers still lingered, holding cups of coffee and talking between themselves. She smiled at each in turn and offered to top off their java, but they respectfully declined and set their cups down on the table and left the room.

Her Aunt Molly had been an employee of MicaTek the day they went under. Aunt Molly had sent her some newspaper clippings of some of the things that were going on including the newspaper of her taking part in a protest outside the courthouse where the case against Richard Forester was dropped due to lack of evidence.

So Alexis was well aware of the facts surrounding the investigation and she also believed that Richard had taken the money and knew where it was. That's why she had gone into his room last night. If only she hadn't bumped into Aaron on the staircase. She knew he could attest to the fact that she was there, and that made her a prime suspect.

Thank God she had the newspaper though. Because it showed someone else there at the protest rally besides her Aunt Molly. And if she had to, she'd use it to clear her own name. She wouldn't even hesitate. *Better him than me* she wryly smiled to herself.

Chapter 31

After Sabrina and the deputy walked out the front door, Aaron let out a big breath. They were knee-deep in it now. He pulled a cell phone out and placed a few calls. He called his mother to see how she was doing as he did every Sunday. Next he called in to his boss and said he had come down with a virus or bacterial infection, and would be out of the loop for a while. Why tell them what was going on? It was just a matter of time before all this blew over anyway and he would be back to normal again. Then he called his wife. He told her that he was going undercover and would not be able to contact her for some time…he didn't know how long. He assured her of his love and asked her to give their 3 year old daughter a kiss for him.

He closed his cell and tapped it thoughtfully against his chin. She must never find out about all of this and about Sabrina. Nobody must ever find out. He hoped that he could find a way to get Sabrina alone. There was much they needed to talk about. He sighed and closed his eyes.

"What a mess," he said to himself.

Chapter 32

Before seeing Doc Meecham and the ambulance off, Sheriff Blackwood asked Mildred to assemble everyone back into the living area again. Mildred made her way back into the Bed & Breakfast from the front porch as the sheriff went down to the parking area. Upon arriving, he gave instructions to the officers gathered there, assigning shifts and positions around the premises. Deputy Moss stood dutifully by his side with a hint of exhilaration in his eyes. Sheriff Blackwood made sure everyone understood their part and then, with the deputy in tow, he walked back to the house.

Everyone was once again in the living area where they were all fingerprinted and photographed. After he was done, Felix and allowed to leave the room to continue his duties in the kitchen. Edna was adamant at having to go through this process in her own home, but she allowed the officer to print her and take her picture. She promptly wiped the ink off of her fingretips and then approached the Sheriff.

"I went to the liberty of preparing this guest list for you Jacob," she informed him. Sheriff Blackwood thanked her and scanned it briefly.

"Has everyone finished their phone calls and gotten everything they needed?" he asked looking up.

Everyone in the room nodded.

"And you all have your forms of identification with you?"

Again nods.

"Please hand those over to Deputy Moss at this time along with all and any portable communication devices you've brought with you. I already have yours, Penny. They were still in your room," Sheriff Blackwood ordered as the deputy circled his way through the room. They all did as directed. When Deputy Moss had accumulated everything, he resumed his position just behind the sheriff.

"Very good," Sheriff Blackwood acknowledged. "The phones in each of your rooms have been disconnected, including yours Alexis. The only phone with a viable connection is the one right here in the living area. Only the Pookotz Sisters, Felix or any of the officers on duty here at the house have permission to call out or answer incoming calls. If you receive a phone call, they'll take a message and relay it on to you. Only in the case of an actual emergency will you be allowed to use this phone. If you're caught using a cell phone, laptop computer or any other portable device, my officers have instructions to confiscate it immediately and put you in handcuffs. We're doing everything we can to work with you, so please extend us the same courtesy. Understood?"

Once more he was answered with nods.

"Okay, then. It looks like Edna has put together a guest list for me here," Sheriff Blackwood continued, looking back down to the paper in his hand. "So let's review it. On the top floor in the Burgundy Room are Sam and Gwen Richards. On the second floor in the Brown Room is Aaron Buchanon. In the Purple Room is Sabrina Riggs. And in the Green Room are Jim and Charlie Frank, although according to a note here, it looks like Charlie will be staying over at Billy Corbitt's home. That's fine. Penny will be moving down into Mildred's room while Mildred will bunk in with Edna. Alexis will be allowed to remain out in her servant's quarters in the building behind the house where Felix also has a small studio apartment. Have I covered everybody?"

"Yes Jacob," Edna confirmed. "That's everyone."

"Alright. Now down to business." Sheriff Blackwood folded the paper and tucked it neatly into his shirt pocket. "I'm imposing a house arrest simply because I don't have the facilities or accommodations for all of you down at the station. We're not a big city. In fact, we're not a city at all. Just a small town in the trees, so this is as new to us as it may seem to you right now. We're also not equipped with tracking devices enough for all of you, so I've posted around the home in strategic places, police officers working overlapping shifts. They have instructions to shoot first and ask questions later. Make no mistake about it. We may be small time here, but we're very efficient."

Sheriff Blackwood paused for a moment to make sure his last statement had fully sunk in and then he continued.

"The Blue Room where Richard's body was discovered is off limits to everyone. And I do mean *everyone*. Which reminds me," he said, looking over to Penny. "Penny, have you been up there to get anything out of the room that you need yet?"

"Not yet," she answered. "I don't know if I can go back in there though."

"It's okay, Penny. You can do it. Deputy Moss will take you up after we're done here so you can get your clothes and personal items," Sheriff Blackwood affirmed.

Penny begrudgingly agreed.

"I'm offering you one more chance to step forward and give yourself up," the sheriff then said, looking at each of them in turn. "I promise it will go a lot easier on you if you do. I beg of you, take advantage of this opportunity."

Everyone assembled there looked uneasily around the room at each other with suspicious eyes and fast beating hearts. But nobody spoke out or stood up. Sheriff Blackwood let out a deep breath.

"Ross, please escort Penny to the room to get her things."

Penny followed the tall, lanky deputy up the stairs for what she hoped would be the last time, dread building within her. After what seemed an eternity, they reached the top floor. Deputy Moss opened the door and admitted Penny into the room. Penny lowered her head and quickly walked over to her suitcase on the table by the window. She hastily threw all her items into the suitcase and slammed the lid shut. Turning, she just as quickly walked back but then stopped dead in her tracks about halfway across. She very slowly twisted her head around to look at the bed. It was empty, the bedspread and sheets showing a slight depression of where Grandpa Dick had been. The pillow case from his pillow was gone. Her eyes welled up and she burst through the doorway, past the startled deputy and down the stairs.

Penny took her seat again in the living area as everyone watched her return. Her features were flushed and she was holding a suitcase close to her chest.

"Are you okay?" Deputy Moss asked, following her in.

Penny didn't respond.

"Do you want to go and lay down, dear?" Mildred offered.

Penny shook her head with a pout. "No. Just leave me alone. I'm okay."

"Are you sure?" Edna probed further.

"Yes."

"Very well, then," Sheriff Blackwood spoke up. "That room is now completely off limits. Along with the officers posted around the house outside, I'll be leaving at least one officer inside with you to make sure everyone behaves themselves. Deputy Moss here will be taking the first shift.

"The investigation and interviewing process will begin tomorrow morning. It's already heading into late afternoon and some of us have families to get back to," the sheriff continued. "You may be talked to in a group or on a one-to-one basis. I *implore* all of you to be truthful in your answers. Are there any questions for me?"

"How long do you think this whole thing is going to take Sheriff?" Aaron returned. "Some of us have families to get back to also." Sabrina shot him a quick look of contempt.

"That will depend entirely on all of you," Sheriff Blackwood answered. "Somebody murdered Richard Forester. Somebody sitting among us right now. I suggest that whoever you are, you come clean and save everyone a lot of trouble."

Nobody said anything.

"This is your absolute final and last chance to come forward on your own recognizance. You won't get another chance to make it easy on yourself like this again," Sheriff Blackwood reinforced.

Again he was met with silence.

The sheriff sadly shook his head. "Until tomorrow then. Good night." Sheriff Blackwood placed his wide brimmed trooper's hat back on his head and turned to leave.

"Wait..."

Surprised, he turned around. Jim Frank stepped forward tentatively.

"Wait," Jim repeated with everyone staring at him.

Sheriff Blackwood raised an eyebrow. "You have something to say Mr. Frank?"

"Yes…yes, I do," Jim hesitated for a moment and then stepped forward one more step.

"It was *you*?" Sabrina asked.

"No!" Jim reacted. "I didn't kill him. But…"

Everyone watched him as he took one more look around the room and then looked back over to Sheriff Blackwood who patiently waited.

"Yes, Mr. Frank?"

With finality, Jim raised his chin and looked at the sheriff and said with confidence, "I didn't kill him. But I know who did. I know who murdered Richard Forester."

"Who? Who murdered him?" Sheriff Blackwood returned.

"It was…" Jim paused and then looked resolutely over to the newlywed couple, Sam and Gwen Richards. "It was *them*!"

Chapter 33

"That's a lie!" Sam burst out. "It's not true!"

"Yes, it is," Jim returned. "Just admit it. You killed him."

"He's lying!" Gwen stood by her husband, heatedly.

"Wait a minute now. Calm down, calm down," Sheriff Blackwood interrupted. "Let's hear what Mr. Frank has to say. Now surely, you have a good reason for accusing Sam and his wife?"

"But it's not true, Sheriff!" Sam protested.

"Let him speak, Sam."

Sam crossed his arms and glowered at Jim. "Fine."

"I do have a good reason," Jim stated.

"Let's hear it then," Sheriff Blackwood replied.

"Last night after dinner," Jim began, "Charlie and I decided to take a walk along the shore of the lake. It was a beautiful night outside, so we took our time and enjoyed some good, father and son time together. It's rare for us to be able to share such quality time together, so we took advantage of it."

"Seriously," Gwen interrupted. "We don't need to hear about his personal family grievances. He just accused us of murder. I don't care if this sounds heartless, but I couldn't really give a rat's ass about his father and son *quality* time!"

Sheriff Blackwood nodded. "Get to the point, Jim."

"On the way back to the house later on," Jim continued, "I saw something. Something that made me stop and look twice, because I couldn't believe I'd actually seen it."

"What did you see?" Sheriff Blackwood queried.

"A dark shape moving around just outside of the third floor window. Richard Forester's window. Somebody was on the roof and making their way around to the back of the house!" Jim responded eagerly.

Sam quietly closed his eyes. He'd been so occupied with getting out of the window and closing it behind him before Penny came back into the room that he hadn't even thought of looking to make sure nobody was outside on the ground first. It was just his bad luck that he'd been seen.

"You saw someone on the roof of *this* house?" Edna asked surprised.

"Yes."

"The roof is at a sharp angle up there!" Edna returned. "It would be suicide for anyone to try and traverse it, especially in the dark of the night."

"Nevertheless," Jim confirmed, "*Somebody* was up there. I saw it with my own eyes."

"Well, *somebody* hardly qualifies the two of us as being murderers," Gwen stipulated.

"I'm afraid I have to agree with Mrs. Richards," Sheriff Blackwood said. "Did you get a good look at who it was? Can you positively identify who was up there?"

Jim looked down and shook his head. "No, I cannot."

"What about Charlie? Did he see them?"

"No."

"Then what makes you so sure it was one of us?" Sam asked.

"Logical deduction," Jim answered looking up.

"Are you kidding me?" Gwen scoffed. Who do you think you are? Sherlock Holmes?"

"Sheriff, this is preposterous!" Sam blurted out. "He says he saw someone up there. A dark shape in the middle of the night that he can't positively identify, but we're guilty of murdering Richard Forester simply because he's logically deduced it! Come on!"

"If you'll let me explain…" Jim cut in.

"Explain? I think you've explained quite enough!" Gwen retaliated.

"No, wait," Aaron interjected. "I want to hear this."

"I do too," Sabrina agreed.

Sheriff Blackwood looked over to Jim. "So do I."

"Why? Surely you can see this is a desperate attempt to pin this on somebody. It's a wild goose chase!" Sam disagreed.

"Because as it so happens," Sheriff Blackwood answered, "I have evidence to suggest that somebody was indeed out there on the roof last night. Therefore, I feel it would be prudent to let Jim finish what he has to say. We should hear him out."

Sam and Gwen stood silently then with frustrated expressions on red faces.

"Ok, Jim. Please explain," the sheriff nodded in his direction.

"Thank you, Sheriff. Well, upon seeing somebody up there, I quickly ran up to the house and to the back where I saw them heading. But when I arrived, nobody was there. And nobody had come down the back way, and they obviously had not doubled back. So there's only one logical explanation to where this person could have gone," Jim said. "And that is the other side of the house and into the other room on the same floor. Their room."

Nobody said a word, but they looked instead at the two newlyweds who both appeared as if they'd swallowed a whole bottle containing syrup of ipecac.

"Sam?" Sheriff Blackwood said then. "Do you have anything to say?"

"No, Sheriff. All I have to say is we're not guilty of murder," Sam responded. "He's proved nothing."

"Okay. Fair enough. But were you in his room? And was that you up on the roof last night?" Sheriff Blackwood queried.

"We have nothing more to say until we have a lawyer present."

"I'm sorry, Sam, but you've waived your right to counsel," the sheriff reminded him. "Answer the question, please."

Sam didn't respond, but sat down instead in a heap on the loveseat. Gwen sat next to him quietly. Sheriff Blackwood sadly shook his head.

"Ross," he called out suddenly. "Go up to their room and bring down every item of clothing they have please."

"You got it, boss."

Sam smiled inwardly. Clothes? That wasn't going to prove anything. All power to him. After a few minutes, the deputy returned carrying an armload full of clothes which he piled on the floor at the sheriff's feet.

"Go ahead, Sheriff," Sam said. "We have nothing to hide. In fact, I'll even show you what I was wearing yesterday." Sam stood up and walked over to the pile of clothes and picked out the t-shirt and jeans he had on the day before and then handed them over. "Like I said," Sam continued, stepping back. "Nothing to hide."

The sheriff quickly inspected the jeans and then tossed them aside. He opened the shirt and looked it over carefully and then stopped and looked up with a wry smile. "Nothing to hide, Sam? Then what is this on your shirt here?"

Sheriff Blackwood held the shirt open before him and showed it to Sam. At first, Sam didn't see anything out of the ordinary and was about to respond in kind but then hesitated. He did see it. Or *them* rather. What he saw were small, blue specs on the fabric of the shirt. Hard to notice at first, but there they were. Sam looked up, confused and shrugged.

"Do you know what that is?" Sheriff Blackwood asked with a raised eyebrow. "Those are blue flakes of paint. The same flakes of paint that we found along the window sill and on the floor of Richard's room today. The blue flakes that resulted from the window being forced open. The window that *you* forced open."

"Oh, goodness!" Mildred exclaimed. "We'd forgotten all about that. Remember, Edna? When Felix painted the window closed and we weren't able to open it anymore?"

Edna rolled her eyes and sat forward. "She's right, Jacob. That bumbling fool had managed to seal the window shut with the paint drying over it and we never did get around to getting it fixed."

Sam faltered and hung his head. There was no sense in trying to deny it any longer. They were good and caught now. The only thing they could do was to just come clean.

"You were in that room last night, weren't you?" Sheriff Blackwood pressed.

Sam slowly nodded his head. "Yes."

"And that *was* you on the roof as well, wasn't it?"

Sam let out a long, deep breath and turned to rejoin his wife on the loveseat. Then looking down ashamedly, he answered. "Yes."

"I knew it," Jim affirmed.

"You know *nothing*!" Gwen spat out angrily in return. "My husband is no murderer. He was in the room and on the roof. But he didn't kill Mr. Forester." Gwen looked intently at Penny. "I swear it to you, Penny. It wasn't us."

"Why did you go in, and why creep around on the roof?" Sheriff Blackwood asked, looking down on the cowering couple.

"Before I say anything," Sam stipulated, "I want Penny to know that I'm ashamed of my behavior. I'm very, *very* sorry for what I've done."

Penny didn't say a word. She wiped a tear from her cheek, folded her slender arms across her chest, leaned back into the couch and just waited.

"Gwen is right, though," Sam continued, sitting forward a little. "We did not kill Mr. Forester. I fully admit that I went into the room while Penny was in the bathroom taking a shower. We thought...well, we hoped that maybe he'd tell us where he'd hidden the money he stole from MicaTek. I believed it was here, somewhere nearby. I mean, why else would someone as sick as he was be in Pleasant Lake so far away from his home or a doctor's care?"

"Grandpa Dick never stole that money," Penny responded. "He was their scapegoat. I've said it and said it and said it time and time again until I've been blue in the face. *He – did – not – steal – that – money*!"

"Yah, well, last night, we fully believed he had," Sam returned.

"Did he tell you what you wanted to know?" Sheriff Blackwood asked with a keen expression on his face.

Sam felt Gwen's grip slowly tighten on his arm before he could answer. He got the message loud and clear. "No," Sam shook his head. "He said he didn't take it."

"Then what? What happened next?" Sheriff Blackwood persisted.

"We heard Penny coming out of the bathroom. Gwen was by the door, so she left the room and made it appear that she'd just come out of our room so that Penny wouldn't know any different. And then...then

I..." but Sam hesitated and hung his head. "I can't. I don't think I can do this."

"You are doing just fine, Sam. Tell us," the sheriff said.

Sam raised his head slightly. He was flustered and near to tears. "I...I didn't want him yelling out or anything, so I reached over to the table and grabbed the Bible sitting there and knocked him out cold with it." Sam suddenly looked up and over to Penny. "Penny, I swear to you that's *all* I did to him. I swear it!"

"And then you forced the window open and crawled out on to the roof of the house," Sheriff Blackwood finished for him.

"Yes," Sam agreed. "I closed the window behind me and then crawled around to the back of the house just as Jim said and around to our window wishing I hadn't done it the whole time. I was hoping he'd wake up and think it was all a bad dream. But he was alive when I left that room. Unconscious...but *alive*." Sam let out a big breath and sank back into the cushions of the loveseat. "There. I've said it. I know it was a stupid thing to do..."

"*Incredibly* stupid!" Edna said then with undisguised anger in her voice. "Do you realize just what it is you have done? Sneaking into a sick man's room and then clubbing him over the head with a Bible? A Bible no less! Such sacrilege." Edna shook her head with a cutting and disapproving look that silenced even Sheriff Blackwood from saying anything. Sam and Gwen sat quietly, shamed all over again.

"I'm sorry," Sam said softly.

"Jim, what time was it when you and Charlie were coming back from your walk? When did you see him up there?" Sheriff Blackwood asked turning to snap his fingers at Deputy Moss and then pointed at the small notepad in the deputy's shirt pocket. Deputy Moss took his queue and pulled out the notepad and a pen and waited for Jim's answer.

"Uh...well, I don't really remember, Sheriff," Jim replied stopping to think. "It was late, but not too late. I guess it was about 10:30 or 10:45 or so."

"Is that about when you got done with your shower Penny?" the sheriff continued.

Penny hesitated for a moment and then nodded. Deputy Moss busily scribbled a few notes down.

"Sam?" Sheriff Blackwood prompted.

"Sounds about right. It was around that time," Sam confirmed.

Gwen looked like she was going to say something, her face in earnest. She stirred restlessly next to her husband, but he reached over and took her hand causing her to stop and look over at him. He slowly shook his head with a serious look in his eye. Gwen, confused, bit her tongue and settled back again.

"Okay then," the sheriff said at last after Deputy Moss had completed his notes and placed the notepad back into this shirt pocket. "I guess that about wraps it up then for this evening unless anyone else has something to add to what has already been disclosed here."

"What?" Aaron burst out flabbergasted. "Surely you aren't buying into their story, Sheriff. Don't tell me you believe them!"

"I don't know what I believe yet, Mr. Buchanon," Sheriff Blackwood pointedly responded.

"You aren't even going to take them under arrest for suspicion of his murder?" Aaron returned incredulous.

"Need I remind you that you're *all* under arrest for suspicion of his death? Look around you, sir. There are police officers posted everywhere around this house. *This* is your jail cell. Sam's and Gwen's too. Remember that."

Aaron could only stare back in disbelief. But he said no more.

"It's hard to believe," Sheriff Blackwood continued, "that only about 24 hours ago I was introducing Richard and Penny to Mildred and Edna just before you all had dinner together. Speaking of which..." The Sheriff looked at his watch. "The time has gotten away from us and Cathy is going to kill me if I don't get home soon. I'll be back in the morning. I advise you all to seriously think about what you're going to tell me when I talk to you individually tomorrow. Nothing has been proven here tonight. Goodnight, everyone."

Sheriff Blackwood turned and grabbed Deputy Moss by the elbow and pulled him out of the room towards the foyer so they could speak privately.

"I'm relying on you to keep a careful watch over things here tonight, Ross," the sheriff reminded him. "Don't take your duty lightly. Remember, one of them is a murderer."

"You can count on me, boss," Deputy Moss hastily assured him.

"Good. I'll be sending Randall Pitchford up here at around midnight to relieve you, so when he arrives, you can go home and then report back to the office at eight o'clock sharp," Sheriff Blackwood instructed him.

"Yes sir."

"You did a fine job today, Ross," Sheriff Blackwood smiled up warmly to his young deputy and patted him approvingly on his shoulder. "You handled yourself well."

"Thank you, boss!" Deputy Moss beamed from ear to ear with obvious pleasure at the compliment.

"You're welcome. You just be sure to keep your head about you now. Understand?"

Deputy Moss vigorously nodded his head still smiling broadly. Sheriff Blackwood nodded and turned to leave.

"Uh, boss?"

"What is it Ross?" Sheriff Blackwood responded turning.

"Do you think Sam was telling you the truth, or do you think he was lying?"

Sheriff Blackwood leaned in and lowered his voice. "Between you and me, Ross, that boy is no killer. They're just a couple of foolish young kids who saw dollar signs before their eyes. He no more murdered Richard Forester than you or I."

"I don't think he did it either."

"However," the sheriff stipulated, "you treat them like anybody else under suspicion. Don't trust anyone until this case has been solved and put to bed."

"You got it, boss."

"And one more thing deputy…"

"Yes, boss?"

"Don't call me boss."

Chapter 34

Jim walked over to Edna after she'd just finished sending Alexis into the kitchen to check with Felix on the preparation of the evening's dinner.

"I'm sorry, Edna," Jim began, "but would it be possible if you could ring down again to see if Charlie is okay? I haven't talked to him since this morning and I'm sure he's wondering about me too."

"I don't see a problem with that, Mr. Frank. Wait here and I'll call the Corbitt's place. I'll be right back," Edna said and then walked over to the phone in the corner of the room.

Jim watched quietly as Edna spoke on the phone over the next couple of minutes until she placed the receiver back down and rejoined him.

"Were you able to reach them?" he asked.

"Charlie is doing fine, Mr. Frank. He's safe and sound at the Corbitt home and getting along famously with Billy. It seems they've become quick friends," Edna assured him. "I have apprised Sharon of the situation and she'll make sure Charlie knows what's going on. She told me to tell you that he'll be well cared for and he's welcome to stay there with them for however long the house arrest will last."

"Thank you. I really do appreciate it."

"No problem at all," Edna replied. Then she paused and looked at him curiously. "Mr. Frank, may I ask you a personal question?"

Jim felt his feathers ruffle a little bit at her tone, but he nodded anyway. "Sure."

"You mentioned your wife's name was Regina."

"Yes."

"I couldn't help but notice a striking resemblance between your son Charlie and the young girl that Mildred and I were talking about earlier," Edna continued. "Her name was Regina too. You know...the girl who we mentioned who used to come here on her summer vacations and help us with the aviary?"

"Oh sure, I remember you mentioning her. What's your question, Edna?" Jim asked already knowing what it was going to be.

"Was your wife's maiden name Saunders? Regina Saunders?"

Jim shook his head even though she had nailed it dead on. That was her maiden name, but he wasn't about to let any skeletons out of the closet just yet. Not with all of this happening around them.

"No, Ma'am. I'm sorry, but the Regina who I married and had Charlie with was Regina Sullivan before she took my name." Jim hoped his lie sounded convincing.

"I see," Edna sounded disappointed. "Well, I'm sorry if I've offended you in any way, but I was just curious. The resemblance is uncanny."

Jim weakly smiled. "It's okay. No harm done." With that, Jim turned and walked away.

Edna saw Penny slowly stand to her feet, wavering with uncertainty for a moment and then make her way over to where Sam and Gwen still sat arm in arm on the loveseat. Sam looked up as she approached them and stood up to face her. He bowed his head.

"Penny...please accept my apolo..."

Penny reached up and slapped him hard across his face before he could finish. The sting of the reproach hurt more than the slap itself and tears welled up in Sam's eyes.

"Apology accepted," Penny replied.

With a darkening red face, Sam quickly brushed past Penny and over to the foyer. They could hear him as he began to ascend the staircase. Gwen hastily jumped to her feet and followed him out. Mildred walked over and put her arm around Penny and sat her down.

Edna for the first time felt really sad for the teenage girl, but she took in a deep breath and announced, "I'm going to go and see what Felix has prepared for us to eat tonight. You all might do well to go and freshen up. It's been a long day; I think it would be nice to put it behind us now and enjoy a good dinner. You'll be joining us, Ross?"

Deputy Moss lifted his head at the sound of his name. "Sure! If it's no bother."

"No bother at all."

Aaron, Sabrina and Jim all agreed and left for their rooms, each giving Penny a parting glance on their way out of the living area. Edna watched as Mildred comforted Penny. Mildred was always good at things like this. Of the two sisters, she was always the one with the big heart, always concerned...always caring. Whereas Edna had always been the organizer, the firm one...the heavy. Edna knew that Mildred could be quite unyielding though when she had to be. But could Edna be as compassionate as her sister was? Sometimes she wondered. Edna shrugged to herself and headed towards the kitchen. They were who they were, and there was dinner to attend to.

Chapter 35

Sam swung the door to the room hard behind him as he entered, but the resounding *slam* that should have followed this action…didn't.

"*Crap Sam!*" Gwen shouted, reacting just in time to catch the door before it hit her right on the nose. "You could've taken my head off!"

Sam didn't seem to care. He was sitting on the edge of their bed with his face buried in his hands. "I'm sorry!" he half-yelled.

Gwen softened a little. "It's okay. Just be careful…"

"I'm sorry! I'm sorry! I'm *so sorry!*"

Gwen realized then that he wasn't talking to her.

"I'm sorry we even came here at all!" Sam exclaimed, looking up. He had tears in reddened eyes. "I'm sorry I even heard of Richard Forester. I'm sorry we came to this stupid bed & breakfast! I'm sorry we…we…"

"We got married?" Gwen finished for him, her voice shaking.

Sam looked up at her with his mouth open, eyes in disbelief. "Oh, no, sweetheart!" He walked over, collecting his young wife into his arms and holding her close. "I'll never be sorry for marrying you. I love you with all my heart."

Gwen let out a sigh of relief and smiled, burying her face into his chest.

"I was just going to say that I'm sorry we ever made up that stupid plan to go into his room in the first place, that's all," Sam explained, now calm.

"Thank God," Gwen said, almost to tears herself now. "I thought you didn't want me anymore."

Sam held her close rubbing her back with the flat of his hand. "No, baby. I would die for you."

Gwen looked up at her husband and then kissed him softly on the lips. "I would die for you too," she breathed.

They parted and he ran his fingers through her dark hair and then slowly turned and returned to the edge of the bed where he sat down again.

"I deserved more," Sam said after a moment.

"What do you mean *deserved more*?" Gwen sat next to him, and held his hand in hers.

"I deserved more than what Penny gave me," he replied. "More than just a slap to the face. I deserved more."

"Honey, don't beat yourself up over this. Please."

"Gwen, I'm ashamed. The man who hit him over the head and knocked him out with a bible…that wasn't me. That isn't who I am," Sam acknowledged.

"I know it isn't," Gwen agreed. "But you need to realize there's a much bigger picture here now than that. In this same house at this very moment, is Richard's murderer."

"Yah and they all think it's me."

"Honestly baby, I don't think the sheriff believes it's us. I feel strongly that if he really believed that, we wouldn't still be here right now."

"Little blue paint flakes on my t-shirt and I handed it right to him," Sam shook his head with incredulity.

"That's hardly evidence of his murder."

"And that's another thing," Sam turned to look at Gwen. "Why tell us what they found? Why did Doc Meecham give us the details surrounding Richard's death? How come he told us about the needle mark, the contusion and the strangle marks on his throat? Didn't you find that odd? I can't imagine they'd normally do that."

"Well," Gwen shrugged, "he was placing us under house arrest. I guess they wanted to make it clear why."

"They could have just said he was found murdered."

"I don't know, hon. But I'm sure they had their reasons."

"I guess." Sam looked back down to the floor.

"The contusion *you* gave him," Gwen offered. "That much is now certain and everyone knows it. But that still leaves the needle mark on his arm and the bruises on his neck. Somebody else was in the room, which you personally witnessed."

"True."

"Which reminds me…"

"You want to know why I stopped you from saying anything about how we overheard Aaron and Sabrina's scheme?" Sam said reading her mind.

Gwen laughed.

"What's so funny?"

"I was just thinking to myself that we really *are* married now, because we're beginning to finish each other's sentences and thoughts," Gwen said.

Sam smiled at her. "Well, if that's true," he replied, "then that means you should already know how I was going to answer that question."

Gwen stopped and then her face lit up. "Actually, I think I *do* know the answer!"

"Let's hear it then."

"You were afraid that they might just think we were trying to shift the blame off of us…like we were desperate."

Sam nodded approvingly. "Not bad! That's pretty close. If you'd told him at that very moment what we overheard, they may not have believed us just like you said. That's why it's more important to find the right

time, so that when we *do* tell him, he'll take it more
seriously and actually look into it."

"So we're going to tell Sheriff Blackwood about it
then?"

"You can count on it."

Gwen kissed him. "I love you."

"I love you too."

Chapter 36

Aaron and Sabrina lingered behind Jim as he climbed up the staircase to the second floor and to his room. Without a word, Jim opened his door and then disappeared on the other side of it, closing it snugly behind him. After making sure nobody was watching, they both quickly entered Aaron's room, the Brown Room, and latched the door shut. Aaron then spun around and placed his index finger to her lips silencing her from being able to say anything. He then leaned in and whispered in her ear.

"If they've taken the time to remove our phones, they could have bugged our rooms as well."

Sabrina nodded her understanding.

Aaron very quickly and deftly checked the room for bugs and after a thorough search, he was satisfied they were okay. He reached out to pull Sabrina close to him, but she pulled away defiantly with a cold look in her eyes.

"Some of us have families to get home to too?" she spat out.

"Come on Sabrina," Aaron sighed. "You know I'm married. I've never kept that from you."

"Yah, but you know how I feel about it, Aaron."

"I'm sorry, Sabrina, but it is what it is."

"I hate that expression!" Sabrina fumed. *"It is what it is."*

"I'm not going to leave my wife and daughter. We've been over this ground before, and this isn't exactly the time to be bringing it up again!" Aaron stated growing upset. "The next thing I know, my wife is going to find a bunny boiled to death on her kitchen stove! *Damn*!"

Sabrina paused and took a deep breath. "Okay. I'm sorry."

Aaron strode over to the dresser on the other side of the room and gripped its corners staring blankly at the wall it rested against.

"They didn't do it," Aaron said after a while.

"What?" Sabrina looked up. "You mean Sam and Gwen, the moronic newlyweds?"

"I went in after they must have because when you pulled Penny from the room, she'd just come from the shower. I know, because the bathroom was still warm and damp with moisture, and the mirror was still steamed over," Aaron explained, and then he let out a short laugh. "Ironic that those two fool kids should come up with the same plan we had…to try and fish the money's location from Richard. What I don't understand is how they beat us to him."

"I would say the point is moot now," Sabrina countered. "But, yah, her hair was still wet. So she'd come from the shower alright."

Aaron pushed himself back from the dresser and turned to face her. "Moot? I don't think so *dear*."

"Why not?"

"Think about it!" Aaron snarled at her, pointing a single finger toward his head. "Those two idiots very well may be the only people alive who know where that $750,000 is hidden."

"But Sam said Richard told him he didn't take it."

"And you believe him?"

"Actually, yah, I do, Aaron," Sabrina admitted. "I think he was telling the truth. You and I have both been in this business long enough to recognize a true confession when we see it, and I believe we saw one tonight."

"Maybe."

"Maybe? C'mon. You just said it yourself. *They didn't do it.* Remember?"

Aaron nodded.

"So why did you say that then?" Sabrina pressed.

"Well, like I said, I went in after they did. The old man was out cold like Sam said. But he was breathing. He was alive. They didn't kill him."

"What about the syringe?"

"I've been thinking about that," Aaron commented. "There are only two possibilities on what could have happened to it. It's either in the hands of the Sheriff and why he chose to keep it from us, I have no idea."

"Or?"

"Or somebody else in this house has it and is keeping it hidden. Also for reasons I can only imagine."

"What do *you* think happened to it?"

"Well," Aaron wrinkled his brow, "while we were in the room checking on Richard, I gave the room a pretty good once over and I didn't see it anywhere. I checked again on the way out, but I'm pretty sure it wasn't there. I'd have gotten a better look though if it weren't for Sam. He caught me trying to..." Aaron then snapped his head around, his eyes blazing. "Wait a minute!"

"What? What is it?"

"Sam and Gwen must have it! Sure...it makes perfect sense!"

"Why do you think they have it?" Sabrina probed.

"It's what he said. He asked me if I was *looking for something*. But it was the *way* he said it that made me remember it. He must have found it, picked it up and kept it."

"How? That isn't possible, Aaron," Sabrina disagreed. "They were in the room before you were. And they wouldn't have been able to go back in afterwards either, because you said that the maid, Alexis was up there right after you'd left. Remember? Add to that the fact that Alexis said she saw Penny coming up the stairs carrying a glass of strawberry milk. So with Penny there after Alexis, they wouldn't have been able to go back in then either. If anyone in this house has it, it would have to be Alexis. Not them."

Aaron mulled it over in his mind. The wheels were turning. Actually, it could have been pretty much anybody. Sheriff Blackwood, Doc Meecham, Alexis...even Penny herself. But he still felt that somehow Sam had it.

"What if it *was* still in the room the next morning and I somehow overlooked it?" he offered. "After Sam asked me that, I left and went downstairs. That's right! He was the last one down. He must have gone in the room after I left, and found it. That little wretch."

"I don't know, Aaron," Sabrina doubtfully shook her head. "That's a pretty big stretch."

"Well, I'll tell you something that isn't a big stretch. Even if they don't have the syringe, they will surely know it belonged to me. As idiotic as they are, it won't be too hard for them to put two and two together to figure out that the missing syringe is what I was looking for."

"I'll give you that. But right now, the missing syringe, as much of a thorn in our side as it is, is not the largest of our worries."

"What do you mean?" Aaron asked.

"They have our ID's. How long before Sheriff Blackwood finds out that you and I are both federal agents?"

Aaron smiled and put his hand on her slender shoulder. "Federal Agents working undercover to bring a suspected criminal, an embezzler to justice. You think that's going to harm us or help us?"

"I see your point," Sabrina relaxed with a small smile of her own. "Yah, you're right. We were just doing our job."

"Exactly. But for now, until they blow the whistle on us, we're still strangers. Agreed?"

"Agreed." Sabrina lowered her face and peered up at him with alluring eyes, a small, mischievous smile playing across her soft lips. "But behind closed doors, we're more than that. *Much* more than that," she said moving close to him, lifting her face to his and then pausing with her lips barely touching his. "Now tell me, Mr. Family Man…how bad do you really want to go home?"

He didn't say a word. Instead he completed the distance between them and kissed her deep and hard. And then he kissed her again.

"That's what I thought," Sabrina purred holding him close.

Aaron slowly pulled away from her, shaking his head.

"What is it?" she asked with a hint of disappointment in her voice.

"Sorry. I only wish I knew what happened with that syringe."

"Are we back to that again?"

"It's just that it's still the one thing that could really mess things up for us."

Sabrina inched forward a step. "You never did tell me what happened in there last night. Did you get the truth out of him? You said he was alive when you went in. The big question is…was he alive when you left?"

Suddenly, three extremely loud raps sounded on the door to the room causing them both to nearly jump out of their skin.

"Mr. Buchanon?" they could hear Edna's muffled voice from the other side of the door. "Are you in there?"

Breathing heavily, Aaron raised a finger to his lips. Sabrina understood.

"Uh, yes. One moment please."

Aaron opened his wardrobe closet and hastily pushed Sabrina inside despite her quiet objections. Then taking in one last deep breath to steady himself, he went over to the door and opened it. Edna stood before him, her hands clasped in front of her.

"Yes?" he addressed her.

"Dinner will be served in ten minutes," Edna informed him. "Have you seen Miss Riggs? She's not answering her door."

"No, Ma'am, but if I do, I'll be sure to let her know," he assured her.

"I just hope she hasn't gone and done anything stupid," Edna admonished with a judgmental eye. "That wouldn't do. Not at all."

"Yes, Ma'am."

"Please, Mr. Buchanon, you can just call me Edna."

Aaron smiled briefly. "Of course. Edna."

"See you downstairs in ten minutes then."

Edna turned and knocked on Jim's door and gave him the same announcement when he answered. He said he'd be there.

Aaron closed the door and let Sabrina out of the closet.

"Thanks for shoving me in there!" she cried.

"We'll have to talk later," Aaron said, ignoring her. "Just play it cool, okay? And keep your eyes and ears open for anything leading to the missing syringe."

Sabrina reluctantly nodded. Aaron cracked the door open. Satisfied that the hallway was clear, he opened it and Sabrina slipped through and into her own room.

Chapter 37

"Felix!"

Felix stopped what he was doing to see Edna standing just inside the kitchen doorway with her hands, knuckles down, on her hips, a scowl on her face, glaring at him.

"I swear you get more and more beautiful every time I see you," Felix said.

"Pffft! I've given everyone a ten minute warning for dinner. I hope you'll be on time tonight...for once!" Edna returned.

"Don't you worry your pretty little self about that," Felix retorted. "Dinner will be served on time. Stop wasting my time and let me get to it!"

Edna ground her teeth and then stopped and looked around.

"Where's Alexis?" she asked. "I told her to come in here and help you get things ready."

"Dining Room!"

"Very well, then."

Edna went to the other side of the kitchen and through the door and into the Dining Room where she found both Mildred and Alexis busily setting places at the table.

"That cantankerous old coot will be the death of me," Edna huffed.

Mildred giggled softly to herself as she floated around the table carefully putting a plate down in front of each chair. "Oh dear!" she suddenly exclaimed when she got to where Richard had sat the night before. She had unwittingly set a place for him without even realizing it.

For a minute, nobody said anything. Edna came over and put her arm around her sister. "It's okay. No harm done," she reassured her. Edna reached down and picked up the plate and handed it over to Alexis. "Return this one to the kitchen, please." Alexis did as she was asked.

"In fact," Edna continued, stepping around to the other side of the table, "I think it would be best to put Penny over here tonight. Charlie's staying over at the Corbitt's place, so she can take his seat. We'll put Ross over there."

"Yes," Mildred agreed, gathering herself together again. "Yes, that would be best."

Within minutes everyone was in the room, sitting where Edna directed them to. The mood was somber and silent, almost as if they were all on death row being shown to their cell. Only Deputy Moss showed any sign of life when Felix wheeled out a tray carefully placed on top of his walker holding pork chops, mashed potatoes, gravy, mixed vegetables and dinner rolls. As the smell of the freshly prepared and hot meal began to permeate the room, everyone finally started to settle down and relax.

Edna looked at her watch and let out a small breath of indignation. *Well*, she thought to herself, *maybe one of these days he will be on time*. But she said nothing as Felix and Alexis served everyone up a healthy plate along with a tall glass of iced tea.

"Oh Felix!" Mildred was the first to speak. "This just looks absolutely wonderful! And I love iced tea. Thank you, Alexis." Alexis finished pouring her iced tea and nodded politely in her direction.

Felix stopped and looked at Edna, waiting for her to say something.

"What Felix? Do you require my stamp of approval?" Edna asked.

"It's never stopped you before!" Felix snapped.

"It does look very nice, Felix, even if it *is* a little late," Edna returned.

"Well!" Felix smiled. "Coming from you, I'll take that as a compliment then."

"Thank you," Edna replied. "And you?"

"And me *what*?"

"Do you have a compliment for me?" Edna continued. "You *do* know how to compliment a lady, don't you Felix?"

Everyone turned and watched as Felix angled his walker so that he was facing Edna straight on. "Of *course,* I know how to compliment a lady!"

Edna sat up prim and proper and waited. "Go on then! Let's hear it."

"Very well. Edna..." Felix paused with a twinkle in his eye. "There is nobody...and I mean *nobody*, in this world who can wear a bun in her hair like you do!"

All tension immediately evaporated with the entire room erupting in laughter as Edna self-conscientiously reached up, almost protectively, to place her hands next to her hair, her face as red as a tomato. Even Penny felt the humor strings being tugged on her own heart as she began to laugh too in spite of herself. For a brief little while, nobody had been murdered...and all was right with the world.

Chapter 38

The rest of the dinner passed by quickly and quietly with very little being said until the last plate had been cleared away. Penny was the first person to leave the table, standing up and stating that she refused to share a dinner with *thieves and murderers*. She snatched up her plate and glass and went into the kitchen to finish her meal with Felix. Nobody objected, and nobody said a word as she left. Penny finished her meal in silence, thanked Felix and then quietly left the kitchen. She entered Mildred's room where she would be sleeping, closed the door behind her and that's where she remained for the rest of the night.

After finishing their dinner, Sam and Gwen left the table where the others, aside from Penny, were all still gathered. Gwen slid her arm inside her husband's and holding each other close, they slowly climbed the staircase to their room on the top floor, entered, and did not come out. Jim was the next person to leave, briefly thanking the two sisters for the dinner, and then he too went straight to his room.

Sabrina wiped her mouth with a napkin and then set it down on the table looking over at Aaron. "Join me in a game of Checkers?" she asked him. Aaron hesitated for a moment and then nodded. "Sure, why not?"

After everyone had finished and proceeded to the living area or their room, Mildred and Edna went to the kitchen to prepare dinner plates for the officers standing guard outside the bed & breakfast. Edna stayed behind to watch over the house with Deputy Moss while

Mildred distributed the meals to the grateful policemen, normally a duty assigned to Alexis. But as she was also under house arrest, it was decided that Mildred should go ahead and see to it.

Alexis busied herself in the kitchen helping Felix to clean and organize the area for the next morning's breakfast. Felix made sure everything looked satisfactory and then exclaimed, "I'm not as young as I used to be!" and left the washing of the dishes to Alexis while he retired to his quarters for the night. Alexis was about to open the dishwasher when Edna appeared.

"No, no, no child!" Edna admonished. "Leave that contraption closed. Fill up the sink instead and wash them by hand. That dishwasher never cleans anything right."

"Yes, Miss," Alexis responded, allowing the dishwasher door to spring shut and proceeded to do as Edna instructed.

"And where is Felix?"

"He went to his room, Miss."

"Alexis," Edna continued, walking over to the sink. "Why don't you let me finish this? You've had a long day and I'm sure you have a lot weighing on your mind with today's events. You may be excused."

"Thank you."

"Be sure to have Deputy Moss escort you out to your quarters though. Don't just go out there skipping along like you don't have a care in the world."

Alexis promised she would and left the room. She found the lanky deputy hovering around in the dining room, still eating a dinner roll.

"I'm ready for bed," she said.

Deputy Moss almost choked on what he was eating and looked back at the attractive maid with a flushed face. "You are?" he managed.

"I'm ready for bed now," she repeated matter-of-factly. "But I can't go to my quarters by myself. I need you to escort me out there so that the other officers won't think I'm trying to make a break for it."

"Ahhh," Deputy Moss relaxed with a sheepish grin. "Sure. No problem. Be happy to." He finished the last of his dinner roll and then wiped his hands clean on the sides of his pants. "This way," Deputy Moss smiled at her and then led her back into the kitchen where Edna was already elbow deep in dishwater.

Edna looked up as they entered.

"Oh Ross," Edna said, "as soon as you're done escorting Alexis to her room could you please come back here? I'd like to discuss a few things with you."

"Sure thing, Miss Pookotz."

Edna returned to her washing while Deputy Moss and Alexis continued through the kitchen and out the back screen door into the growing darkness of the evening outside. The insects were already busy with their nocturnal activities, buzzing and chirping in the air around them as they made their way down the pathway to the servant's quarters. A police officer was sitting on a nearby stump along the edge of the woods to their right and nodded briefly at them. Deputy Moss halted just outside her doorway and Alexis hurried past him. They could hear Felix snoring next door in a deep slumber having decided to go straight to sleep instead of listening to his customary radio shows.

"Well, here you go, safe and sound," Deputy Moss announced with a slight bow.

"Thank you, deputy," Alexis replied with a weak smile and then disappeared on the other side of the door closing it quickly behind her. Deputy Moss stood there for a moment and let out a short sigh. Then turning, he headed back to the house.

Alexis let out a deep breath and flipped the light switch on. Making sure the blinds were drawn, she shed her outfit and slipped on a nightie and a pair of fuzzy bedroom slippers. She sat down on the edge of the bed with a hairbrush and pulled her hair down running the brush through the strands to work out the snags from the day.

Things were starting to get pretty hot and heavy now. She looked over at her nightstand where the phone usually sat, and sure enough, it was gone. Then she had an alarming thought. She stood and padded softly over to her closet and turned on the overhead light inside. She moved aside a few items of clothing and let out a breath of relief to find that the shoebox and its contents were still there.

Chapter 39

The back screen door opened and Deputy Moss entered the kitchen where Edna still labored. "You said you needed to talk to me?" he asked walking towards her.

"Ross," Edna responded without looking up. "Jacob and I didn't get a chance to go over what the arrangements were going to be with the officers assigned to watch the house. I need you to fill me in."

"We'll be working three eight-hour shifts a day," Deputy Moss informed her. "At midnight, we'll be relieved and then at eight a.m. those officers will be relieved. Then again at four in the afternoon..."

"Yes, yes, Ross. I get the picture," Edna interrupted. "How many officers have been assigned to watch the house for each shift?"

"Well, let's see here." Deputy Moss reached up and thoughtfully rubbed his chin. "There will be one officer watching the front door, and another the back. Each side of the house also has an officer watching, as well as one posted by the servant's quarters and still another down in the parking lot to watch the cars. And then, of course, one inside the house. So what is that? Seven? Yes, there will be seven of us posted around the premises at any one time."

"Seven officers for seven suspects," Edna mused. "Fitting, I suppose."

"Seven suspects?" Deputy Moss asked.

"If you think for one minute that Felix, Mildred or I..."

"No, Ma'am," Deputy Moss affirmed. "I was just thinking that it was six, not seven."

"No. Seven."

"We have Sam and Gwen Richards, Aaron Buchanon, Jim Frank, Sabrina Riggs, and your maid Alexis. That makes six."

"And Penny Forester. She makes seven."

"His *granddaughter*?" Deputy Moss returned astonished. "Surely not!"

"Nevertheless," Edna shook her head, "Jacob has named her as a suspect. And why not? She had ample opportunity."

"Opportunity maybe, but no motive."

The door to the kitchen from the dining room swung open and Mildred walked in, her arms loaded with dirty plates, silverware and glasses.

"Just in time," Edna said walking over to help her sister. "I'm ready to wash those now."

"Oh, thank you," Mildred accepted. "Every single one of those dear officers outside were so gracious and kind. They asked me to thank you for the dinner plates, Edna, and Felix too."

"We'll have to thank Felix in the morning," Edna returned, sinking the last remaining dirty plate into the sudsy water. "He's gone on to bed."

"I'm going to go and make my rounds," Deputy Moss said. "Need to check in with the boys outside and inspect inside the house as well. Do you need anything else, Edna?"

"Not right now, Ross," Edna answered. "If we do, we'll be sure to find you."

Deputy Moss tipped his hat in their direction and left.

"Where is everyone?" Mildred inquired picking up a dry towel.

"They've all gone to their rooms. Except for Mr. Buchanon and Miss Riggs. I believe they went to the living area to play a game of Checkers."

Mildred let out a slow breath. "What a long, hard day."

"Yes," Edna agreed. "It's a black day for the Pookotz Bed & Breakfast. Never before in our storied history have we had a house arrest here. Never that is, until today."

"Ironic isn't it?"

Edna looked quizzically over to her younger sister. "What's ironic?"

"It's true that we've never had a house arrest here," Mildred replied. "What's ironic is that there *has* been a murder within these walls before."

"I was trying to forget about that," Edna looked down. "That was well before our time though. And it was never really certain or conclusive that it was murder."

"A mysterious death then."

"Well, the Bed & Breakfast has survived bleak days before and it will survive this as well," Edna said, handing the last scrubbed plate to Mildred who promptly dried and placed it on the shelf with the other clean plates.

Edna reached into the sink, carefully feeling along the bottom for any dishes or silverware she may have missed and then satisfied she'd washed everything, she removed the stopper from the drain and the water began to swirl slowly down.

"We're missing a glass," Mildred announced, standing next to the shelves where all the glasses were stored side-by-side, top down. "Did we forget one over there?"

Edna quickly glanced back down into the sink where all the water had nearly drained out and saw nothing there. She looked over the countertops and scanned the rest of the kitchen, but saw no glass. "It must be out in one of the other rooms. Or one of the officers may still have it with him and just forgot to give it to you when you collected the dirty dishes from them earlier," she replied rinsing out the sink, washing down the last of the suds. "No matter, we'll find it tomorrow."

"Yes, I'm sure we will," Mildred agreed folding her drying towel and laying it softly on the counter top. She let out a small sigh, her eyes remaining downcast. This did not go unnoticed by Edna who stepped over to her sister's side.

"What is it, Mildred?"

Mildred looked up sadly. "I just feel so awful for that poor girl. Her grandfather was all she had left in this world. And to be confined within the same home as his murderer..." She let the sentence go unfinished.

"I saw you with her earlier," Edna confided. "I have to say, I've always admired your caring and warm nature, Mildred. You're a very kind spirit, and I envy you that. I know I used to get down on you for being more responsible over the years, but secretly, I've always wished I was more like you." Edna gave her sister a warm smile.

"Oh Edna!" Mildred beamed with delight. "Thank you! But you *are* a kind and warm spirit. I've never been strong or organized like you. You've always been the one to take charge and get things done around here. And in truth, I've always wished I was more like you!"

The two sisters laughed and hugged each other.

Edna straightened and brought her hand up to her hair and then paused for a moment. Looking back at Mildred, she said, "Do you think maybe I should wear my hair down more?"

Mildred giggled softly and shook her head. "Why? Because of Felix's compliment?"

"Of course not!" Edna retorted with a short snap, her gruff side coming to the fore once more.

"No dear sister, I wouldn't change a thing. This is who you are." Mildred turned to leave. "Meet me in the parlor again for some reading?"

"Be right there. Just going to finish up in here."

"Okay. See you in a bit then," Mildred replied. "And I told you Felix fancies you!" Mildred disappeared through the swinging door before Edna could respond.

"Hmmmph!" Edna grunted crossing her arms over her chest.

Chapter 40

"We need to talk," Sabrina half whispered, sitting in the chair across the game table from Aaron. Aaron was unfolding a checkers board and arranging the pieces and nodding sullenly.

"I know," Aaron replied without looking up. "Just keep an eye out for anyone while we talk, ok?"

Sabrina nodded. "I will."

She waited patiently until Aaron had finished setting up the checkers board and then with a deep breath, he looked up at her.

"You want to know what happened while I was in the room with him."

"Yes," she nodded again. "Sheriff Blackwood will be interviewing us tomorrow. It would be nice to be on the same page going in, don't you think?"

"Yes."

"What *did* happen in there, Aaron?"

"Richard was out cold. Little did I know that he'd just been clobbered over the head with a leather bound bible by that idiot Sam," Aaron began. "I just thought he was out of it…in a deep sleep. My original plan was to wake him up, and get him to tell me where the money was."

"How?"

"Like we discussed in the parking lot at my car. I had enough dirt on him to not only make the rest of his life miserable, but also Penny's," Aaron continued. "If he refused to cooperate, I was going to make sure everybody knew of his dirty little secrets."

"That's right," Sabrina said, remembering. "And the syringe was just supposed to be in case. So what happened? He didn't cooperate?"

"Not exactly."

Aaron stopped and raised a finger. Sabrina froze. After a moment, Aaron relaxed and looked down at the checkers board. "Sorry. I thought someone was coming. We should probably make some moves here. Would look pretty strange to anyone walking in if none of the pieces were moved."

"Who goes first? Red or black?"

"I don't know. It's been years since I've played this game. I think red does. So you can go first."

Sabrina moved a piece forward and then looked back up at Aaron while he moved his first piece. "What do you mean *not exactly?*"

"Well," Aaron answered, looking up briefly, "I suddenly realized that if he was smart enough to fool not only the IRS but also the FBI while in the middle of a full blown investigation, then there was no way he was going to just spill the beans to me. So I decided to inject him with the serum first. Before he woke up. Besides, it wasn't like I had oodles of time."

Sabrina rolled her eyes. "*Oodles?* I've never met anyone who talks like you do, Aaron. *Oodles* of time?"

"I spent a lot of time with my Grandmother when I was young!" Aaron defended himself. "I picked up on a lot of her words and phrases I guess. Now stop giving me a hard time about it!"

"Okay, okay!" Sabrina responded, trying to suppress a laugh. "I'm sorry."

Aaron sat back and let out a long breath. "Do you want to hear this or not?"

"I do. I'm sorry."

He sat back up and moved another piece, not really caring anymore about the game itself. "Okay then. Enough of the grammar corrections."

"I promise. No more grammar corrections. Besides…I think it's kinda cute."

"You would."

"So you got out the syringe and injected him with the serum then?" she asked getting them back on subject.

"Not exactly."

"Aaron that's the second *not exactly* you've told me tonight." Aaron raised his head and began to open his mouth. "That's not a grammar correction!" Sabrina interjected before he could say anything.

"Fine," Aaron stopped short. "No, I didn't inject him. At the moment I was going to inject him with the truth serum, I heard someone coming up the stairs. The creaking of the boards startled me and, stupid me, I dropped the syringe and it fell to the floor. I felt around for it, I looked as long as I dared and then I left the room. That's when I passed Alexis on the stairwell."

"Wait a minute," Sabrina interrupted. "Let me get something straight here. You went into his room and left a needle mark on his arm. A needle mark that the doctor recognized *as* a needle mark, incriminating us in the process. Not only did you lose the syringe, but you didn't inject him? You didn't find out where the money is? And he didn't even know you were there?" Sabrina's voice was growing louder with every word, her face angered.

"Keep your voice down!" Aaron responded in a harsh whisper. "Do you want the whole house to hear?"

"You have got to be kidding me!" Sabrina returned.

"You forgot one more thing that didn't happen."

"Oh really? What else could there be?" Sabrina leaned in.

"I also didn't murder him."

Sabrina's face softened and she grew silent. After a minute, she sagged back into her chair keeping her eyes on Aaron's.

"I didn't murder him," Aaron repeated. "Somebody strangled him, but it wasn't me. And whoever did it, did it after I'd left the room."

"So all you did was to enter the room, put the needle into his arm…and that's it?" Sabrina asked.

"I know, I know. I can see the headlines now. Trained FBI agent botches job. I'm sorry, Sabrina."

"But the syringe…"

"Still puts me in the room and makes us just as much suspect as anyone else," Aaron finished for her. "I know this too. I wish I knew what happened to that damn thing."

"We're not only where we were to begin with," Sabrina mused, "but worse off than when we started. No idea where the money is and under suspicion for a murder we didn't commit."

Aaron solemnly nodded his head. "I'm afraid so."

Sabrina let out a laugh. "Unbelievable."

Aaron smiled in spite of himself. "Yeah."

"So if you didn't kill him, then who did? Sam and Gwen didn't do it. We didn't do it. I dare say it couldn't have been Felix or either of the sisters. It's safe to say it wouldn't have been Charlie either, Jim's son," Sabrina said. "That leaves Jim himself and the maid Alexis."

"And Penny."

"Penny?" was the surprised response. "No. There's no way that girl could've strangled her own grandfather. Besides, even if she had the capacity for such a thing, she wouldn't have the strength to do it."

"I agree. I don't think Penny did it either."

"Then who? Jim?"

"I've been thinking about it," Aaron said, leaning in. "Jim certainly has the strength for it. And possibly the opportunity. But why? What's his motive?"

"Same as the rest of us I suppose. The money."

"Yah, I suppose there's that," Aaron slowly nodded. "But even so, Jim doesn't strike me as the type of guy who'd kill someone else for money. I don't buy it. Not with him."

"So Alexis then? The maid did it?" Sabrina reacted. "You know Aaron, it *still* could be Sam and Gwen. Sam's story about hitting Richard over the head with the bible may be true, but who's to say that Sam didn't get to thinking about it later and got scared. Maybe he went back into the room and killed him to keep him from telling anyone what he'd done. Besides, you might be right. They might know where the money is. And if they do, they wouldn't want anybody else finding out where it is too. What better way to preserve their secret than to bump off the old man."

"I thought of that too," Aaron agreed. "But again, after their confession tonight and how he was towards Penny…no…no, I don't think so. But it's possible."

"I would say it's probable."

"Possible, probable…either way."

"Well that just leaves Alexis then," Sabrina affirmed.

"Yes."

Sabrina lifted an eyebrow. "Are you serious? You think she killed him?"

"It makes sense when you think about it," Aaron answered. "Here she is. A maid in a thankless job, making minimum wage. A pretty young woman like her, stuck here with so much potential to be more than what she is. So why doesn't she just leave? Because she can't afford to. And suddenly, here's this golden opportunity right in front of her. Seven hundred and fifty thousand dollars is an awful lot of money for someone who's looking for a way out. She did pass me going up the stairs. She did lie to me about receiving a text message from Richard. She was alone with him in the room."

"You saw her actually go into the room?"

Aaron stopped short. "Well, no. I kept going down the stairs, but she was in there alright."

"But strangulation?"

"Sure!" Aaron insisted. "She's more than able. A maid used to lifting mattresses, heavy laundry loads, kitchen work, yard work…her hands are strong. Her arms are strong. I have no doubt she could've done it."

"Then that's our play," Sabrina responded leaning forward. "If we're openly accused and come under direct suspicion, we tell the Sheriff about how she lied to you and how she went into the room after you left. I still think she has that syringe too, Aaron."

"I do too now. It's her only card to use against us. If only we could figure out a way to get into her living quarters without being noticed. I'd love to search her room for that syringe."

A sudden noise brought their heads around. Hearts beating fast, the both of them breathed out a sigh of relief when they saw Rufus enter the room wagging his bushy tail.

"We should probably continue this later," Aaron advised. "Just remember, stick to our story tomorrow. You're a freelance photographer. I'm an insurance salesman. We've never met before yesterday. Only if, and I mean *only* if they already know who you are can you discuss the true nature of your identity. Are we agreed?"

"Agreed."

"Good."

Aaron stood to leave.

"Wait," Sabrina said reaching for his arm. "Can I see you tonight?"

"No."

Sabrina sadly lowered her arm and watched as Aaron left the room without another word.

Chapter 41

Deputy Moss slowly made his rounds making sure everything was secure and quiet as the Bed & Breakfast's occupants began to settle down for the night. First, he walked around the outside of the building, making sure that each of the posted officers were doing alright as he made his way. He started from the back, down by the lake shore and then walked over to the servant's quarters where both Felix and Alexis appeared to have turned in for the night. Then he walked along the side of the building, periodically peering up to the roof as he made his way to the front. Satisfied that all was well there, he worked his way over to the other side of the building and made sure that the area was secure. Finally, he walked down to the parking lot to check in with the officer there. When he had finished his rounds, Deputy Moss went back inside the Bed & Breakfast and began his business of making sure all was well and in order between the walls.

He checked the kitchen first and found it vacated, the lights turned off. He checked the lock on the back door and made sure it was closed up tight for the night. Next he went to the dining room and found it empty and dark as well, the table cleared and cleaned. Following the hallway into the parlor, he found Edna and Mildred still up, each in a chair facing the fireplace reading a book. The fire was dying low, so he offered to build it back up for them, but they declined stating that they were about ready to call it day anyway. He wished them a good night and continued into the foyer and down the other side towards the living area. It was empty as well. A checkers board with some checker pieces sat on a table by the window, and a small lamp was turned on. But everything else appeared to be in its place. He walked over to Mildred's room knowing that Penny would be sleeping in there. He knocked softly on the door and, receiving no answer, he quietly cracked the door open and peeked inside. The room was dark, but he could see Penny sleeping soundly underneath the covers. He closed the door and then made his way over to the staircase.

Deputy Moss went up to the second floor. He checked the bathroom to find it was dark and empty. He continued down the small hallway and found the door to Jim Frank's room wide open. He looked inside and found Jim standing quietly by the window on the other side of the room, staring out into the night, the moonlight casting a faint glow over his face.

"Everything okay, Mr. Frank?" Deputy Moss asked, breaking the silence.

Jim didn't reply at first. Then he lowered his head and, without turning, he said, "I was just thinking of Charlie. He's a good boy with a good heart. He takes after his mother you know. He's a bit naïve and innocent in the ways of the world, and I'm not exactly sure how all of this might have an effect on him. I'm thankful that he was able to find a friend, someone his age, to help him through this time though."

Deputy Moss wanted to say something, but remained quiet. It felt as if Jim Frank was talking more to himself than he was to him and he doubted very much that anything he might have to say would be heard anyway.

"Charlie just recently lost his mother," Jim continued, looking back up and out through the window. "It was a very hard time for us both. We found a strength within each other that enabled us to carry on.

I promised him and myself that I'd never let him down, and that I'd always be there for him. But more importantly, I made this promise to his mother before her death. And that's a promise I intend to keep, no matter what."

"Well, I don't have any kids of my own, Mr. Frank," Deputy Moss spoke up then. "In fact, I'm not even married. So I can't even begin to understand what you might be feeling right now, sir, but I believe that you should keep your promise. Family is the most important thing in this life."

Jim turned to look at the lanky deputy. "Yes. Yes, it is. Family is the *most* important thing in this life. Well put, Deputy. Well put."

Deputy Moss smiled.

Jim turned towards the window again, his gaze falling back over the night sky. "I hope that young girl is going to be alright. I think about her too, you know. How drastically her life has just been changed. I pray for her."

"I'm sure I speak for everyone when I say we all pray for her, Mr. Frank."

"Before you leave, Deputy, do you think it would be okay if you called down to the Corbitt's place and allowed me to speak to Charlie for a few minutes?" Jim asked.

"Well, sir, I leave here at midnight. But Officer Pitchford will be relieving me. Perhaps he could call down for you in the morning to check on Charlie. I'll make arrangements with him before I go home if you'd like," Deputy Moss replied. "I don't know if you'll be allowed to speak with him though, that's up to Sheriff Blackwood. You'll have to check with him first."

"Thank you, Deputy. I'd appreciate that."

Deputy Moss nodded in his direction. "I'll leave you be now. Just doing my rounds. If you need anything, just let me know. Goodnight, Mr. Frank."

"Goodnight."

Chapter 42

Deputy Moss turned and continued up to the third floor. The Blue Room had been closed up with yellow strips of police tape crisscrossing over the door from top to bottom. He paused, almost transfixed by the scene. He shook his head. Never before had they had anything like this ever since he could remember in Pleasant Lake. The excitement of the day's activities suddenly seemed to disappear and he felt sad. In fact, he felt ashamed of himself for feeling the way he did when they got the call down at the office. A young girl was sleeping in Mildred's room, a young girl whose grandfather had been murdered less than 24 hours ago. Deputy Moss frowned and moved past the door. The newlywed's room was silent.

Finally, he found himself back down in the living area. He put away the checkers game and lowered the lamp setting to a soft glow. Propping a chair up next to the wall so that he could keep a sharp eye on the door to Mildred's room where Penny was sleeping, he looked at his watch. It was nearly 10:30. Officer Pitchford would be there in about an hour and half. He was certain that everybody in the house would be tucked in for the night by this time, so he sat down and leaned the chair backwards resting his head on the wall behind him.

The Deputy softly hummed a song to himself keeping an eye on the door and the surrounding area. He pulled out his small tablet that he'd been taking notes in through the course of the day's investigation, but soon found himself bored with reading over what meager notes he had. It was a baffling, yet intriguing case. Richard Forester appeared to have been murdered three times, although only one of the attempts was more than an attempt. It was actual murder.

After about twenty minutes, his eyes began to grow heavy, so he forced himself back up to his feet and made another quick check around the house. This lasted all of ten minutes and he was soon back in his chair when he was satisfied everything was still okay. Within fifteen minutes, his eyes grew heavy again and this time, he closed them completely, powerless against his desire for sleep.

Deputy Moss was snoring away when Penny Forester abruptly sat up in her bed and jerked the covers close to her screaming. The piercing scream snapped him back awake and his body jolted in alarm causing the chair to slide from underneath him and he fell, crashing to the floor. He could hear Penny still screaming when a beam of light appeared underneath the neighboring door of Edna's room. He jumped to his feet and began to run over as Edna's door swung open and the tired, but concerned faces of the two sisters appeared.

"What's happening?" Edna demanded.

"I don't know," Deputy Moss gasped, reaching for the doorknob.

He turned the doorknob and burst through into the room. Penny stopped screaming and turned towards him. Mildred reached through the door behind him and turned on the overhead light. Penny's eyes were wide with fright and she was breathing fast and heavy. She had the bedspread clenched close to her chin with tense hands.

"Penny?" Deputy Moss exclaimed, his hand on the pommel of his handgun. "Are you okay? What's wrong?"

Edna and Mildred walked in holding their robes tight.

"Someone was just in here!" Penny blurted out. "I had this feeling...something strange, like somebody was standing over me. I opened my eyes and there it was! A shadow...a person was right there!" Penny turned and pointed to the foot of her bed.

"In this room?" Edna asked.

Penny's eyes watered as she nodded. "I screamed and they went through the window over there." She moved her finger over to indicate the window to her left. The window was open and the night breeze was moving the curtains slightly.

Deputy Moss rushed over to the window and leaned down to look outside. The officer posted on that side of the house was already running over having been alerted by Penny's screams.

"Did you see anybody coming out of this window?" Deputy Moss called out to him.

"Coming out of *that* window?" he called back.

"Yes! Not more than two minutes ago! Did you see anybody? Anybody at all?"

The officer completed the distance and with a confused look he shook his head. "No Ross. Nobody came out of that window that I could see."

"Are you sure?"

"Well, yah...pretty sure."

Deputy Moss shook his head. "I need you to be positive about this," the Deputy stipulated. "Is it possible that someone could have come through here without you seeing them?"

The officer gulped and thought about it. "I suppose it's possible. The moon's bright tonight, but I had my head turned the other direction when I heard the young lady scream. By the time I got over here…well, yah. It would have been possible for someone to have come through the window without me seeing them, Ross."

"Okay then," Deputy Moss let out a breath. He couldn't really be upset. He himself had fallen asleep. "Go get the other officers and search the grounds. It's only been a few minutes. Quickly."

"Yes, sir."

The officer left in a hurry to do as he was told. He'd never seen Ross take charge like this before and it surprised him. It kind of shocked him actually.

The Deputy pulled back through the window and looked over to Penny. Mildred was sitting by her side, her arm wrapped comfortingly around the young girl as she sat shaking.

"Penny…" he started.

Penny looked up with frightened eyes. "It's like a nightmare that will never end," she said in a quivering voice.

Deputy Moss lowered his head. "Penny," he continued, "do you know who it was? Did you see their face? Did they say anything? Do anything? Anything at all that might help us?"

Penny shook her head in the negative. "No. I don't know who it was."

Voices outside the doorway caused them all to look over and find that the other guests had come downstairs as well. Aaron came in first followed by Sabrina; the newlyweds came in next with Jim walking in last. All eyes were on Penny, question marks defining their facial expressions.

"Since you're all here…" Deputy Moss said after a minute.

"Not all of us are here, Ross," Edna interrupted.

"Who are we missing?"

"Alexis."

"Ah, yah," the Deputy nodded.

"I'll check in on her," Edna offered and then left the room.

Penny buried her face into Mildred's robe and cried. "There, there, child," Mildred responded, placing a caring hand on the back of her head.

"What happened?" Aaron asked finally.

"Let's give Edna a moment to bring Alexis here and then I'll tell you," Deputy Moss replied. They didn't have to wait long as Edna soon reappeared with Alexis in tow.

"She was standing in her doorway," Edna said as they entered. "She said she heard the screams out there and they woke her up."

"Did you see anybody besides one of our officers outside, Alexis?" Deputy Moss queried.

"No. When I got out of bed and opened my door, I saw you talking to another officer by the window. Other than that, I didn't see anything," Alexis answered.

"Are you going to tell us what's going on?" Aaron pressed.

"Somebody was in this room not more than fifteen minutes ago," the Deputy answered. "Standing approximately where I am now. Fortunately, Penny woke up and saw them. Or who knows what might have happened."

"I don't get it," Sam offered. "Why come after Penny?"

"Just leave me alone," Penny's muffled voice sounded from Mildred's shoulder. "Grandpa Dick didn't steal the money. I don't know where it is either because he never took it!" Penny looked up glaring at everyone in the room. "Leave me alone!"

Deputy Moss nodded and indicated for everyone to leave the room. Mildred stayed behind while everybody else filtered back out into the living area. Edna closed the door behind her and joined them.

"It appears," Edna stated, "that whichever one of you killed Richard isn't done yet. Quite frankly, it makes my skin crawl to be standing in the same room with a murderer. And whoever you are, you should be ashamed of yourself! Ross?" Deputy Moss lifted his head. "I want a man posted right outside her door and window until we get this resolved."

"I have this well under control, Miss Pookotz," Deputy Moss assured her. "We'll..."

"Under control? Where were you, young man, when this all happened?" Edna returned with a disapproving look on her face, having noticed the overturned chair by the wall. "Fall asleep on the job, did we?"

Deputy Moss cleared his throat but didn't answer.

"Hmmmph!" Edna grunted. "Like I said, Ross, a man outside the door and window at all times while she's in that room. Understood?"

Chagrined, Deputy Moss nodded in agreement. "Yes, Ma'am. Officer Pitchford will be here soon and we'll make all the arrangements."

"As for the rest of you, I hope you're happy. Tonight for the first time in over 35 years, I'm going to have to sleep with the bedroom door locked in my own home! It would behoove you all to do the same." Edna looked at each person in turn. "None of us are safe now. None of us!"

Chapter 43

The rest of the evening passed without incident, though sleep didn't come easy for any of the Bed & Breakfast's occupants. Officer Pitchford arrived a few minutes before midnight and Deputy Moss informed him of the events leading up to the break-in of Penny's room. Arrangements were made to have an officer posted on the door and window leading into her room, though it was suggested by Officer Pitchford that perhaps they should take Penny down to the station and put her in a cell overnight for her own protection. But Penny wouldn't have it, stating she wasn't going to be treated like a criminal. She slammed her door shut and that was the end of that. So the guards were posted with instructions to let nobody in until the next relief showed up at eight a.m. The search that they'd conducted earlier produced no results, so they were no closer now to knowing who'd been in that room than before. Deputy Moss said he was going to be seeing the Sheriff early in the morning and that he'd catch him up to date at that time since everything appeared to be under control at the Bed & Breakfast. They both agreed that they saw no reason to wake him up at this point.

Sam and Gwen disappeared once more behind the door to their room as did Aaron, Sabrina and Jim to their respective rooms. Alexis was ordered by Edna to prepare some coffee for the next shift of officers and then she was escorted to her quarters where she promptly turned off her light, crawled under her covers and tried to sleep. Everyone had completely forgotten about Felix who was still slumbering away as if there weren't a care in the world, undisturbed by the incident. After Edna was advised of Deputy Moss's plans and Mildred had finished tending to Penny, they both retired for the night. Deputy Moss and Officer Pitchford made their final arrangements and then the Deputy left to go home and get some sleep. Everything remained calm and undisturbed until early the next morning when Felix found his way into the kitchen to begin preparing breakfast.

Half an hour later, a fresh shift of officers arrived to take their turn guarding the Bed & Breakfast much to the relief of the previous night's officers who slowly shuffled their way down to the parking lot where their cars were waiting and beyond that, the comfort of their own beds. Edna and Mildred were already up too by that time helping to prepare things for the day while all the other guests still remained in their rooms. Mildred had the guard outside of Penny's door check on her, and he reported she was still sleeping. Edna went out to fetch Alexis and soon the maid was busy assisting Felix with setting up the dining room buffet style as it was the day before.

Meanwhile, Deputy Moss was sitting in Sheriff Blackwood's office, apprising him of all the night's events. The Sheriff listened intently with a darkened expression and a frown on his face; obviously very displeased with the report he was being given. But he allowed his young Deputy to complete his report without interrupting and then he sat quietly for a moment before speaking. Deputy Moss had that empty sick feeling in his stomach...the type of feeling he used to get as a boy when he knew he'd done something wrong and his father was about to discipline him.

"Well," Sheriff Blackwood said at last, "other than the fact that you allowed yourself to fall asleep, you haven't done anything wrong, Ross."

Deputy Moss let out a small breath of relief.

"However, in the future, if anything like this happens again, you call me. I don't care if it is 2:00 in the morning, you call me and wake me up. Not that I was sleeping anyway," the Sheriff stipulated.

"Did you have a hard time falling asleep?"

"No. I fell asleep fine. But I'd taken the bag containing everyone's cell phones into the house last night and one of them got a call in the middle of the night waking Cathy and me up. By the time I located the bag downstairs, it finally stopped ringing so I wasn't able to see which one it was."

"I see."

"Now," the Sheriff continued, "with someone going after Penny last night too, this does change things. You should have brought her down here. In fact, I have half a mind to do that anyway so that she'll be safe."

"Oh, we already thought of that, boss. But she wouldn't have it. We did post a guard outside her door and window."

"Well, there's nothing for it then, I suppose. Here, Ross," Sheriff Blackwood said, reaching for a small plastic bag. "Take their ID's out of this bag and run them for me. Cathy's home sick, so I'll need you to take on a bit more administrative duties today as well. You can use her desk and phone if you need to."

"Sure thing, boss!" Deputy Moss responded, accepting the bag.

"Meanwhile, I'm going to call up to the house and check on things. Rusty Barton will be in charge. I imagine Randall has already gone on home by now. And, Ross?" Sheriff Blackwood paused.

"Yes, boss?"

"Don't call me boss."

While Deputy Moss busied himself calling and verifying everyone's identifications, the Sheriff called up to the Bed & Breakfast and spoke briefly to Rusty. Everybody was accounted for and having their breakfast. There was nothing to report. He informed Rusty that he was going to finish with their ID's and check in with Doc Meecham and then head up there around noon to begin his interviewing process. Rusty asked him if it would be okay to let Jim Frank speak to his son Charlie over the phone and the Sheriff agreed to let him do so. After making his final arrangements, he hung up the phone just as Deputy Moss walked back into his office.

"You're not going to *believe* this!" The Deputy's face was flushed with excitement.

"What? What did you find?"

"Aaron Buchanon is not an insurance salesman. He is Special Agent Buchanon of the Criminal Investigative Division," Deputy Moss replied.

"He's a Fed?" the Sheriff returned, flabbergasted.

"Yep! He's FBI, boss."

"What in the world...." Sheriff Blackwood said, leaning back in his chair.

"But that's not all. It gets better."

"Better?"

"Sabrina Riggs is not a photographer either. Well, actually, yes she is. But not how she led us to believe. She also works for the FBI, same division, as a crime scene photographer. And her real last name isn't Riggs either," Deputy Moss reported. "It's Jackson. Sabrina Jackson."

"You have proof of this?"

Deputy Moss handed him copies of the faxed papers he was reading from. It was legitimate. They were exactly who he said they were.

"I don't believe it."

Deputy Moss smiled. "Told you that you wouldn't."

"They know each other then. But why are they here?"

The Sheriff stood up and walked around to the side of his desk.

"They were here because of Richard. They were following him," the Sheriff answered his own question. "The big question is, why?" He paused. "They were investigating the embezzled funds," he answered his own question again.

"They lied to us, boss," Deputy Moss reminded him.

"Yes they did. They lied to everyone. And that can mean only one of two things, Ross. Either they're on assignment and they lied to protect their cover, or…" Sheriff Blackwood looked over at his young Deputy, "…they're dirty."

"The plot thickens!" Deputy Moss grinned. "Which do you think it is?"

"Well, let's think about it here for a minute," the Sheriff responded. "If they were simply keeping their cover to prevent Richard from knowing who they were, then why didn't they identify themselves after he died? There would really be no reason to have to keep their cover at that point."

"So you think they're dirty then."

"No, now I didn't say that Ross!" the Sheriff returned. "You're always doing that. Going off and making something big out of something small. And while we're on the subject, everything we discuss here this morning stays between us. Okay, Deputy?"

"Okay. I'm sorry, boss. It stays between us."

"Okay then. All I was meaning to imply was that it seems a bit strange that they wouldn't come forward seeing as how the person they were investigating was murdered. If for anything, to clear their own name,"

Sheriff Blackwood surmised. "So I see a couple of possibilities here. Maybe they're also investigating Penny, or someone else up there at the Bed & Breakfast, making it necessary to remain undercover."

"Or they killed him and are trying to stay under the radar," Deputy Moss contributed.

"Yes, that's a distinct possibility," the Sheriff agreed. "But then that begs the question, if they *did* kill Richard, then why not still come forward and use their real identities to try and throw us off suspicion?"

Deputy Moss reached up and scratched his head. "I gotta say, boss, the more we think it over and deliberate it, the more confusing it gets."

Sheriff Blackwood laughed and reached up to clap him on the shoulder. "The mind plays evil games with us, Ross. To try to understand the motives of a killer, you have to try and think like one. I can imagine that's harder for some of us to do than others. But I wouldn't let that worry you too much. You have strong investigative instincts and you know the law inside and out. That's why I hired you to be my Deputy. It takes years of experience to get where I am today, and if you give it the time, then you'll find that it won't be so confusing."

"I hope so."

"How about everyone else up there?"

"Oh, they all check out, boss. Everyone else is exactly who they say they are."

The Sheriff nodded. "Good work, Ross. Go on over to the Pookotz house now. I'll be there shortly. I just want to check in with Doc Meecham first."

"Sure thing..." Deputy Moss hesitated when he saw Sheriff Blackwood raise a finger and open his mouth. "I know, I know. Don't call you, boss," he finished.

The Sheriff smiled and walked out of the office. "See you over there in a bit! And remember, keep this between us for now. Don't let the cat out of the bag!" he yelled over his shoulder.

"Yes, boss."

Hesitating for a moment, the Deputy looked down and then looked back over to where the Sheriff was a moment before and called out, "We don't have a cat!"

Chapter 44

A few minutes later, Sheriff Blackwood pulled up in front of Doc Meecham's clinic just as a nurse walked up to the front entrance. She was about the same age as he was with slightly graying hair pulled back into a long braid that ran down the length of her back to her waist. She wore a snug white nurse's top and skirt, and was in excellent shape for her age.

"Good morning, Nurse Ratched," the Sheriff greeted, getting out of his cruiser.

"Good grief, Sheriff!" the nurse countered. "You know I hate being called that."

"Too many 'Cuckoo's Nest" flashbacks for you?" he smiled.

"Very funny."

"Oh, come on Stephanie, you know I'm just joking. You have to admit that it's extremely ironic that you're a nurse and that your last name just happens to be Ratched," Sheriff Blackwood continued opening the front door for her.

"I admit I find it ironic. I just don't find it amusing! Just call me by my first name like you used to do when we were kids in school."

"I'm sorry, Stephanie." Sheriff Blackwood looked around the front waiting room to the admittance window that she normally occupied. "I know you just got here, but do you know if Doc Meecham is in yet?"

"You just wait here a moment, Sheriff, and I'll go see."

He watched as she hastily placed a purse and shawl on her desk through the window and then she disappeared behind a white swinging door. A few moments later she reappeared with the town physician behind her.

"Mornin,' Sheriff!" Doc Meecham greeted, extending his hand.

"Mornin,' Doc," the Sheriff said, accepting and shaking his hand.

"Oh, Stephanie?" the Doc said, turning to his nurse before she could leave the room. "I know you were running a bit late this morning and that's okay, but we're behind now and really need to concentrate our efforts today."

"I'm sorry, Doc. What do you need me to do?"

"I've already drawn some blood samples from Mr. Forester's body that I need to have tested. Please make sure they're properly sealed and labeled. You'll find the paperwork necessary next to each test tube. You'll also see another test tube with some pink residue in it. This also needs to be tested. Call the courier first thing so they can run them down to the lab in Hemmett," the Doc instructed her. "The sooner the better, we'll need to put a rush on these samples."

"I'll get right on it," she replied, turning to leave.

"Stephanie?" Sheriff Blackwood said.

Stephanie stopped and slowly turned around with a small scowl on her face. "Yes, Sheriff?"

"I'm really sorry about this morning," he smiled. "Just whatever you do, p-p-please d-d-d-don't tell my mo-m-mo-mother what I did. Okay?"

Stephanie gave him an evil eye and, with a huff, she turned and disappeared behind the swinging white door as Sheriff Blackwood let out a laugh.

"Nurse Ratched again, huh?" Doc Meecham looked back from the door to the Sheriff.

"You know I can't resist."

Doc let out a small laugh too. "You're terrible, Jake, just terrible."

"How's the examination coming, Doc?" Sheriff Blackwood asked getting back on point.

"It's coming. Like you already heard me telling Stephanie, the samples are drawn. We just need to have them tested. I'm not equipped for that here, so that's why I am having them sent over to Hemmett. But as soon as I get anything, I'll let you know," Doc replied. "But we do need to get Penny's signatures on some paperwork so I can do this job completely. Are you heading up there today?"

"Heading there right after I leave here. Do you think an autopsy is going to be needed?"

"Pending the results of the lab work, I don't know yet. If I had to close the book on it right now though, I'd have to say death by strangulation. But you know me Jake; I'm very thorough."

"You're a good man, Doc. Keep me posted."

"I will. Talk to you soon. And get Penny's signatures on those release forms I gave you last night."

"I'll do my best."

Chapter 45

Sheriff Blackwood was deep in thought when he arrived at the Bed & Breakfast. The officer posting guard in the parking lot walked over and opened his door for him

"Sheriff," he greeted.

"Anything going on?" Sheriff Blackwood immediately asked.

"Nope. They're getting ready to have a bit of lunch, but everyone's here and accounted for, Sir."

"Is Ross here?"

"He's up in the house," the officer replied.

"Thank you."

Sheriff Blackwood followed the path up to the front door and found Deputy Moss on his way out.

"Hey, boss," Deputy Moss said. "I thought I heard you drive up. I was just on my way down to see you."

"Where is everybody?"

"In the living area having some lunch."

"Take me to them."

"Sure, boss!" the Deputy responded, moving back inside the doorway. "And don't worry. I haven't said a word to anybody about you-know-what."

"That's good, Ross."

The two entered the foyer and then headed down to the right and into the adjoining living area where the Sheriff found everyone gathered as Ross had indicated. They all had plates on their laps with napkins, enjoying a lunch consisting of sandwiches, chips and potato salad.

"Hello, Sheriff," Mildred came up to him with a warm smile.

"Jacob, I'm glad you're here," Edna acknowledged, walking up to stand next to her sister. "Patience is running thin and nerves are on edge," she informed him quietly. Then raising her voice slightly, she said, "Would you like to join us for some lunch?"

Without waiting for his response, she turned to Alexis and instructed her to bring a plate out for him. Alexis left the room to do as she was told. Sheriff Blackwood removed the hat off of his head, much to Edna's approval, and thanked the sisters.

The Sheriff looked around the room for Penny and found her sitting by herself in the corner on the window sill eating some potato chips. She seemed to be completely oblivious to everyone else in the room. He walked over to her.

"Hello, Penny."

"Hi, Sheriff," she responded, looking up at him briefly.

"Ross has told me everything that happened last night and I want you to know I'm sorry. We're going to do everything in our power to make sure whoever did this is apprehended."

"You mean," Sam interjected, "You're going to do everything in your power to make sure that one of *us* is apprehended."

"You're a fine one to talk, Sam," Jim said. "We all know what you did. I still say it was you all along."

"I admit I was in Richard's room. I already came clean on that for the record, but I didn't kill him. I may have been in his room, but I wasn't in Penny's room last night," Sam returned.

"You expect us to believe that?" Jim came back. "You lied about being in the Blue Room to begin with, how can we believe you aren't lying now about being in Penny's too?"

Sam jumped to his feet, nearly spilling the contents of his plate. "I'm NOT lying! I'm speaking honestly!"

"You two *honestly* disgust me," Sabrina said, casting condescending looks at both Jim and Sam. "Will you both knock it off?"

Jim clamped his mouth shut and turned away. Sam looked desperate, but he said nothing else and sat back down next to his wife. Gwen was fidgeting nervously with the fork on her plate, and then she took a deep breath and stood up. Sensing what she was about to do, Sam reached up to stop her but he was too late.

"It's *you* and your boyfriend Aaron over there who disgusts me!" she shouted. "All this time we've been coming under fire for his murder, but we're innocent. Why don't you tell us the truth about that night, Sabrina? Aaron? What really happened?"

"What are you talking about?" Sabrina responded with a dark glare. Aaron shifted uneasily next to her.

"Sheriff," Gwen said, turning to face him. "We heard it all. Sam and I. We heard Aaron and Sabrina in the parking lot plotting to kill Richard for his money."

"That's hogwash!" Aaron said, sitting forward.

Everyone looked at him for a minute. Suddenly, he became self-conscious. "Okay, okay! I get it! I talk funny. But it *is* hogwash. They're just saying this to put the blame on somebody else."

"No we aren't. I swear, Sheriff, it's the truth," Gwen continued. She turned to face Sabrina and Aaron. "Don't you wish that you'd walked over to the right car in the first place, Aaron? Who do you think was in the backseat of the other car?" Everyone shifted their gaze back over to Gwen. "Hey," she added with a blush, "we're newlyweds. It's allowed."

Sabrina's and Aaron's faces clouded over. Sheriff Blackwood registered their reactions and with a lifted eyebrow he stepped forward. He'd remained quiet up to this point hoping this would lead to something. And apparently, it had.

"Tell us what you heard, Gwen," he said at last.

"We heard them say how Sabrina was going to lure Penny out of the room while Aaron would go in and find out from Richard where the money was hidden," she explained.

Aaron and Sabrina remained silent.

"Then Aaron was going to kill him. Make it look like it was because he was already sick. Don't know how they would do that unless..." Gwen stopped short and then her eyes opened wide. "Unless he had a syringe of something he was going to inject him with. Yah, that makes sense! The doctor said he found a needle mark on his arm."

Aaron looked like he was going to explode, while Sabrina's face lowered quietly. Her arms hung heavy at her sides.

"And these two have been playing us for fools too," Gwen added, reveling in the moment. "They're lovers. They've known each other since before coming here. That was obvious in the parking lot."

"It's not true," Sabrina breathed.

"She's right," Penny said from the corner. She stood up and walked over to stand next to the Sheriff. "Sabrina did come up to my room and she did ask to talk to me. I thought it was strange at the time, but I took her for her word. I believed she was trying to be my friend. But all she was doing was helping someone else to murder Grandpa Dick." Her words were hard. Sabrina didn't look up, but she could feel the contempt behind the teenager's eyes.

"That's all well and good," Aaron finally replied, "but that doesn't prove a thing. Those are only words."

"Sheriff?" Alexis had her hand raised slightly.

"You have something to say Alexis?" Sheriff Blackwood acknowledged.

"I saw Mr. Buchanon coming down the stairs from the third floor that night. I was going up to check on Mr. Forester and Penny when I saw him coming down from their level. Penny wasn't there, so he could have been in the room with Mr. Forester alone," Alexis informed them.

"Why didn't you say anything before now about that, Alexis?" Edna demanded.

"Begging your pardon, Miss, but it didn't seem relevant until now," Alexis replied respectfully.

"Well, what of that, Mr. Buchanon?" Sheriff Blackwood inquired. "Isn't your room on the second floor? Why were you up there?"

"I told her why!" Aaron said. "The bathroom on the second floor was being used. So I went up to use the bathroom on the third floor."

"But why the third floor? Surely the one downstairs is just as easily accessible and maybe even easier to get to," Sheriff Blackwood pressed.

"I don't know why. I just decided to use that bathroom."

"Who was using the second floor bathroom?" Edna asked. "Was it you Sam?"

"No, Ma'am," Sam answered. "Our room is on the third floor. We've only used that bathroom since we've been here."

"Was it you, Mr. Frank?" Edna continued.

"No," Jim shook his head. "Charlie and I spent most of the evening outside until I saw Sam up on the roof."

"But this happened after that," Sabrina added.

"Well, that's true," Jim recalled. "But no, Charlie and I went straight to bed. Neither one of us were in that bathroom."

"We know it wasn't Sabrina or Penny, because they were together talking at that time. It wasn't Alexis or Felix; they have their own bathrooms. And I can attest to the fact the neither Mildred or I ever use the bathrooms up on the second or third floors," Edna concluded. "So, again, Mr. Buchanon, who could have been in that bathroom causing you to go upstairs? Rufus perhaps?"

"I don't know!" Aaron blurted out. "All I know is that the door was closed, the light was on and somebody was in there."

"Oh this is just ridiculous!" Gwen exclaimed. "He's *lying*! Sam and I heard them planning his death, Alexis saw him coming down from his room. They are your murderers, Sheriff!"

"Yah, what about that?" Aaron said, perplexed. "Alexis told me she'd just been paged by Richard and that was why she was going up there. That's total B.S.! He didn't page her."

"That's not what I said," Alexis intervened.

"It most certainly is so."

"No, Mr. Buchanon," Alexis continued. "What I said was that I was going up to make sure they *had* my pager number should they need me for anything and to check on him. He was sick and I was just making sure they were going to be okay for the night."

"That's a lie!" Aaron burst out.

"It seems to me the only person who's doing any lying here is you, Mr. Buchanon," Sheriff Blackwood stipulated.

"How do you mean?" Aaron asked.

"What I mean is this. How would you know that Richard couldn't have paged Alexis...unless you were in the room there with him?"

Chapter 46

Aaron looked like he'd just swallowed a frog.

Sabrina reached over and placed her hand on his arm. "Sit down Aaron," she softly said. "You've said enough."

Aaron sat down and hung his head.

"Sheriff," Sabrina took over, standing up, "the truth of the matter is that Aaron and I are Special Agents on assignment from the FBI. We were sent to follow Richard Forester from our department in Criminal Investigations to find out what had happened to the $750,000 that was embezzled from MicaTek. I'm sure by now you've had a chance to run checks on our identifications?"

"I have indeed, Miss Jackson," Sheriff Blackwood replied.

Sabrina caught her breath. "You just called me Miss Jackson."

"Yes I did."

"Well, then, you already know who we are."

"Is that true?" Mildred asked.

"It's true, Mildred," Sheriff Blackwood confirmed. "They really are with the FBI. As for their story about why they're here, I guess that's yet to be determined."

"I knew there was something more about you two than you professed to be. Especially you, young lady," Edna added, looking shrewdly at Sabrina.

"Okay, I understand all that. And now it makes sense why you two are here, even though I thought the investigation was closed. But it still doesn't explain why you were in our room," Penny said.

"What Sabrina is trying to tell you is that we were here on assignment. We had to remain undercover and that's why we both gave you fake stories. It was imperative that we find out what Richard knew about the embezzled funds and we couldn't afford to blow our cover. That's the only reason we're here. Nothing else," Aaron interrupted, having calmed down substantially. "Sabrina asked to speak to Penny so I could approach Richard alone. So yes, I was in the room with him while Sabrina and Penny were talking, but it wasn't to kill him. I had brought with me a syringe that contained Sodium Pentathol."

"What's that?" Sam asked.

"Basically, it's a truth serum," Aaron explained. "I was going to inject Richard with it and then have him confess to me first off that he had taken the money, and secondly where he'd stashed it. I actually had the needle in his arm ready to inject when I heard Alexis coming up the stairs. It startled me and I dropped the needle. I wasn't able to find it. I still don't know where it is. But I swear to you all, Richard was still alive when I left that room. He was breathing, he had a pulse. He never even knew I was there."

"That still doesn't explain what Sam and I heard them saying in the parking lot, Sheriff," Gwen redirected. "They were going to kill him."

"So you overheard us, little missy!" Sabrina shot back. "But he just finished telling you that we didn't kill him. And we didn't. Everything we said is the complete truth."

"Just like when you told us you were a freelance photographer?" Jim asserted.

"I am a photographer," Sabrina returned. "For the Federal Bureau of Investigations."

"I don't believe them," Gwen kept on. "I know what we heard! They did it. They had to have done it!"

Everyone grew quiet then. After a moment, Edna stood up.

"No. They may have schemed to kill him just like you and your husband did. But they didn't kill him," Edna said, facing her maid. "Isn't that right, Alexis?"

Chapter 47

Alexis cowered into the cushions of the couch she was sitting on.

"Miss?"

"You went into the room right after Aaron left," Edna stated.

"Yes, Miss."

"So if Aaron had killed Mr. Forester, then why didn't you alert us? Why didn't you call out?" Edna finally asked.

All eyes were on Alexis at that point.

"Because...because..." Alexis stuttered.

"Because he was still alive!" Edna affirmed. "Isn't that *right,* child?"

Alexis slowly nodded. "Yes, Miss. He was still alive."

"Thank you!" Aaron threw his hands up into the air. "Told you, I didn't do it. Do you have my syringe?"

"No," Alexis responded. "I found no syringe."

"Why is this syringe so important to you anyway?" Sam asked.

"Because it would prove I'm telling the truth. If you find that syringe, then you'd find it's still full. None of its contents were emptied out."

"So what happened when you were in the room with Richard alone, Alexis?" Sheriff Blackwood queried.

"And why did you lie to me about him paging you?" Aaron added.

"Nothing happened," Alexis replied. "I only lied because well..."

"You were going to ask him about the money too weren't you?" Sam asked.

Alexis nodded.

"Alexis!" Mildred exclaimed with a saddened expression on her face. "And you seemed like such a nice girl."

"And?" Sheriff Blackwood waited.

"Like I said, nothing happened. I wanted to ask him about the money, but he was sleeping so peacefully....well, I just decided to....I got scared and I chickened out," Alexis answered.

"You chickened out?" Sam repeated.

"I left the room. I saw Penny going back up to the room with a glass of strawberry milk for her grandfather. I wished her a good night and then I went to bed," Alexis finished. "It's true. That's all that happened."

"Well, then, Penny, it comes over to you," the Sheriff said, turning to face the young girl. "Was your grandfather still alive when you entered the room after you passed Alexis?"

"I don't know."

"You don't know?"

"I thought he was. He was lying there so quietly and peacefully. I didn't want to disturb him so I set the milk down on the nightstand and pulled a pillow and some blankets down to the floor next to the bed and slept there. But honestly Sheriff, I don't know. He could have been alive, or he could have already been..." Penny began to choke up.

"Then it seems we still have an unexplained murder on our hands, although our list of suspects is narrowing down. We're also no closer to finding out who was in Penny's room last night either or why," Sheriff Blackwood concluded. "And please, everybody sit down," he indicated with his hand. "Please."

Everyone settled back into their seats, casting nervous glances around the room at each other. Alexis looked up and saw Edna shaking her head disapprovingly at her. She looked down ashamed.

"I have to admit," Sheriff Blackwood began again, "that this is one of the most bizarre cases I've ever worked on. We have three different people aside from Penny admittedly having been alone with Richard in the room, and all three professing their innocence. Sam was there first and clobbered him over the head with a bible, knocking him out cold. He escaped out the side window and shimmied along the rooftop to his own room where Jim saw him as he was returning from a walk with his son. Then Sabrina coaxed Penny out of the room where Aaron had a needle stuck into his arm ready to inject him with Sodium Pentathol which was foiled by Alexis who was on her way up to try and find out where the money was hidden as well, but upon arriving, she chickened out or so she says and left the room. Penny returned carrying a glass of strawberry milk but seeing the unmoving figure of her grandfather, she figured him for resting deeply and soundly and therefore did not wish to disturb him. So she stayed away from him, electing to sleep on the floor. But truth be known, he *could* have been dead. Have I pretty much covered it to this point?"

He was answered by nods all around.

"So, it's safe to say that sometime *after* Alexis entered the room, Richard was strangled whereupon Penny found him when she woke up the next morning," the Sheriff said. "I'm sorry, Alexis, but that leaves you as the primary suspect at this point."

"Me?" Alexis exclaimed. "I couldn't have strangled him to death."

"Why not?" Aaron asked. "A sick old man, possibly already lying on his death bed and you, used to the heavy chores around here…that's an awful lot of money for someone in your stature."

"I didn't kill Mr. Forester, but I can prove to you all who did."

"What are you talking about, Alexis?" Edna responded.

"You know who the murderer is?" Mildred asked.

Alexis nodded.

"Where is this proof, Alexis?" Sheriff Blackwood prodded.

Alexis turned to look at Deputy Moss who was sitting off to the side taking notes. His eyes opened wide as everyone shifted their gaze over to him.

"Ross Moss, could you please escort me to my room?" she asked.

Chapter 48

While the Deputy waited for her in the doorway, Alexis went straight to her closet and removed the shoebox and its contents from the top shelf. Things had escalated much faster than she'd expected, but she was ready for it. This newspaper would clear things up in a hurry. She knew that no matter what the results of today's events would be, she was out of a job. There could be no doubting that. But she had to clear her name. That's all that mattered right now.

"Need some help?" Deputy Moss asked.

Alexis clutched the box to her chest and took a deep breath. Turning, she shook her head. "No. I have what I need. We can go back now."

Deputy Moss led her down the path to the main house and back into the living area where the others waited patiently. She nervously re-entered the room, still clutching her shoebox close to her.

"You better go ahead and say what it is you have to say, Alexis," Edna admonished.

"Yes, Miss."

Alexis resumed her seat and lifted the shoebox cover and removed the newspaper. She cleared her throat and began.

"My Aunt Molly sent me this newspaper some time ago. She used to work for MicaTek and lost her job when the money was discovered stolen and the plant was shut down. On the day of the court hearing, she and some other protesters showed up outside the courthouse carrying signs and a newspaper photographer was onsite taking pictures, one of which was used in this newspaper article. My Aunt Molly was in the picture, so she sent me a copy of the article. I don't know why, but I've kept it all this time." Alexis paused for a moment and then she continued. "But when I took another look at this photo a couple of nights ago, I recognized somebody else. There was another protester there that day. His sign reads 'An Eye for an Eye.' He used to work for MicaTek too, apparently, and he's here in this room right now."

"Who is it, child?" Mildred probed.

"It's Mr. Frank," Alexis responded holding out the newspaper to the Sheriff. This was met by an audible gasp and all eyes turned on Jim.

Chapter 49

Sheriff Blackwood walked over to retrieve the newspaper and, placing a pair of reading glasses over his eyes, he took a close look. It was a picture of Richard Forester walking down the steps to the courthouse and, standing off to the side with a sign, as Alexis indicated, was Jim Frank. The Sheriff removed his glasses and studied the newly accused who sat still and said nothing.

"So it seems you had a motive, Mr. Frank," the Sheriff stated. "Why didn't you say anything about your having worked there?"

Jim remained still and kept his mouth shut.

"If Mr. Frank did indeed strangle Mr. Forester, that means he would have to have been alone with him after Penny had returned from her conversation with Sabrina," the Sheriff continued. "Penny, did you leave the room at any other time during the night?"

"I did wake up about a quarter to two," Penny replied. "Grandpa Dick appeared to still be sleeping. I left the room to go downstairs and outside for some fresh air. I took the glass back down with me."

"The glass?" Sheriff Blackwood asked.

"Yes, he must have woke up while I was sleeping and saw it sitting there because it was almost empty."

"Well, that proves he was alive after I left the room!" Alexis exclaimed. "He couldn't have drunk the milk if I'd killed him."

"And there were strawberry milk stains on his pillow case too, boss," Deputy Moss offered.

"Well it would appear that's correct," the Sheriff assessed. "So assuming that nobody else entered the room while you slept up until 1:45 and then left again, your grandfather must have still been alive."

"Yeah, he must've been," Penny agreed. "I'd forgotten about the empty glass."

"So what did you do after you the left the room?"

"Well, like I said, I went outside to take in some fresh air. I took a little walk down by the lake shore. I came back in after about twenty minutes or so, I guess, and went into the kitchen. I was washing out the glass when a huge bug, like a cockroach went into the sink. It scared me, so I washed it down the drain and then I turned on the garbage disposal to kill it. I *hate* bugs," Penny explained.

"Sheriff, if I may," Mildred interrupted.

"Yes, Mildred?"

"Edna and I did hear the garbage disposal at about 2:15 that morning. It woke us up in fact," Mildred offered. Edna nodded with the memory.

"That confirms then that Penny was outside of her room at that time," Sheriff Blackwood said. "Then what, Penny?"

"Well, I dried the glass and put it on the shelf with the others. But then I heard the dog howl. I hoped I hadn't woke anybody up, so I turned off the light and went back to my room. Grandpa Dick was like I'd left him. So I covered myself up on the floor and went back to sleep. The next time I woke up..." Penny stopped short.

"It's okay, Penny," the Sheriff said. "So you were back in your room about 2:20 or so?"

Penny nodded.

"That leaves a space of about 35 minutes that Penny wasn't in the room. More than enough time for someone else to enter and strangle Mr. Forester,"

Sheriff Blackwood paused and looked back down at Jim Frank. "Are you the strangler, Mr. Frank?"

Still, Jim remained silent, unmoving.

"Ross," the Sheriff called over to the Deputy.

"Yes, boss?"

"Go search Jim Frank's room."

"You don't have a right to do that," Jim said finally. "It's my room!"

"But it is *our* Bed & Breakfast," Edna stipulated. "And I have no problem with a search being conducted on the premises."

"Go search it, Ross," Sheriff Blackwood repeated.

"Sure thing, boss."

Deputy Moss left to do as instructed. Jim's temples began to pound. Within minutes, the lanky Deputy returned carrying a small object. As he drew nearer, everyone could see that what he held in his hand was a syringe. And it was full of liquid.

"I'll bet you anything that's Mr. Buchanon's syringe and that it contains Sodium Pentathol," Sheriff Blackwood commented, watching Jim for his reaction. "The fact that Ross found it among your possessions puts you in the room with Richard Forester, wouldn't you agree, Mr. Frank?"

Jim remained stolid.

"This isn't getting us anywhere!" Sam burst out.

"Jacob, one moment please," Edna said and, standing, she walked out of the room. She returned a minute later carrying a framed picture and handed it down to Jim. He reluctantly accepted it and looked at the image it contained. It was a faded image of his beloved wife as a teenager, and abruptly he closed his eyes, his heart overflowing with sorrow. He pressed his forehead to the glass pane of the picture and began to weep uncontrollably.

Chapter 50

"Regina…my sweet, sweet Regina," he whispered.

Nobody said a word as they watched Jim grieve over his lost wife.

"That bastard took everything from me," Jim sobbed. "Because of him, my beautiful wife lies dead today. She had cancer and because of his actions, she couldn't get the treatment she needed. Oh, Regina….I couldn't let this stand, could I? Could I?"

Jim looked imploringly at each in turn.

"I watched and I waited. Waited until Penny left her room and I just *knew* it was a sign from above that she was leaving the room so that I could make it all right again," he continued. "I stood above him then, in the darkness. How could he rest so easily when my Regina had been taken from me? When Charlie's mother had been taken from him? So I did it. I strangled him! I choked every bit of life out of him and sent it to my sweet angel watching from above. I gave Regina life again through his death. An eye for an eye as the Good Book says. An eye for an eye."

Jim bowed his head and tears streamed down his face. His hands wilted and the framed picture fell to the floor. "I'm so sorry, Charlie. I'm sorry."

With sad eyes, Sheriff Blackwood looked over at his Deputy and motioned for him to go over to Jim. Deputy Moss removed the handcuffs from his belt and gently helped Jim to his feet. Jim made no attempt to resist as his hands were cuffed behind him. With a shaking voice, Deputy Moss read him his rights while the Sheriff guided Jim out of the room and down the walkway to the parking lot beyond. The others filed out behind them following them down to the parking area, watching in stunned silence as Jim was helped into the backseat of the Sheriff's cruiser.

Right at that moment, Charlie rode up on bikes with Billy Corbitt and upon seeing his father handcuffed and in the back of the cruiser, he immediately dropped his bike and ran over.

"Dad? What happened? Why are you being arrested? Dad?" he exclaimed, placing the palms of his hands on the window.

Jim looked up at him with tears in his eyes. "Forgive me, Charlie. Please forgive me."

Sheriff Blackwood got into the front seat and started up the engine. "Make sure nobody leaves yet," he instructed Deputy Moss. "We still have a few more odds and ends to take care of first. I'm going to run Mr. Frank down to the station and book him for Richard's murder. I'll call back up here shortly."

The Deputy nodded and stepped away from the car as the Sheriff drove away. Charlie ran after the car for a short distance, calling out to his father, and then stopped as he began to cry. Mildred walked over and comforted the boy while the Deputy directed everyone back into the house.

Edna approached Penny who stood still watching the cruiser disappear down the road. "Are you okay, Penny?"

Penny slowly nodded.

"Now Grandpa Dick can truly rest. He will suffer no more." Penny turned and joined the others as they walked up the pathway to the Bed & Breakfast.

Edna slowly turned and followed them.

Chapter 51

Later that evening, Sheriff Blackwood made his way back over to the Bed & Breakfast. The mood was somber, almost depressing among everyone there. He returned all the ID's and cell phones and informed everyone that they'd be free to leave in the morning if they wished. He further explained that Jim Frank had given an official confession and that his young boy Charlie would be staying with the Corbitt's for the night until his uncle could come and retrieve him the next day. He spoke individually to each person and then he sent the officers posted around the premises home. The Bed & Breakfast was no longer under house arrest.

As was expected, Alexis was let go and she was busy packing her things back in her living quarters. This caused Felix's ire to go up as this would "just cause more work" for him as he put it. Mildred busied herself taking care of Alexis's normal duties while Edna found her way to the Sheriff and pulled him aside.

"So what's going to happen now, Jacob?" she asked him.

"Jim signed a confession. He killed Richard Forester, but it wasn't for anything as mundane as money. It was a crime of passion. It was out of grief for his wife," he replied.

He then went on to tell Edna his story, and how he and his son Charlie were here to scatter Regina's ashes on the lake by her request. The fact that Richard Forester happened to be here at the same time was pure coincidence. Nothing more. Edna was sad to hear how

Regina had died and she explained how she noticed a strong resemblance to her in Charlie. But she knew there had to be another reason why they were here because fishing season hadn't opened yet. She remembered how Regina used to love it up here as a teenager and she found a picture of her hanging in the hallway from a summer trip years ago. It was that same picture that she'd shown to Jim.

He commended her for her quick thinking and then went on to explain that Sam confirmed seeing somebody up in Richard's room through the window at a little after two a.m., that, along with the syringe having been found in his room, would be strong enough to hold up in any court of law when coupled with his confession. Edna asked how he came by the syringe. Sheriff Blackwood further explained that after he'd strangled Richard, Jim walked over to the window and looked out of it because he thought he'd heard something outside. He had heard something. It was Sam trying to hide by his car. When he turned to leave, he felt something poke him in the foot and found the syringe lying there by the window. He picked it up and took it with him not knowing exactly why or the consequences that action would bring him.

"What about the others, Jacob? They still broke the law," Edna queried.

"Well, Alexis didn't break any laws Edna. What she did wasn't right, but she didn't cross any legal lines. Besides it's my understanding that you've terminated her services here anyway," Sheriff Blackwood answered. When Edna nodded her agreement, the Sheriff continued. "I think our two FBI Special Agents Aaron Buchanon and Sabrina Riggs, a.k.a. Sabrina Jackson will have their hands full for a while. I've spoken to their superiors and advised them of their participation in what took place here over the past few days. They'll be getting a copy of my official report as well. Suffice it to say, they were not happy. Not happy at all with what they heard. As for our lovebirds, I could charge Sam with assault, but to be completely honest with you here, Edna, they are good kids. They just got married and are getting started in life. I believe they've learned a hard lesson. If they can make it through this together, then I wish them God Speed. Penny has already said she wouldn't care to press charges against them either."

"I suppose so, Jacob," Edna acquiesced. "If you think it's best. There's no excuse for their actions though."

"No, there's not. I agree with you on that point, but I think they'll learn and grow from this experience. Sometimes the best discipline a person can receive is the one they give themselves. I can see how Sam is beating himself up over this. I don't believe any further action is necessary. However," he paused, "something still seems to be a bit off with those two. So I'm going to have a couple of officers follow them over the next couple of days to see if it leads us to anything. How's Penny taking all of this?"

"Hard as can be expected, but she appears to be okay. She'll be staying here with Mildred and I for a few days while she figures out what she's going to do next."

"That's good. I still have some papers I need to have her sign, but I can wait for a little while longer," the Sheriff replied.

"Will you be joining us for dinner tonight, Jacob?"

Sheriff Blackwood hesitated and then smiled. "Yes. Tonight I think I will. I'd be delighted. I just need to call over to Cathy to let her know first if that's okay?"

"Of course! We have all the phones back in their rooms, so take your pick of which one you'd like to use," Edna smiled back.

The Sheriff removed his hat and followed Edna inside.

Chapter 52

Felix served another fine meal, "On time for once!" Edna acknowledged. After a few minutes of complete silence in the room, Penny looked up and around the table.

"I just want to say that I'm sorry to all of you if I said or did anything over the last few days that may have been inappropriate or wrong. I didn't mean for anything to be personal and I didn't mean to hurt anyone's feelings," Penny said.

All eyes turned to her in surprise.

"Oh, honey," Sabrina reacted. "It's we who should be apologizing to you. *We're* the ones who acted inappropriate, not you. And for that matter, you have my deepest apologies and condolences for your grandfather."

"Mine too," Aaron agreed with a sad smile.

"Ours too, Penny," Sam added. Gwen smiled and nodded her agreement.

"And you have ours too, Sweetie," Mildred confirmed with a warm smile.

"Same here, Penny," Sheriff Blackwood said.

The tears welled up in Penny's eyes. "Thank you."

"Listen up," Sabrina announced, standing up. She raised her glass in toast. "Tomorrow, we all get to face the reality of our actions. But tonight, let's enjoy this dinner and each other's company. I propose a toast. To Penny! May she have a long, happy and prosperous life!"

"To Penny!" everyone echoed with raised glasses.

The dinner passed and soon everyone got ready for their last night in the Bed & Breakfast. Penny walked out the back door and down the pathway to the servant's quarters hoping to see Alexis. But the former maid had already left. Penny peeked inside the window and saw a piece of paper on the bare bed. She turned the doorknob and the door swung wide open. Making her way over to the bed, she picked up the piece of paper and found a note scribbled on it.

Tell Penny I'm sorry. Alexis.

Chapter 53

The next morning was a busy one. Felix was grumbling as usual, Edna was barking orders as usual and all of the occupants, except for Penny, were busy loading luggage into their cars. Everybody said their 'goodbyes' and returned to their lives.

After a light breakfast, Mildred took Penny out to the aviary and showed her where they used to keep the birds before it finally went uncared for. She again offered for Penny to stay on and help rebuild the aviary until she could figure out what she wanted to do. Penny thanked her and said she'd think it over.

Mildred found her sister inside the Dining Room clearing away the morning's dishes and promptly helped her with the chore.

"Maybe we were a little bit hasty in letting Alexis go," Mildred said.

"After what she did?" Edna replied. "How could we ever trust her in this house again?"

"I suppose you're right," Mildred agreed. "I'll put up a posting in town for another maid later today down at Grogan's on the information board."

"Call up Mr. Randolph at the newspaper too to see if he can post a wanted ad for us," Edna suggested.

"Good idea. I'll do that."

"Where's Penny?" Edna asked.

"She's over in the aviary looking around," Mildred confirmed. "She has some things to sort out, poor girl. But she's considering our offer to stay."

"Very good," Edna nodded. "I'll be right back. Going to the kitchen for a minute."

Edna left the Dining Room and entered the kitchen to find Felix busy cleaning the counter tops. He looked up briefly and then returned to his cleaning.

"Mildred is going to be posting a want ad for another maid today, Felix, so hopefully we'll have some help for you soon," Edna informed him.

"Good! I'm not as young as I used to be you know!"

"How could we *not* know, you old codger? You keep reminding us!"

Felix grumbled under his breath but said nothing else.

"Felix," Edna continued, walking over to the pantry. "We appear to be running low on supplies too."

"After feeding every policeman in town for the last two days, that comes as no surprise to me," Felix replied.

"Yes well, could you please run a quick inventory and prepare a list of things we need?" Edna continued, looking through the items stacked on the shelves.

"Sure, sure," Felix responded.

"And be sure to add some more strawberry mix to the list. I don't see any in here. Penny must have used up the last of it the other night."

"Did you say strawberry mix?" Felix perked up.

"Yes! Strawberry milk mix," Edna said, placing a hand on her hip. "Don't you have hearing aids you can wear?"

"We haven't had strawberry mix in this house for years! Nobody drinks the stuff, so I stopped stocking it. It seems silly to buy something that will just waste away on the shelf!"

Edna felt a lump go up in her throat. "What did you say?"

"Oh! So I'm the one who needs hearing aids, huh?" Felix grunted. "I said that I never stock strawberry mix. There isn't any in that pantry today, because there hasn't been any in that pantry for years!"

Chapter 54

A few days later, Penny had her things packed and loaded in the Camry ready to depart the Pookotz Bed & Breakfast for home. She stood on the front pathway between the house and the gate. It was a beautiful day outside. Edna, Mildred, and even Felix had come out to see her off. She walked over and hugged each one in turn, thanking them for their hospitality.

"It was our pleasure to have you here," Mildred said. "Please come see us again, Penny. Hopefully, it will be under much better circumstances next time."

"Thank you, Mildred," Penny replied with a smile. "Thank you, Edna, for helping me and allowing me to stay as long as you have."

"It was the least we could do," Edna assured her.

"And thank you too, Felix, for such wonderful food. You're a great cook!"

"It's nice to see that *somebody* appreciates my efforts around here!" Felix returned as Edna let out a small huff. "You're quite welcome, Miss."

"Are you sure you won't stay a little while longer?" Mildred offered.

"No. It's time I left now. I have to go back home and take care of things there. Grandpa Dick's body has already been flown back and I need to arrange for his cremation. I can't afford a decent burial, so I'll have him cremated instead," Penny replied. "He really loved it here. Maybe I'll bring him back again someday where he found his final peace."

"That would be nice," Mildred nodded.

"Well...I guess that's it then," Penny announced with a small shrug.

"Take care, Penny Forester," Edna said.

"Thank you. You too."

Penny turned and, taking a deep breath, she smiled to herself and took a step forward.

"Oh, Penny, dear," she heard Mildred say behind her. "You almost forgot something!"

Penny stopped and turned around. Mildred was holding up a dirty, empty glass. She frowned and looked at Mildred.

"I don't understand."

Edna brought an arm from around her back. In her hand was an Azalea which she placed stem down inside the glass. She locked her knowing eyes on the girl's and gave her a sad smile.

"*Now* do you?" Edna asked.

Penny's face went as white as a sheet and she began trembling. Edna noticed the reaction and nodded with satisfaction. "I thought so," she said. "Jacob will be here shortly to collect you, Penny. But first, I want to know why? Why did you do it?"

"Do?" Penny stammered. "I've...I did nothing...Jim Frank killed Grandpa Dick. He confessed."

"Oh yes!" Edna responded, walking forward. "Jim Frank thought he'd killed your grandfather. He really believed he had. The only problem here, Penny, is, by the time Jim got to your grandfather, he was already dead, wasn't he?"

Penny was frozen, her eyes beginning to glaze over. "What?" she gasped with a forced smile. "That's crazy!"

"I wish it were, sweetheart," Mildred said with saddened eyes. "But the truth of the matter is, your grandfather was suffering *so* much that it became unbearable for you, didn't it? You couldn't stand to see him in so much pain and agony."

"I have to hand it to you Penny," Edna said. "You almost got away with it. You even had me fooled, and that's a hard thing to do."

"Edna may be many things Penny," Felix contributed. "But she's *no* fool!"

Edna stopped and looked at Felix in surprise. "Why, thank you, Felix! I believe that's the nicest thing you've ever said about me."

Felix grumbled under his breath but said nothing else.

"I didn't kill Grandpa Dick! I could never do that!" Penny retaliated, regaining some of her composure.

"Let's go over the events of that evening, shall we?" Edna prompted. She placed her hands on her hips and slowly walked back over to rejoin her sister. "When you and your grandfather arrived that night, it was obvious he was in a great deal of pain. It didn't take a medical genius to be able to see he was gravely ill. It was also equally obvious that you had a great deal of love for your grandfather. You two were close. Why when they started accusing him of taking that money at the dinner table, you were right there by his side defending him to the last! I admired you for that.

"While everybody else was off scheming to get your grandfather's money, you decided, for reasons unknown to me, to ease his pain, so to speak. You had determined in your own heart to help him fall asleep. Permanently. To end his suffering so that he could finally find peace. The trick was…how? How would you do this without bringing suspicion back on yourself? You couldn't do anything so crass as to suffocate him; after all, you still loved him very much. So then what? He was very ill. If you found him dead the next morning, who wouldn't believe that his cancer

had done him in? After all, you'd just confided in
Sabrina that same night of his condition. So the logical
conclusion would be to poison him. And nobody would
be the wiser for it. How am I doing so far?"

Penny frowned but said nothing.

"Let's skip to the part where you said you brought
some strawberry milk up to your grandfather to ease his
stomach," Edna continued. "A seemingly innocent act
in of itself. The only problem with that is....Felix?
What's the problem with that?"

"I never keep any strawberry mix in the house,"
Felix answered.

"What?" Penny responded. "You heard me say the
first morning in the living area that I brought my
grandfather some strawberry milk! Why didn't you say
anything then?"

"I didn't hear *half* of anything that was said that
morning!" Felix grunted. "Or believe me, I would have.
You're lucky I'm even hearing you coherently right
now!"

"Blunt excrement, remember, dear?" Mildred
reminded her.

"So when Felix informed me that we've never had
strawberry mix in the house, I knew then you'd been
lying," Edna surmised. "The question then became
why? The obvious answer was that you'd murdered
your own grandfather. So if that wasn't strawberry mix
in the milk glass, then what was it?"

Edna paused and took the glass from Mildred's hand
and wiggled it in the air with the Azalea going from
side to side. "Am I still doing good?"

Penny's lips quivered and her eyes were downcast.
"But how…" Penny started.

"How did we know to look for an Azalea?" Edna
finished for her. "Do you remember when you said you

had washed the bug down the sink drain and then turned on the garbage disposal to kill it?"

Penny nodded sullenly.

"When Mildred and I entered the kitchen to investigate," Edna explained, "Mildred remembered smelling a faint scent in the air although at the time she couldn't place it. But then a couple of days later while she was serving food to the officers posted around the house, she noticed some displaced soil in her flower garden. Somebody had uprooted some of her flowers. Lying on the ground was an Azalea. She picked it up and once again, she caught the scent. It wouldn't be until a few days later that she would put two and two together. It was the same scent both times. What was disposed of that night in the garbage disposal were Azalea flowers."

Edna paused to look at Penny. She remained frozen like a statue.

"Did you know, Penny, that if you were to grind up some Azalea flower petals and mix them into a glass of milk that it could pass for strawberry? The color resemblance is amazing! I know, because we actually did it just to see what would happen," Edna stated, keeping her eyes on the young teenager. "Did you also know that if ingested, Azaleas are toxic to humans? Especially to someone with a weakened heart and with a fatal illness such as your grandfather's? This we also know because we called over to Doc Meecham's office and asked him. But more about Doc Meecham in a minute. First, let's talk about what *really* happened with the garbage disposal and the events leading up to it.

"After you had returned to your room with the milk, you had to assist your grandfather in drinking down your little pink concoction. You had to assist him, because he was still groggy from being clobbered over the head with a bible. Of course, you couldn't have known that and assumed this was due to his sickness. While you did that, some of the milk must have dribbled down onto his pillow case where it remained to be found the next morning. Then you set your cell phone alarm for 1:45 in the morning, judging this to be more than a long enough time for the poison to work its way through his system. And besides, everybody would safely be asleep by this time. We know this, because you'd forgotten to turn the alarm setting off before all the cell phones were collected and it woke Sheriff Blackwood and his wife up the next night. He thought it was an incoming call, but in actuality, it was just your alarm going off again at 1:45.

"When you woke up at 1:45, you checked your grandfather and, satisfied that he was dead, you took the empty glass and went downstairs to rid yourself of all the evidence. But somehow, Rufus found his way into the house and you must have heard him coming in through the front door. e's done that before in the past and like he's done on previous occasions, he just trotted right over and plopped himself down right in front of my door. This startled you, so you headed out the back door and hung out by the lake shore until you were positive that the coast was clear again and headed back to the kitchen, still carrying the glass. *This* glass," Edna indicated holding up the glass once more in her hand.

"That wasn't all you had with you though, was it?" Edna paused for a second. "You still had some left over Azalea petals too. Truth be known, if you'd just tossed them out over the surface of the lake, they would have been lost forever. But you thought you'd be clever by destroying them using a different method. That was a mistake you made only because you *over*-thought it. There was no oversized bug. It was Azalea petals you used the garbage disposal on. Mildred and I heard you in there and it woke us up. In fact, when I stepped on poor Rufus's tail in the darkness, he let up such a pitiful howl of pain that I was surprised the whole house hadn't heard it. You'd just finished destroying the petals in the disposal when you heard Rufus howl. But you still had the glass! You wouldn't have time to wash it before someone walked through that door. So what did you do? You opened the dishwasher and you placed it inside figuring that it would be washed along with all the other dirty dishes the next day, therefore effectively cleaning the last of the evidence. A great plan except for one thing."

"Edna never uses the dishwasher, child," Mildred said.

"I always insist on hand washing the dishes because that dishwasher can never clean them right," Edna confirmed. "Mildred noticed the next evening that a glass was missing from the shelf. We searched everywhere for the missing glass. We looked in all the rooms, except for the Blue Room of course. We looked outside, thinking one of the officers might have left it out there, but after a frugal search, we came up with nothing. That's because it was sitting in the dishwasher the whole time, and neither of us even thought of looking in there. Not until we figured out that it wasn't strawberry milk you were bringing to your grandfather to drink, that is."

Penny was visibly trembling. "But…but what about the person who broke into my room? What about that?"

"What about that?" Edna responded with an eyebrow lifted. "Okay, let's talk about that for a minute. You said that you woke up and saw the dark shadow of someone standing right at the foot of your bed. It was too dark to see who it was."

"That's right," Penny replied.

"That's right. Fine," Edna proceeded. "Mildred and I conducted a little experiment last night while you were eating in the kitchen with Felix. I lay down in the bed where you were and left my eyes closed for a solid five minutes, allowing my eyes to adjust. Then I sat up and looked straight to the foot of the bed where Mildred was standing, and recognized her almost instantly."

"But you were expecting to see her!" Penny retorted.

"The point is, child, that I could make out her shape in the darkness and I knew it was her. And I dare say your eyes are probably in better shape than mine!" Edna returned. "What I'm saying is that there's no way you would not have recognized who was standing right there in front of you at the foot of your bed, even in the darkness of the room. There was plenty of light coming through the window from the moon when I saw Mildred standing there, just like it was the night you said someone had broke into your room. I spoke as well to the officer who conducted the search for this mysterious intruder that night and he told me they found nothing. Not even any footprints in the soil underneath your window…which to me is very odd considering it was freshly laid soil where Mildred was planning on planting some flowers."

"Azaleas in fact," Mildred added.

"There were no footprints, because there wasn't anybody who'd actually made them. Which means you made the whole thing up," Edna concluded.

"Why would I make that up?" Penny returned.

"Why indeed?" Edna questioned. "Earlier that day Jacob informed you that you were considered a suspect and were to remain under the provisions of the house arrest just like everyone else. You didn't take to that very well if I remember correctly. So why would you make that up? To throw suspicion off of yourself. You were, after all, every bit as much a victim in this whole thing as your grandfather. So, you waited for things to calm down. You watched through a crack in the door until you were sure that Ross had fallen asleep, and then you went over to the window and opened it. You checked for the officer outside and saw he was turned away. You crawled back into your bed and screamed bloody murder. Job well done."

"I didn't do it," Penny said in a weak voice, sounding less and less convincing as the time wore on.

"Sweet, child," Mildred said, moving forward. "We know you did it. Doc Meecham informed us of the results of the blood samples he took as well as the milk stain residue they took off the pillow case. The poison in both matched. Your grandfather died due to poisoning. With the amount of poison in his system coupled with his weakened condition, he estimated his time of death to be between twelve midnight and one in the morning. Well before Jim Frank even got to him. Poor Mr. Frank was so delirious with emotion, that he didn't even realize he was strangling a man who was already dead. He actually believed that he'd killed him."

"But he didn't, Penny," Edna established. "Because you already had."

"You have no physical proof," Penny countered.

"You mean like the fingerprints on the glass here?" Edna returned, tapping her fingernail against its surface. "Jacob has already run the prints off of this glass against another glass you used just last night that we gave him. It was a perfect match. And the residue taken from this glass matches that on the pillow case. It matches the Azalea toxin found in your grandfather's system Penny. You are good and caught child. I'm sorry."

Penny dropped her head and started crying. Mildred walked over to stand before the teenage girl and placed her hand under her chin, lifting her face until Penny's eyes were level with her own. "Why Penny? Why did you take this upon yourself, child?"

Tears gushed from Penny's eyes and she nearly yelled back in reply, "Because I couldn't *take* it anymore! Grandpa Dick was in so much pain! He was coughing up blood, he was doubled over. It was awful! It was terrible! He told me that he loved it here. He told me that if he could choose a place to die, it would be right here! I had to take the pain away from him. I had to stop his suffering and agony. Grandpa Dick's last words to me were that I needed to be *strong*. That I needed to be *capable*. So I did what I had to do! I brought him relief and peace. I was strong and I was capable! For him!"

"Well, you certainly are capable," Mildred agreed. She stepped back with a sharp, disapproving look in her eyes. "But you're not strong. A strong person would have stood by his side and helped him through. She would have held his hand to the very last, giving him the love and support he needed, even if it meant digging deeper inside of herself than she'd ever done before to provide him with the kind of strength that he depended on. A strong person doesn't murder someone who's experiencing that kind of pain, Penny. I want you to ask yourself something. And I want you to *really* think about your answer, child. When you killed your grandfather, was it to relieve him of his pain…or to relieve you of yours?"

Penny dropped her head and slumped to the ground just as the flashing lights of the approaching police cars filled the parking area. Mildred backed away and stood by her sister who took her by the arm and hugged her close. Sheriff Blackwood soon appeared on the pathway with a couple more officers and they took Penny into custody. Penny stood as they cuffed her and led her away.

Sheriff Blackwood walked up to the Pookotz Sisters and removed his hat, and humbly nodded to each of them. They smiled warmly back at him.

"I have no words for you two," the Sheriff said. "Thank you. I'm indebted to you both. You've done a very, very good thing here today. I have to admit, she had me completely fooled."

"She had us all fooled, Jacob," Edna responded kindly. "She even fooled herself."

"So, did Richard embezzle the $750,000?" Mildred asked.

"I'm glad you asked me. Edna, do you remember when I said I was going to have Sam and Gwen followed?" Sheriff Blackwood responded.

"Yes," Edna replied. "Did it lead to something?"

"Did it ever! They followed our newlywed couple all the way to Portland International Airport. Sam and Gwen went to the storage locker area and tried to open a locker with a key. But the locker wouldn't open. Finally, after Sam starting banging on the locker and putting up such a fuss, my officers had to control the situation. Sam and Gwen finally admitted that the key was Richard's and that the money was supposedly inside of the locker. Airport security detained Sam and Gwen until members of the FBI could arrive to question them."

"So the key was to a different locker?" Mildred asked.

"Yes," Sheriff Blackwood answered. "After Sam and Gwen were taken away, one of the FBI agents noticed that the key was labeled 'E-28'. Well, the locker was indeed locker number 28. He tried the key himself, but again, it wouldn't open. The agent pulled an airport worker aside and asked him if he was in the right area. The worker looked at the key and informed the agent that the key was for locker number 28 on the eastern side of the airport. The locker the agent was trying to open was 'W-28', in the western storage area. When the agent used the key on locker 28 on the other side of the airport, it opened right up. And guess what he found inside?"

"$750,000?" Edna submitted.

"No."

"No?" Mildred countered. "Then what did he find?"

"He found a case containing nearly $1,200,000."

Their jaws dropped.

"Over a *million* dollars?" Edna exclaimed. "So Mr. Forester *did* embezzle that money after all?"

"It would appear so. Only it was about $450,000 more than what they originally thought. The FBI are investigating it further now. Sam and Gwen are in their custody currently until everything is cleared up."

"It just goes to show you that you can never tell with some people," Mildred commented.

"I don't understand it. Why would Richard freely give that up to Sam? It doesn't make sense," Edna said.

"Honestly, Edna, we don't understand it either. The only thing we could come up with is that perhaps Richard wasn't completely coherent or that he was starting to lose his mental awareness and ability. I'm afraid that part of the mystery will more than likely remain unsolved."

"Do you think Penny knows about this locker?" Edna asked.

"Doubtful. But we will question her on it."

"What about Mr. Frank? What is to become of him?" Mildred asked.

"Jim Frank is a free man again and he's eternally grateful to you two. He's going to be taking some counseling and starting over with his son Charlie. He'll be fine, once he learns how to deal with the loss of his wife," Sheriff Blackwood affirmed.

"Hopefully Jim and Charlie will find the strength within each other to help cope with her loss," Mildred said.

"You be sure and tell Jim that he's welcome to come back here when he's ready to scatter Regina's ashes," Edna added. "There will always be a place for him and Charlie at the Pookotz Bed & Breakfast."

"I certainly will," Sheriff Blackwood agreed. "Well, I have some business to attend to. Thank you again. Edna. Mildred."

"Jacob," Edna replied.

"Good day." Sheriff Blackwood turned and walked back down the pathway to his cruiser. Within a few minutes, the parking area was once again clear leaving the Pookotz Sisters and Felix once again standing by themselves.

"Felix!" Edna exclaimed, turning to face him. "Why aren't you on the phone ordering more supplies? Don't you know we have a new maid starting here on Monday?"

"I know we have a new maid starting here on Monday!" Felix snorted. "I'll have enough supplies here to feed an entire army by five o'clock this evening if you want, you old hen!"

"Old hen?!?" Edna shouted.

"See?" Felix returned. "Lookie there! Yer feathers are already getting ruffled!"

"I swear you'll be the death of me, you ornery, old coot!"

Felix turned his walker and grumbled his way up the pathway back into the house with Edna following, her hands hefting the sides of her long dress up as she climbed the front porch steps.

"I should have gotten rid of you long ago!" Edna continued.

"I should be so lucky!" Felix said as they went into the front door.

Mildred watched them disappear into the Bed & Breakfast and, shaking her head, she laughed to herself.

"No doubt about it. Those two are in love!"

ABOUT THE AUTHOR

Bart J. Gilbertson is the author of the Pookotz Sisters Mystery series. Although he was born in Wisconsin, he spent most of his youth and later years in the rocky mountain state of Idaho. He has been all over the northwest and it is his love for the lush green state of Oregon that inspired the setting for Pleasant Lake and its inhabitants. *Deathbed & Breakfast* is his first novel. He attended ITT Tech and received an Associate in Applied Science Degree for Computer Networking Systems and graduated with honors. Bart has worn many hats over his lifetime career, but the one he is most proud of is that of being a writer. He currently resides in O'Neill, NE. He has two children.